THE Engagement EMBARGO

By
Samantha
Chase

Cover Design: Kari March/Kari March Designs

Editing: Jillian Rivera Editing

PRAISE FOR SAMANTHA CHASE

"If you can't get enough of stories that get inside your heart and soul and stay there long after you've read the last page, then Samantha Chase is for you!"

-NY Times & USA Today Bestselling Author **Melanie Shawn**

"A fun, flirty, sweet romance filled with romance and character growth and a perfect happily ever after."

-NY Times & USA Today Bestselling Author **Carly Phillips**

"Samantha Chase writes my kind of happily ever after!"

-NY Times & USA Today Bestselling Author **Erin Nicholas**

"The openness between the lovers is refreshing, and their interactions are a balanced blend of sweet and spice. The planets may not have aligned, but the elements of this winning romance are definitely in sync."

- *Publishers Weekly, STARRED review*

"A true romantic delight, *A Sky Full of Stars* is one of the top gems of romance this year."

- *Night Owl Reviews, TOP PICK*

"Great writing, a winsome ensemble, and the perfect blend of heart and sass."

CHAPTER 1

Love is like a hole; once you fall in, it's hard to get out.

UNKNOWN

"We have wilting sunflowers over here!" Skylar Jennings called out. "Wilting sunflowers, people!" She looked around frantically. "Can someone please replace these with cheery, non-wilting ones?" With a huff, she continued to scan the large banquet room and felt a sense of pride. The theme for the wedding was country chic–lots of mason jars and sunflowers. It was very rustic and charming. The colors made it feel like you were walking in the mountains during the fall foliage–very trendy. It was the only thing the bride had contributed to the plans.

Wedding planning was her life–even though she had gone to college and graduated with a psychology degree–but it didn't take long for her to realize it wasn't her passion. Luckily, she had a plan B to fall back on. After starting up the business three years ago with her two best friends, Josie and Leanna, Meet Me at the Altar Wedding Services had finally started to become a success. Skye loved helping couples plan their big day, and it was always so rewarding to see the look on their faces when they saw how she brought their vision to life and made their day exactly what they wanted.

Today was the first time she found zero joy in it.

"Why are there wilted sunflowers?" a voice called out, and when she turned, she saw one of her partners, Josie, walking toward her.

"I'm already working on it," Skye assured her. "We have plenty of extras in the cooler so we'll just swap them out. No big deal." Then she looked at Josie and started to smirk. "Nice outfit."

Looking down at herself, Josie frowned. She was in a pair of purple sweatpants, an oversized white buttoned shirt, gray slipper booties, and there were several large rollers in her hair. "We're in the middle of getting ready and I was too fidgety to stand still so I figured I'd come out and see how things were going."

"You're a bridesmaid today," Skye gently reminded her. "And not one of the wedding planners. We've been over this a million times. I've got it all under control."

Another frown from Josie. "This isn't right."

Skye looked around frantically. "What? What isn't right? This looks exactly like the picture Tracy printed out for us from her Pinterest board!"

"That's not what I mean. This wedding as a whole. It's just...it's wrong." She sighed and looked at Skye sadly. "My brother is making a huge mistake."

Actually, her brother was on his fourth mistake, but who was counting?

This wasn't a topic Skye particularly wanted to discuss, so she simply nodded and let her friend talk.

"Think about it," Josie went on. "We've dealt with dozens of brides in the last few years, and when did one ever hand us a picture off the internet and say, 'Do this' and then have no interest in anything else, huh? It was weird and it's wrong and...I just can't believe he doesn't see it!"

"I get why you're concerned, and yes, it was a little strange, but...not every bride is all about the details. Plus, Elliott was more than happy to fill in the gaps and he had enough enthusiasm for both of them."

"Elliott is an idiot."

Skye fought a smirk. "That's your brother you're talking about, and you know he's not an idiot. He's a borderline genius." She shrugged. "He just happens to be in love with being in love. You can't fault him for it. Isn't that something we all want? To be in love and have someone love us back?"

I know I wouldn't mind that...

"Skye, this is his fourth engagement..."

"But only the first to get to the wedding day, so..."

They were silent for several minutes as they watched their staff scurry around putting finishing touches on the room–including replacing the wilting flowers. "I just don't like seeing him get hurt."

"He's not going to get hurt," Skye softly replied. "This is what he's always wanted. If anything, he's floating on a cloud of happiness right now. This is his day and you need to be happy for him."

"Maybe."

"No maybes about it. Now go and change out of that outfit, put on your gown, and let's do this."

And with a small groan, Josie agreed and made her way out of the room and back to the bridal suite.

"Okay, another crisis averted." And she prayed it was the last.

So far, it had been a fairly uneventful day. It seemed like everyone was on their best behavior today since Elliott was family. Everyone knew and loved him and were excited to be a part of his big day.

Except Skye.

Right now, she'd give anything to be anywhere else in the world.

It was a good thing she was the one in charge today and could easily distract herself from having to stand there and watch the man she'd been in love with since she was twelve years old marry someone else.

Yeah, today was definitely going to suck.

When Josie had suggested them bringing in someone else to handle overseeing everything so Skye could be a guest, she shut it down fast. There was no way she could sit in a chair and watch Elliott and Tracy say their vows to promise to love each other and all that other crap without either standing up and speaking her piece or sitting there and losing her mind.

Neither were great options, so playing the part of the too-busy-to-be-a-guest wedding planner was her role for the day.

And she planned on spending a lot of time in the kitchen.

Or crying in the coat closet.

Forcing herself to focus on the wedding as an event and not the people getting married, she made her way to the kitchen to check on everything there.

As expected, it was controlled chaos. The catering staff

was amazing and their head chef Patricia was famous for her signature dishes. Skye knew she never had to worry about the menu when Patricia was in charge. With a smile and wave, she continued to walk around and check on progress, and back in the far corner of the kitchen was her other partner, Leanna, who was also their on-staff baker.

"If you're coming over to steal some frosting, I've already set a bowl aside for you over there," Leanna said without looking up from the cake she was decorating. Honestly, the woman worked magic with cakes of all shapes and sizes, and it never ceased to amaze her.

"Is it chocolate?"

This time Leanna stopped and shot her a patient stare. "Would I put anything else aside for you?"

"You're right. Sorry." And because it would be rude not to try it, Skye settled onto a stool in the corner with her bowl and let out a small sigh.

"You doing okay?" Leanna asked as she went back to work on placing delicate sugar flowers on the cake.

"Of course. Why?"

"The sigh, for starters." She placed another flower on the cake–an edible sunflower this time–before she straightened and turned around to face Skye. "And the fact that this is Elliott's wedding." Leanna was the only person in the world who knew how Skye really felt and it was good to have someone to talk to about it.

"I'm not loving it," she admitted. "I thought I was okay with the whole thing. I mean, it's not like he's ever shown any interest in me at all, ever, so..." She sighed again and it was longer and louder. "But now that the day is here? I just don't know what I'm going to do when I see him. Them. All of it."

Leanna walked over and gave her a hug. "I'm so sorry. I

can't even imagine what you're feeling." When she pulled away, she grabbed one of the other stools and sat down beside her. "I think once the ceremony starts, you should go. I can handle things. I've got a change of clothes with me and I can walk around and make sure everything's under control. My assistants can handle setting up the cake and desserts."

"I can't ask you to do that. I'm a grown woman and I've accepted the fact that Elliott is getting married."

"Yeah, but that doesn't mean you should have to stay and watch it happen. Seriously, Skye, don't torture yourself. If it were me, I would have called in sick or taken advantage of hiring someone else to oversee this event like Josie suggested."

"Maybe I'm just a glutton for punishment and figured by being here and seeing it all happen that I'd force myself to get over him."

They sat in silence for several minutes before Leanna stood. "I have to finish getting the flowers on this cake. Eat your frosting."

With a small laugh, Skye looked down at the bowl and smiled. "Is it buttercream or whipped?"

"I find it insulting that you even ask," Leanna murmured as she focused on another edible sunflower.

Taking a small spoonful of the decadent frosting, Skye licked it and hummed with appreciation. "Any chance you have a bucket of this to send home with me? I have a feeling I'm going to need it."

"There's definitely some extra, but not a bucketful. And if anything, I'd rather send it home with you than with me. Lord knows if it's sitting around, I'll eat it and then where will I be?"

"Oh, stop. I can't believe you don't eat more of this stuff. I know I would if it was around me all day."

"Yeah, but you have a great metabolism and could probably eat a bucketful of icing and not gain a pound. I'm gaining weight as we speak just talking about the icing."

Skye shook her head and took another spoonful of frosting. "That's ridiculous and you know it. You're beautiful and there's nothing wrong with you."

"Tell that to my pants that are feeling mighty squeezy right now."

It was an argument she would never win. Leanna struggled with her weight for years and it didn't seem to matter what anyone said to her or how beautiful they all told her she was—she never believed it.

"Whatever icing is left, I'll take it," she said around yet another spoonful of chocolate. "And between this, some wine, and the yoga pants and hoodie I plan on putting on when I get home, my pathetic look should be complete."

"You're not pathetic, Skye. You're just sad and there's nothing wrong with that." She put her tools down and faced her. "You should crash at my place tonight. We can be sad together."

Her eyes went wide. "What are you sad about? I thought things were going well."

She shrugged. "My sister's baby shower is in two weeks. You know what that's going to be like, right?"

Sadly, she did.

"Your family is awesome and everyone loves you and if they want to give you any grief about being single, simply pop a cupcake in their mouth and tell them to go..."

"I get what you're saying," Leanne quickly interrupted. "No need to break out the potty mouth."

Unable to help herself, she laughed. Leanne was incredibly sweet and sometimes it was fun to just mess with her by threatening a swear word. "Okay, then. No feeling sorry for yourself."

"Skye..."

"And hey, there's still a couple of weeks so maybe you'll meet a great guy and you'll tell everyone about him and how happy you are!"

"Right," she replied dryly. "Because things like that happen to me all the time. You'd think on one of these jobs– a wedding, an engagement party, any of them–that I'd meet a cute, eligible single guy. But do I? No."

"Right there with you."

"Elliott's got some cute friends. Maybe..."

"Don't you dare even say it! There is no way I'd even consider hooking up with one of his friends! Cute, eligible, or otherwise!" Groaning, she put the near-empty bowl of frosting down. "Maybe I should go. If I'm this much of a mess before the ceremony, I can't even imagine what I'll be like after it."

"Good plan. I've got this covered."

"Thanks, Lea. I appreciate it." Standing, she looked around. "I'm just going to do one last walk-through of the room, but I'll let you know when I'm definitely on my way out." They hugged before Leanna went back to putting flowers on the cake.

Resigning herself to being a coward, Skye walked back out to the banquet room and did a final check on everything. She spotted two servers lingering near the hall of the groom's suite and her curiosity was piqued. When she got closer, she whispered, "What's going on?" They both jumped and she could tell they were afraid of getting in trouble, so she put their minds at ease. "Everything okay back there?"

Dot, who had been with Meet Me at the Altar since the beginning, gave her a nervous smile. "It sounds like the groom and best man are arguing, and we sort of got sucked in while trying to hear what they're saying."

Elliott and Tyler were arguing? That didn't seem like a thing.

And now she had to stop and try to listen too.

"Um...if you need us to go and finish straightening chairs..."

Raised voices hit Skye and all she could do was shush Dot and step a little farther into the hallway and pray no one else caught what they were doing.

Within minutes, the girls were gone and Skye was holding her breath outside the door of the groom's suite.

"Look, all I'm saying, El, is that I want you to be sure."

Straightening his tie and staring at his reflection in the mirror in the tiny groom's suite, Elliott gave his best friend Tyler an easy smile. "We've been over this before. I'm sure."

"You were sure three other times..."

"Those were nothing like this."

"Okay, fine. This is the first time you're walking down the aisle. It's just that..."

"Is this really the conversation we should be having right now? The wedding is about to start," he said with a huff. Running a hand through his hair, he cursed the fact that no matter how hard he tried, it never looked completely neat.

Maybe I should have gotten it cut yesterday instead of last week...

Stepping in front of him and blocking his reflection,

Tyler's smile was more than a little forced. "How long have we known each other?"

"I don't know. Pre-school or something," Elliott replied as he took a step back to try to put some space between them. He loved Tyler like a brother, but close-talking was definitely not something he enjoyed.

"Exactly. Since forever. I know you and I know what you're doing."

"Um...trying not to be late for my own wedding? Yeah." But when he went to move, Tyler stopped him.

"Tracy's a nice girl. She's sweet and funny and...a good friend."

"But...?"

"But...I don't see this as the great love for either of you. Are you sure you're getting married because you're in love with her or just because you want to get married?"

Now he'd had enough. "Why is everyone so down on marriage?" Elliott snapped, storming across the small room. "I mean, maybe it's not right for everyone, but that doesn't mean it isn't right for someone! For *me*! I don't understand why everyone is on my case about this!"

"Elliott..."

"No! You need to understand where I'm coming from. I *want* to be married and I want to be married to Tracy! I believe in falling in love and starting a family and going through all the highs and lows that go along with that! I want to live with someone who loves me and gets me and who completes me! Is it wrong to want to sleep beside the perfect person for the rest of your life? Is it wrong to want to enjoy inane conversations at two in the morning over...over...I don't know...whether or not there's a sale on lawn mowers?"

"Elliott, you're spiraling."

"Can you blame me? We're standing here, ten minutes before my wedding, arguing over whether or not I should be doing this! If this is how you felt, why would you wait until today to bring it up?"

He was about to say more when Skylar seemed to crash through the door. "Oh, my God! I'm sorry!" she said. "I...I...was doing final check and lost my balance at the door and...and..."

Her eyes went wide when they landed on him, and Elliott's immediate thought was how adorable she looked when she was flustered. She was dressed in a very nondescript navy blue dress with her honey-blonde hair pulled back in a sleek ponytail. Very professional looking. And yet he still saw traces of the girl he grew up with. It was an odd observation, but...there it was. He was about to ask if she needed anything, but she seemed to realize she had interrupted something and took a step back.

Clearing her throat, she muttered another apology before leaving the room. It took all of three seconds for Tyler to start talking.

"Believe me, I wanted to say something sooner, but...I don't know...there never seemed to be the right time!"

"And you suddenly thought this was it?"

"Okay, I get it. The timing sucks," Tyler conceded. "It wasn't intentional, I swear!" He paused and seemed to collect his thoughts. "No one's saying anything bad about marriage, Elliott. This is about marrying the right person for the right reasons! Honestly, I think you love the idea of marriage so much that you're a little blind to who you're marrying!"

"And what's that supposed to mean?" he demanded, more than a little offended.

"It means," he paused and let out a long breath. "I don't think Tracy loves you. Not the way you love her."

"You don't know what you're talking about," he argued.

"El, I've been around you enough to know that you guys act more like people hanging out together than a real couple. She's like a friend or..."

"Marrying someone you're friends with is a good thing, Ty. At the end of the day, you should genuinely like the person you're married to."

"Oh, I agree, but there should be more. There should be...you know...all the other stuff. The romantic crap."

"I am not taking relationship advice from someone who says romantic crap." And before Tyler could object, he raked a hand through his hair and went on. "And what do you even know about this? Tracy and I do a ton of romantic stuff!"

"No, you do a lot of romantic stuff *for* Tracy."

"That's not..."

Wait...was that true?

Clearly Tyler caught his hesitation and decided to run with it. "Think about it, Elliott. All the romantic stuff that the two of you do is initiated by you." He paused. "What did you do for her birthday?"

"Took her to Napa and did the hot air balloon ride with a champagne picnic afterwards. Why?"

"And what did she do for your birthday?"

"Um...you know...we did the uh...the thing," he stammered vaguely.

"Dude, she bought you those custom car mats! And she didn't even wrap the box!"

"But I wanted them so–if you think about it, it was a very thoughtful gift!"

"Fine, you wanted them. How about for your anniversary? What did you do?"

"I surprised her with a trip to Asheville where we went for that spa retreat. It was something for both of us."

Tyler stared at him hard. "And what did she give you?"

Dammit.

"She uh...she forgot that it was our anniversary."

"How are you not seeing a pattern here?!" Tyler cried. "For all your talk about wanting what your parents have and what your grandparents have and all that happy horseshit, you are clearly settling here!"

"*I'm not!*"

"Yes, you are! Because that girl is nothing even close to what you say you want! There are no shared hobbies, no cute trips or inside jokes...none of it! If anything, she just seems content to hang out and let you take her places! Why are you settling?"

"I get that you don't agree with the way I think and that's okay. You don't have to."

"Elliott, can you really stand here and tell me this relationship is perfect? That there isn't *anything* about Tracy that you would change? Or anything about the relationship that doesn't check all your boxes? Because I'm going to tell you, I can see that there are things that just don't...I don't know...fit."

Letting out a long breath, he pinched the bridge of his nose and silently counted to ten because–sadly–Tyler had a point.

If he were being honest, there were *some* aspects of his relationship with Tracy that weren't as romantic as he'd hoped. But that came with time, right? All the examples Tyler just gave were things he had brushed off as no big deal, but...maybe they were. He just attributed it to her laid-back attitude and was hopeful that once they were married, things would change.

"And what about this wedding?" Tyler asked, breaking into his thoughts.

"What about it?"

"Most women dream of and plan their wedding for years! This was sort of put together in a matter of months and..."

"And what?"

"And it just seems to me like it was treated as just an everyday kind of event rather than the biggest day of her life."

"Since when do you know anything about planning a wedding?" he snapped.

"Since I have three sisters who I had to sit through wedding planning hell with! Trust me, each of those weddings took a minimum of a year to plan and they were all super obsessed with every little detail. Tracy just went on Pinterest and said, 'Here. Do this.' I mean, that's not normal, Elliott."

Okay, so maybe she didn't show as much *enthusiasm* for the wedding as brides usually do, but maybe that was just nerves. Maybe...

Just as he was about to explain some of this to Tyler, Skylar popped her head into the room and announced it was time. "Thanks, Skye. We'll be right there," he said with a smile. Then, without a word, he walked back over to the mirror to make sure he looked okay. Standing beside him, Tyler asked him one more time if he was sure about this, and Elliott told him he was.

And in that moment, he truly believed it.

When he was in front of the room and looking out at all his family and friends, he felt good. Confident. At peace.

The music began to play and the next thing he knew, Tracy waltzed toward him–a beautiful vision in white–and he thought about how lucky he was–how fortunate. She looked so happy–happier than he'd seen her in weeks! Her smile told him her earlier lackluster reaction to the wedding really was just about nerves. Now that their big day was finally here, she was just as excited as he was, and her radiant smile was the sign he needed to truly relax. Yes, a radiant smile that was...

Not quite directed at him.

Hmm...

Looking over his shoulder, Elliott caught a glimpse of their officiant–Tracy's best friend, Daniel St. James. Somewhere in the wedding planning process, the idea of having one of their friends officiate came up and it seemed like a good idea at the time. He had expected it to be one of his friends, not hers, and certainly not this guy.

Yeah, he wasn't overly thrilled with Daniel stepping up to do the ceremony, but Tracy convinced him it was the perfect personal touch to their big day.

However, looking at the smile Daniel was currently directing at Tracy, he wasn't quite so sure.

Once Tracy was at his side, she did smile at him and– for a moment–Elliott relaxed. Why was he looking for trouble or letting his mind wander toward things that didn't even matter? Daniel and Tracy were friends and rather than looking at this as a bad thing, he should be thankful that he cared enough to want to be a part of their big day. Taking her arm and looping it through his, he faced forward with confidence.

Here we go...

"Family and friends, welcome," Daniel began.

Elliott studied him and tried to relax but...he frowned.

Daniel looked like he had just stepped off the cover of *GQ* while Elliott looked a little...well...*not* like the cover of *GQ*. They were both wearing tuxedos, but Daniel's had a more custom fit to it while Elliott's was definitely of the rental variety.

And it didn't end there.

Here's the thing–Elliott had no problem with who he was. He knew he was tall and good-looking–but not overly so. He was a hard worker, loved to volunteer his time wherever it was needed, and cared deeply about the people in his life. Maybe he was a little on the quiet and reserved side and he enjoyed the simpler things in life, but that made him happy.

He made a good living as a software engineer and had been the fastest climbing one in the company! And while some called him nerdy-looking–he was one of those people who enjoyed wearing glasses–he never felt inferior to anyone.

Until right now.

"You know, when Tracy and I first met, I knew we were going to hit it off," Daniel was saying and Elliott forced himself to focus. "I remember the first time we hung out on the playground in fourth grade," he went on with a small laugh and then proceeded to tell a story of the two of them bonding over peanut butter cookies–Tracy's favorite.

Okay, that was sort of new information...

"I think back at all the amazing times we've had together–the trips to the Bahamas, the cruise to Mexico..."

Wait...when was this?

"Do you remember the time we got stuck in the rain when we were camping and had to share a sleeping bag in my tent?" Daniel asked while flashing his model-worthy dimples.

Is this even an appropriate story for a wedding service?

Elliott discreetly tried to clear his throat to get the point across that he was *not* amused with the direction of this speech, but no one seemed to notice.

"Tracy, you are my best friend and the most amazing woman in the world," Daniel went on. "And you deserve every happiness and all that is good in this world because *you* are everything that is good and perfect and wonderful. We are all better people for knowing you." He paused. "At least, I know I am."

O-kay...

"Marriage is about the joining of two lives and making them one. About commitments and the future and building something together. Something special." He let out a long, soft breath, and his gaze never left Tracy's. "And every time I think of that for you, I know that the only way to make sure that happens, is if you're with me."

Elliott felt the collective gasp in the room all the way to his soul.

Say what now?

Tracy went to pull her arm from his, but for some reason, Elliott held firm.

"Daniel," she began, her voice trembling slightly. "What? I mean..."

And then, the six-foot Adonis stepped forward and it was like something out of one of those damn rom-coms Elliott secretly enjoyed watching. The guy had the perfect amount of shame and confidence that made you want to cheer for him.

Your typical romantic hero.

Except...he was the bad guy here! No one should be cheering for Daniel because he–*Elliott*–was supposed to be the hero today! This was his day! His moment! How could he not...

"Maybe I should have said something sooner, but...I couldn't. I thought I was doing the right thing," Daniel explained, his eyes never leaving Tracy's. "You are the only person in this world who makes everything right, and I know the timing of this really isn't ideal..."

Did everyone think it was appropriate to bring their feelings up today?!

"But I wanted you to know—*needed* you to know—before you say 'I do' to another man, that...well...I would love the chance to prove to you how perfect we can be together."

Next thing Elliott knew, he was stepping aside and watching his fiancée kiss her best friend.

*This can**not** be my life!*

As he stood there stunned, he wondered just what exactly he was supposed to do—should he break them apart? Yell? Scream? Just what is the appropriate reaction to having your wedding hijacked in such a dramatic fashion?

Before he could figure it out, Tracy and Daniel looked at him. "Elliott, I'm sorry, man. I really thought I'd be okay with this," Daniel said and, dammit, he sounded sincere.

"Me, too," Tracy said. "I'm so sorry, but...I always hoped one day Daniel would feel for me what I felt for him. I just thought it wasn't meant to be." And then she had the nerve to smile at him.

A pitying smile.

"I never wanted to hurt you; you have to believe me. But...this is something I have to do, Elliott. I hope you understand."

His mouth was moving—he knew it was—and yet no words came out, and in the blink of an eye, the happy couple was running down the aisle and away from him.

You could have heard a pin drop in the room.

A hand on his shoulder reminded him that he was indeed awake–that this wasn't some sort of crazy dream or a nightmare.

This was his life.

"El, man," Tyler began. "I don't even know what to say."

That made two of them.

Wordlessly, the two of them walked back to the very room they had stood in just moments ago while the throngs of people left–undoubtedly wondering what they were all supposed to do.

Collapsing in the first chair he spotted, Elliott pulled his tie loose and let out a long breath. He had no idea if he was angry, sad, or simply confused. The only thing he did know was that he was numb. Letting his head fall back, he closed his eyes and just tried to focus on breathing and embracing the silence. Maybe if he could just have a few minutes to try to make sense out of this disaster, he'd start to feel a little better.

Or at least like he could breathe.

Sadly, the silence didn't last long because it seemed like his entire family had followed him and instead of wrapping him in their arms and telling him how sorry they were, they sort of surrounded him and waited for him to straighten in his seat.

"Um..."

"Elliott," his father said somberly, authoritatively, "it's time we had the talk."

Great. Just what he needed right now.

CHAPTER 2

Love is like heaven, but it can hurt like hell.

UNKNOWN

"No, I'm not sure what we're supposed to do with three hundred crab cakes, Pat," Skye said with more than a hint of annoyance, smoothing a hand over her sleek ponytail. "Let's give the family a few minutes to let the dust clear before we start freaking out about food!"

Normally, Skye was known for keeping her cool and never getting upset, but this wasn't an ordinary wedding. Right now, she wished she could be a fly on the wall in the groom's suite rather than being the responsible wedding planner and business owner who had to figure out how to deal with this mess.

Her emotions were all over the place and she felt a twinge of guilt for being happy Tracy left Elliott at the altar. But then her heart broke for him because she just watched his life essentially get destroyed in front of a hundred and fifty guests.

Was he okay? Devastated? Relieved?

Yeah, that last one played on her mind the most because of the conversation she overheard before the ceremony. But no matter how much she wanted to, there was no way she could go and listen at the door again.

"Skye," Leanna said as she walked over, interrupting her thoughts. "This is a nightmare! Have you talked to Josie? What are we supposed to do? We've never had a wedding fall apart like this! What if we're left holding the bag because their precious daughter ran off with the preacher?"

Doing her best not to roll her eyes, Skye leveled her friend with a glare. "First of all, he wasn't a preacher. He was just a friend who went and got ordained online to do this wedding."

"Are we sure? I don't remember Josie saying that."

"I would think it was obvious. I mean, you heard the speech, right? That was definitely coming from a friend." Then she paused. "Or at least...I hope he's not a preacher. That would make this even worse. Although, I guess he could still be a friend who was a preacher or..."

"Okay, I've lost interest. Does it even matter? What's our plan here?"

"I can't even imagine what Elliott is thinking right now or how he's feeling. This has to be the worst day of his life. There's no way to bounce back from something like this. At least, not quickly."

"Um...hello? I get that you're in love with the guy and probably wishing you could just step into Tracy's shoes, but we've got bigger problems here," Lea reminded her. "We've got enough food here for almost 200 people and since there isn't going to be a reception, what are we supposed to do with all of it? And the cake? I spent days on that beast!"

"We don't know that there isn't going to be a reception. For all we know, runaway bride and creepy officiant could decide to roll with it and be the ones to get married today."

"I don't think that's going to happen. It would be really tacky for them to do that, don't you think?"

"Thank God we got paid before the ceremony, but... what if they put a stop on the check?"

Now she did roll her eyes and turned her head. "First of all, we have a contract. No one is stiffing us for the bill. We might not get the money today, but the law will be on our side. The worst-case scenario here is that we're going to be eating three hundred crab cakes and more because we don't have enough takeout containers for all this stuff."

"Okay, but..."

"I'm just giving them a few minutes to discuss before going out there and talking to them. I'm sure they're just trying to figure out what to do, as well. After all, it's not every day that your daughter walks out in the middle of her wedding like that. I doubt they had any idea or even considered the possibility of this happening." She paused. "I don't imagine this sort of thing happens very often."

"But maybe..."

Crossing her arms, Skye scanned the beautifully-decorated event room and shook her head. "Of course, they could just go on with the party and celebrate...something. It would be a shame to let it all go to waste. Or maybe the bride and the preacher really did run off to get married and this could be their reception."

"I thought we agreed he wasn't a preacher and that it would be tacky?" Leanna commented, seeming to calm down. From her spot beside Skye, she looked around the room too. "Although...if it meant we get paid and people get fed, who am I to judge? Someone's got to have a birthday or something, right? That would be a lot more palatable than substituting one groom for another."

Just the thought of it put a bad taste in Skye's mouth.

As if on cue, the parents of the bride walked in and she quickly excused herself. "Please be good news," she whispered to herself as she plastered a smile on her face. "Mr. and Mrs. Burrows, tell me what I can do for you."

For the next twenty minutes, it was extremely tense and Leanna joined her midway through to make sure everything was going to be okay. The Burrows' were visibly distraught by what their daughter had done and hated to be out the money for a reception that wasn't happening, but fortunately they weren't taking it out on Skye and the business.

"I'm not quite sure what the protocol is on something like this," Mr. Burrows said with a weary sigh. "It's not like Tracy to be this impulsive, but..."

"Skylar," Mrs. Burrows said with an equally tired tone. "What are our options?"

There was a question about event insurance–something Meet Me at the Altar did offer, but the family turned down–and it was painful to remind them of that. However, the insurance would have only applied if an act of God or nature caused the cancelation, not a runaway bride.

Is there such a thing as runaway bride insurance? Do we need to add that to the contracts?

They did try to haggle a discount, but Skye rejected it and was thankful Josie hadn't come out to see what was going on.

Either way, Mr. Burrows asked for all the food to be donated to the local homeless shelter.

Once they were out of the room, Skye and Leanna

sagged against each other with relief. "Oh, my goodness," Leanna said, pulling a chair away from one of the fully-set tables and sitting down. "That was rough."

Pulling up a chair to join her, Skye sat down with a weary sigh. "You can't blame them for trying to get a deal, but we still have to pay the staff and cover the cost of everything." Her head leaned back. "At least they were decent enough to want to donate the food. We need to make some calls and see who can take it and if there are any restrictions."

"I'm on it," Leanna said. "But I need to sit for a few minutes. This whole day has been exhausting."

"Tell me about it."

"I'm so happy you were still here. I don't know what I would have done if I had to handle this alone." She paused before glancing Skye's way. "And...why didn't you leave?"

"Morbid curiosity," she murmured. And rather than engage in more conversation, she simply closed her eyes and wondered what they should do next. They had to break down the room they'd just set up, load everything up in the truck and take it back to their warehouse-slash-office. It was going to be tedious, and they were still going to have to wash everything even though they didn't use it, but...health codes prevailed.

She had no doubt that everyone was going to want to talk about what happened and she hoped Josie didn't want to come and join in to help.

Everyone knew not to let Skye help because she had a reputation for being a bit of a klutz. And because of it, she had never worked in the food service industry–not in high school, not in college, just...never. Even thinking about it was enough to make her shudder.

The food, the mess, the noise, the risk of dropping a tray of food on someone...yeah, totally not her thing.

So when it was time to gather the crew and tell them how the rest of this day was going to go, they would already know she'd be the one directing, not helping.

And Skye would get to that in another few minutes. She just needed a little more time to let the events of the last few minutes really sink in. Beside her, Leanna let out a long breath and stood up.

"I'm going to go and call around about the donations. First, I'm going to feed the staff, and then we'll talk to them about how we're going to break down the room. Is that okay with you?"

"Absolutely. Thanks, Lea." Once her friend walked through the kitchen doors, Skye let out a long breath of her own and glanced around the room that looked so festive and yet would see no celebration today.

That's when her psychology-major mind kicked in.

What would make someone do what the officiant did? Why would he wait until the ceremony to profess his love like that? If he was close enough to Tracy and Elliott to volunteer to perform the service–if that was even the way it was–why not say something sooner? What has to be going through someone's mind to think that the actual ceremony was the proper time and place to make a declaration like that?

"I mean, for the love of it, wouldn't it have been better to go speak to the bride before she walked down the aisle?" she murmured as she reached over onto the table and picked up one of the place cards, absently studying it. With a flick of the wrist, she tossed it aside as anger simmered just below the surface.

What kind of woman can just walk away from the man

she is supposed to love and marry? How can a few words from some...some...guy, make her issue a flimsy apology before she runs off? Did she even love Elliott at all or was this wedding an excuse to get away from her parents or some other kind of cry for help?

"I hate people like that," she said, touching a silk sunflower in one of the centerpieces. "Did she even give poor Elliott more than a cursory thought before turning and running?" She paused. "All I can say is good luck to the new groom, because if she was heartless enough to walk away from one man, she more than likely won't have any problem walking away from you."

"Did you say something, Skye?" one of the servers said as she walked by.

"What? Oh...um, sorry. Talking to myself." And with a smile, she stood and walked toward the back of the room and gazed longingly at the exit. While Skye knew Leanna would totally be fine if she left now, it just didn't sit right with her to dump everything on other people. There was still no sign of Josie and this was something they'd never had to deal with before so she'd suck it up and do her job because...well, just because.

It was a toss-up whether to go right to the kitchen or to head down the hall to the groom's suite and see what was going on. No one would question her being there now. She and Josie had been best friends since the sixth grade and she was practically family. There had been a long line of people who followed after Elliott once he made his exit and she doubted he'd even notice if one more person showed up to offer him...what? Advice? Condolences? What was the proper etiquette for someone getting left at the altar?

That's when it hit her how wrong it was for her to go back there. To know that all his family and friends just witnessed what was probably the lowest point in his life... she now wanted to go and shoo them all away. He must have felt like he was punched in the gut and now had an audience around him when he probably wanted to be alone. She couldn't imagine that he had seen this coming.

But Tyler *was* warning him...

Still, even if it wasn't Elliott, no one deserved to have something like this happen to them–especially when they're good and decent, like Elliott. He was one of the good ones, and she'd like nothing more than to get five minutes alone with Tracy to put her in her place. After all, how could she possibly look at such a sweet face and then leave him?

And Elliott had a really sweet face.

A kind face.

Sandy brown hair, gray-blue eyes, and black-rimmed glasses...he had kind of a sexy geek vibe about him.

And that was just the tip of the iceberg. Elliott Sullivan was the total package and didn't deserve to be humiliated like this.

The poor guy...

Wistfully, Skye looked around the room one last time and felt an overwhelming sense of sadness that no one was going to enjoy the beautiful décor and the food or celebrate the union of two people.

It was a little heartbreaking.

And as she made her way toward the kitchen, she wished someone would come out and give her an update so she could know if Elliott was okay.

"An embargo?"

"Yup."

"But doesn't that normally deal with government or trading goods or..."

"Stop being so literal, Elliott!" his father cried out before taking a moment to compose himself. "All I'm saying is that maybe...enough is enough. For right now, at least."

Scanning the worried faces staring at him, Elliott had to wonder how long they had all been waiting to have this kind of talk with him.

"But...Dad..."

Holding up a hand to stop him, Martin Sullivan stood tall and gave his son the stance that never failed to put him in his place. "Son, we have watched you valiantly search for that perfect someone for years. You wear your heart on your sleeve and there was a time when it was admirable and sweet. But even you have to admit that something just isn't working here."

Sighing, he nodded. Why deny it?

"All we're saying is that it's time for you to take a step back and maybe re-evaluate some things in your life."

His eyes instantly went to his mother. She was always his biggest champion–his biggest supporter and the one who always believed in him. She looked so pretty in the plum-colored gown she had finally decided on. For months she searched and conducted surveys in the family to help her pick. They had all celebrated her decision and now look where they were–in a tiny groom's suite celebrating nothing. He could see the weariness in her eyes–the sadness.

The pity.

Damn.

"So what exactly is it you're saying here, Dad?" he asked, rubbing a hand over his face and wishing he could simply be alone. Having so many witnesses to his humiliation certainly wasn't helping anything right now. And who thought it was okay for his entire extended family to come in here?

His mother was the one who responded, however. "Elliott, you need some time where you aren't thinking about being in a relationship. A little time where you focus on yourself and realize it's okay to be alone."

Seriously?

"Oh, I'm pretty sure I'm going to be focused on being alone right now, Mom," he said wearily. "As a matter of fact, I can guarantee when I get home later, it will be blazingly obvious that I'm alone."

"Again, you're being too literal," his father said, crouching down in front of him as if Elliott were a child. "Your whole life, you've been searching for someone to be with–your other half–and because of that I don't think you truly know yourself or how to be alone. You've got this vision of who you would be as part of a pair. I think it's time for you to figure out who you are as just yourself."

But Elliott already knew the answer to that.

Lonely.

"I get what you're saying, Dad. I do. But being alone isn't all it's cracked up to be. Trust me."

"Maybe you should take up a hobby!" his aunt Ruth chimed in. She was eighty-eight and had hair as yellow as the sunflowers in the centerpieces and always seemed to have something to say.

Like now.

"Um..."

"Maybe you can take up yoga or learn origami!" she suggested.

"Aunt Ruth, I don't really think origami..."

"I know I always adore getting one of those little paper creatures," she interrupted. "I once had a friend who made me an origami frog that could actually leap!" She laughed softly. "It was such a beautiful little frog. So sweet."

Groaning, Elliott was about to respond when someone else spoke up.

"No, he needs something a little manlier–like knife making or glass blowing!" his sister Josie called out and when he looked up at her, she winked and he knew she was trying to lighten the mood.

"Don't be ridiculous," someone else called out. "Elliott's not the kind of guy who's going to build weapons. He needs something that's a little more his speed–maybe bird-watching or model train building?"

Okay, now he wanted to know who said that! Jumping to his feet, he scanned the group and saw his cousin Nick was the smartass. "Model trains? Seriously?"

All his cousin did was smirk.

Next thing he knew, everyone was throwing out suggestions–most of them equally ridiculous–so he stood up on his chair, stuck his fingers in his mouth, and whistled as loud as he could until the room went silent. With fifty pairs of eyes on him, his shoulders sagged.

"Look, I appreciate all of you and how you're looking out for my best interests here, but...this is just all a bit much to think about right now." Stepping down, he did his best to put a smile on his face as he turned toward his parents. "I get what you're saying, and I promise to think about it."

That should have been it.

But it wasn't.

Clearly, there were some strong feelings about what was going to happen next.

"I'm sorry, Elliott, but we're all in agreement here," his father said sternly. "You are not allowed to date, get involved with, or ask anyone to marry you for at least a year."

"*Not allowed*?" he cried. "Are you serious?"

"As a heart attack."

Doing his best to remain calm, Elliott tried to reason with him. "Dad, I am a grown man. You can't just...forbid me from dating! Now I'll admit that I am going to need some time to move on, but..."

"A year, Elliott," his mother said. "You've tried things your way and it hasn't worked out for you. Maybe take some advice from others who have had...let's just say...more success in their relationships. I think we know what we're talking about."

And then fifty heads seemed to nod in unison.

Damn them.

"We are all actively committed to making sure you stick to this," his father continued. "So plan on seeing a lot of us– all of us–over the next year. We're doing this for your own good." He placed a hand on Elliott's shoulder. "Because we love you and we don't want to see you get hurt again."

"Maybe you should get a dog? Or some fish?" Aunt Ruth called out.

He couldn't hold back the sigh. There was no way he was going to win this argument right now, so rather than try, he simply thanked everyone for coming out and said he needed to be alone.

Amazingly enough, they all listened and walked out of the room together after hugging and kissing him goodbye. Josie was the last one to leave and she hugged him extra hard. "I'm so sorry this happened." When she pulled back, she gave him a weak smile. "I'm here for you if you need to talk." They were only eleven months apart and more like twins than anything, and he always turned to her for support but right now, he seriously just wanted to be alone.

When it was down to just Tyler in the room, Elliott sat back down.

"Man, that was...intense," he murmured.

"Which part?" Tyler joked, sitting beside him. "Seriously, you okay?"

He shrugged. "I'm still a little shell-shocked."

"I'm so sorry, Elliott. Really. Now I feel even worse about the things I said before the ceremony. Although, if you think about it..."

"Not the time for that," he quickly interrupted. Because...yeah. He'd already thought about it.

They sat in silence for several minutes before Tyler spoke again. "C'mon, let's get out of here. We'll go grab a beer and a burger and just chill. What do you say?"

It sounded good, but...

"I appreciate it, but I really just want to go home and... be. Rain check?"

"Yeah. Sure. I'll drive you home."

Right. Because he didn't have his car here because he and Tracy were supposed to be taking a limo to the airport later to go on their honeymoon to Belize.

Daniel was probably buying himself a ticket and packing his suitcase right now.

The bastard.

Together, they walked out of the room and Elliott noticed the catering staff scurrying around cleaning up the room. Hopefully they all got paid and would be happy to be able to go home early rather than hanging out all day serving wedding guests.

Then he wondered how much the average server made. Did they get paid by the hour? By the gig? Were they getting shorted on their pay since there wasn't a reception? His mind was spiraling but at least he wasn't simply thinking of himself right now.

Unlike some people...

Damn Tracy and Mr. *GQ*.

No one made eye contact with him and he wasn't offended. The last thing he wanted was more sympathetic glances. He had a feeling he'd be seeing an abundance of them in the coming days and weeks so if he could avoid a few right now, he'd take it. When they were outside by Tyler's car, Elliott stopped.

"You know what? I think I left my phone back in the suite."

"Want me to go grab it for you?"

But Elliott waved him off. "You go ahead. I'll go grab it and I think I'm gonna just walk around for a while and then grab an Uber or something. Or maybe ask Josie for a ride. I'm sure she's going to hang around with her staff for a while."

"Dude, don't just wander around the city in your tux. That's just sad."

"Yeah, well...kind of fitting, don't you think?"

"Don't do this," Tyler pled. "Get your phone and we'll get out of here. I hate thinking of you being alone right now. It's not good for you."

"Maybe not, but honestly, it's what I need. I'll call you tomorrow, okay?"

With a silent nod, Tyler waved and climbed into his car, and for the first time in over an hour, he felt like he could breathe.

Pulling his tie from around his neck, he stuffed it in his pocket and opened the top button of his shirt before heading back into the catering hall. Making his way across the event space, he wondered if this kind of thing had ever happened before to anyone else. He was fairly certain it had, but...he kind of wished he had some idea of what he was supposed to do or how he was supposed to feel. Was there a support group he could join to find out what he should be doing next?

Other than being forced into an embargo.

He snorted at the thought. *Embargo*. It was ridiculous. No one could honestly expect him to just change who he was and stop wanting to be involved with a woman for a year, could they? Of course, there was some merit to the idea–after all, it wouldn't be the *worst* thing in the world to take on a new hobby or find something new to do. If anything, it would be a great way to meet someone new.

"Ugh...just stop," he muttered, spotting someone walking into the groom's suite. He saw the swish of a long, blonde ponytail and immediately knew it was Skylar. She was probably just doing her job–cleaning up another spot after an event.

When he stepped into the doorway, he stopped in his tracks. She wasn't cleaning up.

She was looking through his phone! Seriously, could this day just stop already??

Storming into the room, he yelled, "What the hell, Skylar?" and then watched in horror as the phone slipped from her hand and crashed to the floor.

She gasped.

Elliott froze.

And he heard the distinct sound of glass breaking.

Why didn't I get the screen protector when the salesman told me to?!

Rushing across the room, he crouched down and went

to pick up the phone. Unfortunately, so did she, and their heads crashed together.

"Ow!"

"Dammit!"

Steadying himself, Elliott reached out to do the same for her. With his hand on her arm, he asked, "Are you okay?"

Rubbing a hand over her forehead, she nodded. "Yeah. Sorry."

Releasing her, he picked up his phone and stood before extending a hand to her again. Once she was on her feet, he looked at her with annoyance, then down at his phone.

And its cracked screen.

"I am *so* sorry," she said breathlessly. "I was cleaning up in here and saw the phone and was trying to see if I could tell who it belonged to. I swear I was going to come out and try to find you!"

It sounded plausible, but he wasn't in a particularly trusting mood right now. He knew he was seconds away from a complete breakdown and decided to just take his busted phone and go. He'd made it all of three steps before she spoke.

"Hey, I said I was sorry." And then she was standing in front of him looking sincere. "Please, I'll even pay to replace it, Elliott."

All he could do was stare.

"I'm serious," she went on, as if sensing that he was having a hard time believing what she was saying. "I mean, it was an accident, but I could have been more careful. I know I tend to be a klutz sometimes and I try to avoid handling things that aren't mine, so..."

"It's fine, Skye. Really. I just want to go." He made it two steps farther before she called out to him again.

"And I'm sorry about what happened out there. I can't

imagine how you're feeling, but...at least you were surrounded by so many people who care about you."

"Yeah. Lucky me." And then he stepped around her and started toward the door again.

And she was in front of him in the blink of an eye.

"Look, I get it. You're having a crappy day."

"Ya think?" he asked, hating his own snarky tone.

"But...let me be the one person today who maybe does the right thing for you," she said softly and damn if her big brown eyes didn't convince him. "I didn't mean to break your phone and I'm sorry that it all happened the way it did. I'm sure this is like the proverbial straw that broke the camel's back for you right now."

"Something like that."

"So...can I please fix your phone? Or replace it? It would really make me feel better."

"I don't see why," he commented. "It was an accident. If I had been paying more attention, I wouldn't have left it in here. So really, it's okay. You're not responsible. I'll take care of it."

"But..."

This time Elliott stood a little taller and did his best to sound firm. "We're good." And then he stepped around her and finally–*finally!*–walked out the door. He avoided talking to anyone and breathed a sigh of relief when he was outside and no one was talking to him. Looking around, he wondered where he should go and what he should do and... nothing came to him. Going home seemed like the obvious choice, but the thought of being alone was suddenly beyond unappealing. He could walk around but...Tyler was right; walking around the city in his tux just seemed a bit pathetic.

"So now what?" With a weary sigh, he found himself standing on the sidewalk watching the traffic speed by.

Then he continued to stand there and lost all track of time–not that it mattered; he had nowhere to go and no one was waiting for him.

And that was the way it was going to be for at least the next year, thanks to his family.

CHAPTER 3

I never fall in love, because everything that falls breaks.

UNKNOWN

"You broke his phone?" Josie cried.

"I broke his phone."

"What is wrong with you? How could you do something like that? Hasn't the poor guy been through enough?"

Groaning, Skye rubbed her temples and willed herself not to lose her patience. "It wasn't like I did it on purpose! I went to clean up the room, saw the phone, and knew it had to belong to him. I had just seen him walk out a few minutes earlier, and I figured I'd slip it into my pocket and go after him."

"So why didn't you?"

"Because he came back first, yelled, and scared the crap out of me! I dropped it! It was an accident, for crying out loud! It wasn't like I found the phone and deliberately smashed it on the ground. Sheesh. Give me a little credit here."

Josie studied her for a long moment. "Okay, sorry. Everything is just…I'm frazzled, that's all. I still can't believe this all happened." She sighed. "And I'm doubly stressing out because not only was this a job for us but this was my brother's wedding! The look on his face was just…"

"I'm sure," Skye gently interrupted because she didn't even want to think about it. She had seen it and it broke her heart.

"And then you go and break his phone…"

"Okay, for the record, it's not like I dropped the cake and ruined the wedding. This party had derailed way before I dropped Elliott's phone."

"Still, you certainly didn't help matters."

Yeah, she knew that and still felt wildly awful about it. If he had simply let her pay to fix or replace his phone, she knew she would have felt much better–less guilty. The last thing she wanted was to be the reason Elliott had even more negative thoughts about this day.

And towards her.

Hopefully she hadn't pushed him over the edge…

Although, in the grand scheme of things, a busted phone was nothing compared to getting dumped at the altar.

"Skye?"

"Hmm?"

"Look, I'm sorry I snapped. I'm just worried about my brother and being that I can't snap at Tracy, I took it out on you." She paused. "I'm going to go change out of this dress and then help with getting everything in order here."

All she could do was nod.

"But I need you to do me a favor."

"Of course. Anything."

"Here," Josie said, thrusting a large paper shopping bag into her hands.

"What's this?"

"This is enough meals for a few days. For Elliott."

She eyed the bag suspiciously. "O-kay..."

"He said he wanted to be alone, and he seemed annoyed with the family after the whole embargo thing..."

"The what?"

Josie then explained what went down in the groom's suite and Skye felt her jaw drop and her eyes go wide. "It's for his own good," she explained. "He'll realize that in the long run."

There were no words and yet a million thoughts raced through her mind. "That just seems a little..."

"Drastic? Yeah, I know. But we all talked about this when he and Tracy first got engaged. I honestly thought we were never going to have to use it, but...here we are."

Again, her psychology-degree mind was going wild but there was no way she was going to get into it with Josie.

Not today anyway.

"And why are you giving me his doggie bag?"

"Like I said, family members are probably the last people he wants to see. But you? You're neutral and it won't bother him if you show up and give him a bag of food. We both know he's probably not going to want to cook for himself, and considering he should be heading off on his honeymoon, I greatly doubt he even has food in his house."

"There's always takeout..."

"Sure, but this way I can feel good knowing he's at least going to have a few homemade meals. There's crab cakes, champagne chicken, a couple of lamb chops, mashed potatoes, some baby quiche bites, and a plate of shrimp. All his favorites."

"Jos, do you really think he wants food from the wedding reception? Don't you think that's going to be a little strange? Plus, this food should be going to the shelter," she protested, pushing the bag back.

"Oh, please! That family owes my brother for what their heartless daughter did to him! If I thought he had room, I'd send all the food to him!"

"It was a good menu..."

Before she knew it, another bag was thrust into her arms. "And a bag for you since you're doing me a favor."

"Okay, but let me help with the cleanup and..."

"You've already broken a phone," Josie said with a hint of a grin. "Besides, I have a lot of rage to get out so I am more than happy to stay and bark orders at everyone."

"Yeah, I'm not so sure that's a good thing."

"I promise not to make anyone cry," she promised. "Please just go and check on Elliott and text me later, okay?"

It was the last thing she wanted to do, but how could she say no without alerting her friend to there being so much more to the whole situation? Leanna was the only one who knew about her feelings and telling Josie certainly wouldn't help.

Especially now that there was an embargo in play.

Which was utterly ridiculous.

Once she had her things, Skye waved to the servers she passed on her way out and once she stepped outside, she wondered how she was going to handle all of this. Elliott was clearly annoyed with her and she probably wasn't going to be any more welcome than his family. Hopefully she could just hand him the bag and go without upsetting him even more.

"I had *one* chance to be the one to maybe make him feel better, and instead I made things worse," she murmured as she walked toward her car.

Halfway across the parking lot, she froze.

Elliott was standing on the sidewalk looking more than a little lost.

Hanging her head, she knew there was no way she could just get in her car and go. How was it possible his family and friends just left him here? She glanced over her shoulder toward the building and considered going to get Josie, but immediately reconsidered.

"What have I gotten myself into?" she wondered as she made her way toward him. If he heard her approach, he didn't let on. When she was beside him, she asked, "Are you waiting for a ride?"

Glancing at her, he held up his phone. "That was the plan, but I can't get the app to work. So I was just trying to figure out what my plan B should be."

Hanging her head, Skye knew she was in for a little more self-torture. "C'mon. Let me give you a ride."

He may not have said any words, but his face said it all.

Laughing softly, she said, "I'm being serious, El. Josie asked me to bring you some food so you were going to be seeing me anyway. Might as well let me do this for you or I'll just show up at your place later." When he didn't respond, she rambled on. "And really, is that what you want? You could be settled in and all cozy and comfortable and then I'll come banging on the door–probably trip and hurt myself in some way–and then spill all this food on your floor. And with my luck, you'll have white carpet or something and the only thing that will spill will have a red sauce." She let out a long breath. "Then you'll have to be reminded of me every single time you walk in or out your front door because...you know...red sauce stains. Is that really what you want?"

And then the most amazing thing happened.

He laughed.

An honest-to-goodness, genuine laugh.

And for the first time all day, Skye had hope–for both of them.

"So what do you say?" She motioned back toward the parking lot. "Can I give you a ride?"

Nodding, he turned to follow her.

"Let me take the bags," he said, and when she turned to hand them to him, their hands brushed and it was the first time she had ever touched him. His skin was warm and a little rough and it felt really good.

She murmured a thanks to him and did her best not to make eye contact. They walked in companionable silence until they reached her sporty little Hyundai SUV. Using her key fob, Skye unlocked the doors and watched as he put the bags in the back seat before climbing in. Once she was seated, she noticed Elliott simply sitting and looking down at his hands.

It took her less than five seconds to realize she needed to say something.

"Can I say something?" she asked, even though she knew she was going to talk no matter what.

He shrugged.

"Did you have any idea that this guy–you know, the officiant guy–had feelings for Tracy?"

His eyes went wide when he looked at her and sputtered for a moment before responding. "That's more of a question than an observation."

"Who said I was going to make an observation?"

"It was kind of implied. You asked if you could say something, not ask something. Say implied an observation."

She never knew he was quite so literal.

"Okay, fine. Hey, Elliott, can I *ask* you something?"

"Not with that attitude." With a snort of disgust, he turned his attention out the window.

Luckily, she wasn't deterred. Sure, he may resent the question right now, but she knew he needed to talk about what happened today.

Whether he realized it or not.

Turning the car on, she adjusted the air before twisting in her seat to face him and repeated the question. "You can't ignore the situation, Elliott. The fact is, I'm not going to be the only person to ask about this. Why not start talking about it? What have you got to lose?"

His head snapped around and he winced. "I don't see where this is any of your business. If you ask me, it's a little macabre to want to know–like morbid curiosity–and frankly, I'm offended."

Nice speech, she thought, but again, she wasn't deterred.

"I'd say that response will work a couple of times," she said levelly. "It's a good distraction and some people will pull back and possibly apologize, but I'm here to tell you, you need to talk about this."

Another snort. "No, I really don't. And certainly not with you."

"Why? What's wrong with me?"

"Other than the fact that you're my sister's best friend and you're probably going to run back and tell her everything I said? Oh, and maybe because you have no idea what you're talking about? Or maybe..."

"Actually, I am the perfect person for you to talk to right now," she countered.

Clearly Elliott was a snorter–something else she never knew–because it was the third time he had that initial response to something she said. "Now this I've got to hear."

"I'm kind of a neutral party," she explained. "I have no real connection to you…"

"Josie's your best friend…

"Or your fiancée…"

"Ex-fiancée," he corrected.

"Right. Ex," she agreed. "So you can say whatever it is that you're feeling and I'm not going to tell you you're wrong or that you should have seen this or that. I'm just someone who is willing to sit here and listen to you."

"I have friends who can do that," he grumbled, but she could tell he wasn't nearly as offended by her offer as he was a minute ago.

"I'm sure you do. But at some point, someone's going to try to tell you that you should have seen this coming or that they did and tried to warn you or…"

"Were you listening to my conversation with Tyler before the wedding?" he asked incredulously.

"What?! No!"

"Then why would you say that?"

"Say what?"

"About someone trying to warn me…"

"*Was* he trying to warn you?" she countered and quickly realized this was getting them nowhere. Now he was going to be defensive and honestly, that was the last thing she wanted.

"Oh, my God! You sound like a damn psychiatrist! Can we please just go?" he asked. "Had I known accepting a ride was going to involve a therapy session…"

"Who said this was a therapy session?" she asked, feeling a little defensive herself. If anything, she was doing her best to make this *not* feel like a therapy session! "I'm just trying to help, that's all."

"Well don't," he grumbled. "I just...maybe drop me off at the Verizon store or something so I can replace my phone."

"You sure you want to do that? While you're all...you know...in a tux?"

Looking down at himself, he shook his head and muttered a curse. "Can you just seriously give me a break here, Skye?"

"Fine. But know this–if we go to the Verizon store, I'm coming in with you and I'll tell the salespeople that I'm paying for the repair or the replacement or whatever it is that you're going to do. Are you prepared for that? Huh?"

He groaned.

"I have a counteroffer for you," she said with a smile.

"Oh good..."

"Let's go grab something to eat. My treat."

"Skylar..."

"Well, we do have those doggie bags, compliments of Josie. But I'm not sure you want any of it."

"I did help plan the menu," he said begrudgingly.

And she felt a small flutter in her tummy at his words. He was opening up a little. "Oh yeah? What were your choices?"

He shrugged. "The crab cakes."

"Got some."

He studied her for a moment. "The lamb chops."

"Got some of them too."

Twisting slightly in his seat, he eyed the bag in the back. "And the mashed potatoes."

"Josie assured me they were in there too. Hopefully she put some in my bag..."

"How much food did she give you?" he asked with a hint of a smile.

"Let's just say she made sure you have enough for a few meals." She shook her head and laughed. "My bag doesn't look nearly as full, so..."

He nodded. "What else is in there?"

"Some shrimp, quiche bites, and the chicken. What do you think?"

"I think I don't like mushrooms and the chicken has mushrooms." His smile grew.

"Tell you what, you can have my lamb if she gave me any and you can give me the chicken and mushrooms. What do you say? We can go eat at your place or just drive to the nearest park and do this picnic style!"

"You got any plates or silverware?"

"Oh. I didn't think of that." She paused. "So...shall I drive you home and we can continue this conversation?"

For a minute, she simply held her breath because she knew she was pushing–even though she had told herself not to. The poor guy probably just wanted to be alone and here she was all up in his business. In her defense, however, she was driving him home and bringing him food, so that had to count for something, right?

"What do you say, Elliott?" she nudged, hoping she sounded casual.

He raked a hand through his hair and let out a low, husky laugh. "I can't believe I'm saying this, but...sure. Why not? It's not like things could get any worse for me, right?"

"Um...wow. That was a little hurtful."

His eyes went wide. "What? Oh, sorry. I didn't mean..."

Laughing, she playfully swatted at him before straightening in her seat. "Stop! I'm just teasing–trying to lighten the mood. For all you know, this could be the exact thing you need today! Someone to just hang out with." She backed out of the parking spot. "We could talk about what went down today–or not. Maybe play some video games–if that's what you're into. Or maybe we can just eat and wish each other a nice life. It's up to you."

He laughed again. "Are you sure? Because you've kind of been up in my business since the phone incident."

"If you had just let me fix it..."

"Yeah, yeah, yeah. I know. This is my punishment."

"I don't think anyone's ever referred to me quite like that, but...whatever."

"Skye?"

"Yeah?"

"Can you please just drive?" he asked, resting his head back against the seat.

"Sure."

"So where was the mother of the bride?"

"Well, when we found her, she was...shall we say...in a very compromising position with the best man!"

"No! At her daughter's wedding?"

"At the church!"

Elliott laughed hard and had to admit, Skye was doing a great job of keeping him entertained. She had been telling him wedding horror stories–which really should have been the last thing he wanted to hear–but listening to her made him realize he wasn't alone.

And who knew there was so much drama in the wedding world?

They had polished off quite a bit of the food and he was feeling pretty good, all things considered. Once they had gotten back to his house, Elliott changed out of his tux and Skye pulled her gym bag from the car and changed into yoga pants and an oversized t-shirt. They were both comfortable and laughing and for a day that was incredibly crappy, right now things didn't seem quite so bleak.

Still...he knew this was all a great distraction, and eventually he was going to have to be alone to process everything. So when all their food was eaten or put away and the conversation started to slow down, he looked over at Skye and smiled.

"Thanks for drawing the short straw today."

She looked at him oddly. "Um...what?"

"You know, Josie sending you here to check on me. I appreciate it. Honestly, I don't think I could have dealt with my family."

"Oh, well...you're welcome." The silence was slightly awkward, but they seemed to be on the same page. Standing, she went and got her purse and her gym bag and smiled at him. "I guess I'll get going then. Is there anything else you need?"

Sliding his hands into his pockets, Elliott shook his head. "I'm going to be fine." Then he let out a mirthless laugh. "Eventually."

The instant the word was out of his mouth, he knew his mistake. Skylar's face went from serene to sad–or pity, take your pick–and as much as he hated it, he was smart enough to know he needed to get used to it. Everyone he knew was going to be looking at him like that for the foreseeable future.

"Skye..."

The smile was back on her face and he appreciated her

restraint from offering him pointless words of encouragement. "If you'd like, I'll tell your sister that you're fine and
well-fed, and to wait for your call." Then she leaned in a
little closer as if telling him a secret. "You know, otherwise
she'll be calling you every day to check on you." She walked
over to the door and looked over her shoulder at him and he
could tell she wanted to say more, but simply went with,
"Take care of yourself, Elliott," before leaving.

He stared at the closed door for a solid minute before he
allowed himself to turn around and walk over to the sofa.
Collapsing down on it, he let out a long, weary breath. Now
what? Skye coming home with him was definitely a blessing, and for all his carrying on about wanting to be alone, he
already hated it. Glancing at his watch, he saw it was just
after eight. Right now, they would be cutting the cake at the
reception. By nine, he and Tracy were supposed to head out
to the hotel near the airport for their wedding night. And at
eight tomorrow morning, they'd be leaving on their
honeymoon.

Instead, Tracy was going to be sunning herself with
Daniel, and Elliott was stuck eating leftovers and sleeping
alone in his own bed.

It took a few minutes of shifting around for him to get
comfortable and his eyes closed as his mind seemed to be in
overdrive with thoughts of what his future held. Just
thinking about the things his father and the rest of his
family said to him and what they expected of him for the
next year was enough to overwhelm him.

An embargo.

Who does that?

Who even *thinks* like that?

But the sad reality was that he had been so hyper-
focused on pursuing what he wanted for himself with his

whole heart, that he didn't realize how that looked to other people.

Not that it should matter; it was his life, not theirs. But clearly he had hit a point where everyone thought they knew better and...maybe they did.

Maybe it was time to throw in the towel and just give up and get used to being single forever. Hell, some guys actually wanted that.

He just never thought he'd be one of them.

"Well, this is going to suck," he murmured.

There was his job to keep him busy, and he did have a lot of close friends he knew he could turn to and hang out with to keep his mind off of his crappy life, but if any of them felt like Tyler had, it was going to be a long time before he felt comfortable hanging out with them.

"And I'm back to being alone."

Yeah, things weren't looking particularly good at the moment and he wished he knew when it was going to change. There was no way he could simply stay cocooned in his house indefinitely just to avoid the lectures or *I told you so*'s. They were going to happen no matter what and the sad part was, even if any of them had spoken up sooner–like before today's wedding massacre–Elliott knew he wouldn't have listened. He still would have pushed for this wedding because he thought he knew better.

How messed up was that?

"I should seriously get therapy."

Then a thought hit him–Skylar. While not a practicing therapist, she did have a psychology degree and talking with her today once they got here to his house, had helped him to feel a little better. Maybe she would be open to meeting with him once a week just to hang out and talk? It would be less intimidating than finding a therapist and having to admit to a stranger how pathetic he was. Considering he and Skye had known each other for years and she knew his family dynamics, he wouldn't have to go through the whole process of explaining it to someone. She knew just enough that they could simply jump in and start talking.

The idea definitely had merit.

The big question was could she keep what was said between them just between them and not go back and tell his sister? That was definitely something to think about. Right now, he'd have to hope that she could and the next few days would really be the first test. If his sister called–or anyone in his family–and repeated anything specific he and Skylar talked about, then he'd know he couldn't trust her.

But if everyone behaved?

Then he was definitely going to reach out.

Skylar was safe–a friend. No one was going to condemn him for hanging out with her. There was no way she was included in the embargo, so...

All around, spending some time with her was going to be a good thing.

CHAPTER 4

Sometimes the person you fall for isn't ready to catch you.

UNKNOWN

"Why would you send Skylar to go home with your brother?" Skye heard Mrs. Sullivan yelling at Josie on Monday morning as she walked into the office.

"Mom, relax. It's just Skye. She doesn't count in the whole embargo thing. She's family."

"She is a single woman and you know how your brother is! Why would you throw temptation right there in his path?"

Skye stopped in her tracks and held her breath. No one had seen or heard her come in, and she desperately wanted to know where this conversation was going.

"It's not like that, Mom," Josie patiently explained. "Seriously, Skye looks at Elliott like a brother and I'm sure he looks at her like a sister. He clearly didn't want any of us checking on him and I knew I could trust her to make sure he was okay. This isn't a bad thing."

"I don't know. I'm afraid he's going to be looking for a rebound no matter what we all said to him."

Josie was quiet for a moment. "It's too soon for that. Even for Elliott. Besides, it was one dinner. They don't ever see each other except when he stops by here and I have a feeling it's going to be a while before he wants to come anywhere near this place."

It actually took an entire month before Skye saw Elliott again.

That wasn't exactly unusual, but she had hoped to see him again after she'd driven him home and had dinner with him after the whole wedding fiasco. Josie had kept her up to date on how he was doing, but only briefly, and there was no way she could push for more information because her friend would have eventually gotten suspicious.

So here she was on a Wednesday evening still at the Meet Me at the Altar office when Elliott walked in.

Her heart skipped a beat before it started to race at the mere sight of him.

I have it so bad…

She looked up and smiled at him but didn't attempt to stand. Undoubtedly she'd trip or do something stupid, and it was just safer to have the desk between them. "Hey, Elliott!" she said cheerily. "What brings you here?"

He was dressed like he'd just left work, in navy trousers and a white button-down shirt with the sleeves rolled up to his elbows. His forearms were tanned and had just a light smattering of hair and add that to his large hands and you had…

Arm porn.

Seriously, I have it so bad...

"Is Josie around?" he asked from where he stood in the doorway, and Skye felt mildly disappointed. Of course he'd be here to see his sister...

"Oh, sorry. She's gone for the day. I'm sure you can call her. I think she was going straight home. Maybe you can catch her there."

Then he took a tentative step into the office. "Actually, I'm here to see you, but I wanted to make sure she wasn't here first."

Skye was pretty sure her lips were moving, but no words were coming out.

He walked fully into the room and sat down in one of the upholstered chairs directly in front of her desk. "So, how are you?"

"I...I'm good," she stammered and cursed the silly tremble in her voice. "Good. And you?"

He shrugged. "I'm doing okay. Every day gets a little better, so...I can't really complain."

"Good. That's good," she said and then groaned. "I swear I know more words than this."

His smile was sweet and completely disarming. He'd never directed that smile at her before and her tummy fluttered and she knew she needed to pull herself together because she was looking more and more like an idiot.

"So what can I do for you?"

"When we last spoke, you told me about getting your degree in psychology," he began slowly. "And I was curious if you ever considered using that degree."

Okay, that was not at all what she was expecting, and it seemed like a really odd question. "You mean like taking on patients?"

Nodding, he said, "Yes, exactly like that."

"Um...not really. Plus, I never went back for my master's or anything. I'm not even sure I could take on patients." Then she let out a low laugh. "Although, I feel like I'm a therapist to my friends and family sometimes. Everyone is always looking for someone to talk to about one problem or another, and I'm always ready to listen."

He nodded again and seemed to consider his words. "How would you feel about taking on another friend?"

Her eyes went wide, her jaw dropped, and for a moment, Skye thought she was having a stroke. He couldn't be serious, could he? Or maybe he wasn't talking about himself. Maybe there was someone else he was referring to and she was jumping to conclusions.

What if it's Tracy? Did he honestly think she'd want to talk to his mean girl of an ex? What is wrong with him? Why would he ask that of her? It was ridiculous and rude and...

"Um...Skye?"

"Hmm?"

"I think I lost you there for a minute. You sort of zoned out."

"Oh, right," she said, smoothing a hand over her ponytail. It was a nervous move she did and she knew that, but... sometimes it helped her to take a moment. "Sorry. So who would you like me to talk to?"

"Me."

"What?"

He nodded yet again. "Me. I'd like to know if you would possibly consider informally talking with me and helping me figure out what is wrong with me since I keep making these terrible decisions with my personal life." Then he shook his head. "And...I'm kind of in an angry phase and I already know that can't be good."

Swallowing hard, Skye tried to think of all the reasons why this was a bad idea–a terrible idea–the *worst* idea. But the selfish part of her–the part that genuinely cared about this man–really wanted to help him.

Even if it meant torturing herself.

But...

"Elliott, I'm not sure I'm the right person for this."

"The day of my wedding you told me you were the perfect person for this," he challenged with a small smile.

Grimacing, she murmured, "Oh, you remembered that, huh?"

And when he let out a low chuckle, Skye knew she was in trouble.

"Yeah, I remembered."

For a minute, all she could do was stare at him because she had no idea what to say. It was one thing to offer to talk to him the day of the wedding; it was obviously the right thing to do. But a month later, what could she possibly say? And did she really want to know why he found it so easy to fall in love?

With everyone except me?

Okay, yeah. She was definitely going to have to get over that one because there was no way she could possibly sit and talk with him–help him–if she only focused on her own feelings of rejection.

"Listen, Elliott," she began carefully, "I really wish I could help you, but...I don't think it's a good idea."

His expression turned somber and it felt like she had kicked a puppy. "May I ask why?"

Ugh...where do I even begin?

Fidgeting in her seat, she frantically searched for the right excuse. "For starters, I'm not a therapist. I may have gone to school for psychology, but that doesn't mean I'm qualified to help you. Plus, you're my best friend's brother and that's definitely a conflict of interest."

"You said that didn't matter."

"Well, that day it really didn't. I wasn't talking with you as a therapist. We were talking as friends and...I don't know...this just seems like something you really need a professional for."

He studied her for a long moment before leaning forward in his chair. "Here's the thing, Skylar, I don't want to sit and talk to a professional. It's embarrassing enough sitting and talking to you about this."

"You're embarrassed?"

He nodded.

"Why? We've known each other for years! If anything, talking to a stranger would probably be a lot easier."

"I disagree. I don't want to have to explain my entire family dynamic to a stranger and waste time. You know all the players involved and it will make this whole therapy thing–for lack of a better word–go much faster."

"Elliott, therapy isn't about getting things done faster. It takes time to delve into the human psyche. You need to be willing to put in the work and peel back the layers and..."

"My family put an embargo on me!" he blurted out.

"Um...yeah," she replied quietly. "I heard."

In that moment, he looked utterly defeated. He leaned back and then slouched slightly in his seat, raking a hand through his hair. And when he looked up at her, she saw so much pain there. "I'm a joke to my family and friends, Skye. Hell, just thinking about it pisses me off. I have a year to figure some things out and...please. I just need someone to cut me a break and help me."

She knew she was going to regret this.

And she knew she was going to end up needing to see a therapist herself.

But even if she didn't factor in her feelings for Elliott, she couldn't stand to see someone hurting and not try to help. So…

"I'll do it," she said quietly.

He straightened. "You will?"

"I will."

Elliott jumped to his feet, a genuine smile on his face. "Skye…I…you have no idea how much this means to me! When can we start? Are you busy now? Can I take you to dinner?" He glanced around. "Or we can get takeout and go to my place or…"

He was rambling at this point and Skye knew she was going to have to reel him in and take control of the situation.

It was the only way she was going to survive it.

Holding up her hand, she cut him off. "How about this– we meet up on Saturday morning for coffee? Someplace neutral. And we'll do this once a week."

His shoulders sagged and he was back to looking dejected. "But…that's several days away."

"Elliott, you just sprung this on me and I think if we're going to do this, we need to keep it on at least a slightly professional basis."

"Okay, but weekends are your busy time. I just thought…"

Crap. She hadn't even taken that into consideration. "You're right." She pulled up her calendar and glanced at it. "Are there any mornings where you're free?"

"I need to be in the office by eight and I'm not sure either of us is up for a sunrise therapy session."

"Hmm, good point." This was way more difficult than

she would have thought. "I don't always have a set schedule, but..."

"How about tomorrow night then? We can meet every Thursday night and I know you want to keep this professional but...I think meeting at my place would be best. I'll take care of dinner. It's the least I can do since you're helping me out."

Again, he had a point.

"Fine. Tomorrow night. Seven o'clock. Your house."

His face lit up as he smiled at her. "Thanks, Skye. You're a lifesaver."

"Don't say that yet. We don't even know if this is going to help."

"It will," he said confidently. "I have every faith in you."

At least one of us does...

Elliott looked at his watch for the tenth time in as many minutes and frowned.

How fitting would it be if his therapist stood him up too?

Groaning, he walked around his house and wondered what he was supposed to do. He picked up Chinese food on the way home, all the pillows on his sofa were fluffed, and every surface had been dusted.

All that was missing was Skylar.

It wasn't like she was overly late, but...it was 7:05 so technically, still late.

He paced some more and wondered–not for the first time–if he was doing the right thing. Therapy was not something he was comfortable with, but talking with someone he knew seemed a little more palatable.

Was it going to help? He had no idea. But he had to try, and he had nothing but time on his hands thanks to his family.

Although...he was a grown man. It wasn't like anyone could really enforce it if he did happen to meet someone and...

The doorbell rang and Elliott practically sagged with relief. When he opened the door, Skylar looked more than a little uncomfortable.

Not a good sign for their first meeting.

She was dressed casually–faded jeans, an oversized sweatshirt, and her hair in the ever-present ponytail–and for some reason she looked more like the girl he remembered from when they were growing up than the woman running a successful business with his sister.

"Hey," she said, a little breathless. "Sorry I'm late."

Elliott motioned for her to come in. "Everything okay?"

Skye stepped into the house, stood to the side, and waited for him to lead her–which seemed a little odd too. Was she really this uncomfortable with the whole thing?

"Um...we're dealing with a bit of a bridezilla and her parents are equally aggressive. Basically, it's a nightmare. They came in this afternoon for a cake tasting and made poor Leanna cry." They walked into the living room and she sat down on the sofa and let out a weary sigh. "Josie was ready to snap so I sent her to check on Leanna and I had to play peacekeeper to the clients and...ugh, it was awful. Like, I don't understand why people are so hateful."

"Wow, that had to suck. I'm sorry." He sat down beside her and wasn't sure what to do or say to make her feel better.

"For the most part, we're used to clients being extremely particular in what they want and they should be. A wedding is a big deal and it's supposed to be a once-in-a-lifetime event so it's only natural to want everything to be perfect. And we can give them that perfect day without anyone getting mean." She leaned back and let her head fall against the cushions. "Mean people just suck."

"Yes, they do," he agreed, mimicking her pose. They sat like that for several minutes before Elliott turned his head to look at her. "Would Chinese food help?"

Her eyes were closed as she asked, "Are there dumplings?"

"There are."

"Any chance you also got some lo mein?"

"The house kind so everything's in it."

Smiling, she turned her head to face him. "I can't say it will make everything all better, but it's certainly a good place to start."

Standing, he held out his hand to her and watched as she looked mildly horrified before standing on her own.

Okay, that was definitely weird...

Conversation was fairly basic as they sat down to eat. Elliott wanted to make sure Skye was relaxed and comfortable with him before they jumped into discussing why his life was such a mess. So they talked about how Leanna was after the bridezilla incident and some of their upcoming events and then they discussed his job and what it entailed and by the time they were done eating, it seemed like everything was okay and Skye looked and sounded much more at ease.

They worked together to clean up and Skye was telling him about a trip she took last year to the beach with a couple of her cousins. He wasn't sure how they got on that topic, but he enjoyed listening to her talk about how she learned to surf, fish, and how much she simply enjoyed sitting on the sand and meditating in her own way.

"What does that mean–in your own way?"

She shrugged as she picked up her glass and walked toward the living room. "It's really just me sitting peacefully and clearing my mind while taking in the sounds and scents around me. It's so freeing and I try to replicate it at home with a sound machine, but it's not the same. Hopefully I'll get to go back in the fall and experience it again."

"I hope you do too." Elliott looked at where she was sitting on the sofa and decided to sit in the oversized matching chair opposite her. After all, if he were in a therapist's office, they wouldn't be sitting together, so... "So," he began.

"So." That apprehensive look was back on her face and that's when he knew this wasn't going to work.

"Okay, let's call this a failed experiment," he said flatly.

"Already? Why?"

"Skye, if you could see what I'm seeing, then you'd know why. You're clearly uncomfortable with this and I'm sorry that I put you in this position. I just..." He sighed. "Talking with you really did help and I just thought that it would again. I apologize. Really. This was very selfish of me."

And now he felt awful. Skye was a good friend and practically family and he didn't want to do anything to jeopardize that relationship. She'd been a part of his life for so long and if she wasn't his sister's best friend, he probably would be looking at her differently.

And would have acted on it long ago.

But no. They'd known each other for too long for him to ruin things like this.

"For what it's worth, I don't think you're being selfish,

Elliott," she said, her voice soft and sweet. "I think you're genuinely trying to work through something difficult and no one likes to do that. It's painful and it makes us take a hard look at ourselves and sometimes we end up not liking what we see."

With a nod, he sat back. "So...what do you think I should do?"

She studied him for several moments. "Can I ask you something?"

"Of course."

"How are you doing? In general."

He shrugged. "For the most part, I'm okay. I'm working and doing all my normal stuff."

"Have you heard from Tracy?"

Another nod. "A week after...you know...she called and came over to get her stuff. She hadn't really moved in yet. It was just a lot of boxes we planned on dealing with after the honeymoon."

"Did the two of you talk?"

"We did. She showed up alone and we spent an hour together before her father and brothers showed up to help move everything." He paused. "And before you ask, Daniel wasn't with her."

This time Skye nodded. "Did you feel it was helpful to talk to her? Did the two of you settle things?"

"I don't think there was really anything to settle. She apologized multiple times and the thing is, I understood. Was I disappointed in how it all went down? Yes. Was I humiliated? Definitely. But...I realized it was better for it to happen before we got married than after. That would have been a huge betrayal."

She went silent again and seemed to consider his words. "Okay, I think that's a very healthy way of looking at it, but...maybe you should realize that this is a blessing in disguise."

"What do you mean?"

"Elliott, if you had truly been in love with Tracy, you wouldn't be this chill about it. You'd be angry and hurt and brokenhearted. It seems to me you're more upset about how everyone is looking at you than about Tracy leaving you."

"I wouldn't say..." But then he stopped and thought about it and...she was right. He was more upset about the way his family talked to him afterwards than he was about the relationship ending. "Oh, shit."

And when he looked at Skye, she was nodding. "And that's just the first step. How do you feel?"

"Honestly? Even more foolish," he gruffly admitted. "How did everyone see it but me?"

"I don't know, but that's really just the tip of the iceberg. It would be doing you a great disservice for me to meet with you as a pseudo therapist. You need someone who really knows what they're doing. Trust me."

He wanted to be offended or at least upset, but...she was right. It didn't matter how much he wanted to fast-track all of this and figure out what he was doing wrong, this wasn't going to be a quick fix.

Dammit.

They sat in silence for several minutes before he spoke again. "I appreciate your honesty and your willingness to do this even though you didn't want to."

"We're friends, Elliott, and I hate to see you hurting. And as your friend, it's my place to tell you the truth about what I think you need. If this had been Josie or Leanna, I would have suggested the same thing. It's one thing to hang out and have a bit of a bitch session over a couple of glasses of wine, maybe a little kickboxing or something to get out some aggression...but for something deeper, I would only recommend seeing a professional."

"Wait...say that again."

"What? How I would recommend seeing a professional?"

"No, before that. The whole getting out the aggression."

A small smile played at her lips. "I can't speak for everyone, but I happen to find some aggression therapy very helpful."

Elliott stood and said, "Follow me," before leading her down to his basement where he had a small home gym set up. He had an elliptical, some free weights, and a punching bag. "Would this work?"

Her eyes lit up. "Oh, my goodness! I wish we had a setup like this at the office for days like today! This is amazing!"

While she looked around, Elliott pulled out two pairs of gloves. "I can't believe I didn't think of this before. I could have been feeling a lot less rage by now."

Skye turned and looked at him with surprise when he held out the second pair of gloves to her. "Um...I'm not really dressed for this."

"Then go grab your bag out of your car. I know you always carry a comfy outfit to change into."

"Oh, really? How do you know that?"

"Because you told me about it the last time you were here," he said with a grin. "You go do that and I'm going to go change and we'll meet back down here in five." When he turned to go, Skye called out and stopped him. "What?"

"This is crazy! You don't need me here to do this. If anything, you'll probably feel a lot better if you're alone."

"I disagree. I need someone to talk to me and force me

to deal with this anger I've got and keep me focused. That would be you."

"Great," she murmured.

"C'mon! This is better than sitting upstairs and doing the whole psychology thing, isn't it?" When she didn't respond, he pushed a little more. "Plus, you'll get a chance at the bag and get out some of your aggression from the mean clients today."

"Ugh...I hate how appealing that is," she grumbled. "Fine. We'll punch things and get angry and hopefully feel better."

When they were back upstairs and she was heading out to her car, he yelled out, *Eye of the Tiger*, Skye! *Eye of the Tiger!*" And when he heard her laugh, he knew this was probably the first time he was looking forward to any form of therapy.

Ten minutes later, they were back downstairs and he was helping her lace up her gloves.

"You know," she began, "I said kickboxing. We never wear gloves in kickboxing."

"Yeah, well...I'm not big on kicking. I'd rather punch so...here we are." Once they were ready, he took a step back. "You want to throw the first punch?"

Her eyes went wide and she laughed. "At you or the bag?"

"Ha, ha. Very funny. The bag."

"Well, considering this night was about your therapy, I think I'll just go stand over against the wall and let you get things going."

Nodding, he waited until she was a safe distance away and...punched.

And felt...nothing.

He stared at the bag and hit it again.

Still nothing.

"Um...I know I'm no authority on boxing or punching things but shouldn't you be hitting it harder and...you know...more?"

"I get what you're saying, but...I'm not feeling it."

"Okay, I was hoping not to have to do this, but..." She paused and let out a long breath before speaking again. "Elliott Sullivan! What is wrong with you?" she yelled, and he was a little taken aback by how loud and fierce she sounded. "Quit sitting around feeling sorry for yourself and being a baby! Stop letting your exes walk all over you and making your family step in to ban you from dating! Is this the life you want?"

And oddly enough, that worked.

Rearing back, he threw one punch. And then another. And another until he was pounding on the bag. His body got warm and then hot; sweat began to pour off of him as he continued one punch after another and beside him, Skylar was egging him on about his family and the embargo. After a while, he wasn't so much paying attention to what she was saying as he was to her tone.

His arms began to ache and he was starting to get breathless when...

"You must be a really crappy boyfriend or bad in bed for this to keep happening to you!" she was yelling when he stopped punching.

"Hey!" he snapped, and the bag hit him hard enough to make him stumble. "That was a cheap shot!"

"Oh, right. Sorry," she said as she blushed. "I guess I got carried away."

"Yeah, just a little," he murmured and stepped aside. "You're up."

"Oh, I don't think so. All that yelling really seemed to help me a lot. I'm good."

"Nuh-uh. That wasn't the deal." Walking over, he took her by the shoulders and gave her a playful shove toward the bag. "Go on. Give it a good punch."

She did punch, but somehow missed the bag.

"Wow."

"Like we didn't already know that I'm not athletic or coordinated? Really?"

Actually, he did know that and felt a little bad about making her do this.

"No, you can do this, Skye. Trust me." Then he stood behind the bag and held it steady. "Go ahead. Try again."

"Elliott..."

"You can do this. Come on. Pretend this bag is the person who made Leanna cry."

Her expression turned fierce and she reared back and swung her arm.

And somehow managed to trip and fall.

"Skye, come on. You can't be this bad at this. It's like you're not even trying."

When she stood up, she glared at him and he knew this was going to be the one. She was going to hit the bag and stay standing up. He went to steady the bag when she punched him in the arm. Hard.

"Ow! What the hell?"

"I do not appreciate you mocking me!" she said, stomping her food to accentuate her point.

"That wasn't mocking; that was encouraging. And it was no different from what you were doing for me. Teamwork, Skye. It's all about teamwork."

"Ugh...this is the worst. And now I'm not even remembering the mean clients because now I'm mad at you!"

"Whatever it takes to get that aggression out. Come on! Do it again!" He held the bag firmly. "And this time, hit the bag and not me."

"Whatever." This time she *did* hit the bag several times and she kept going with tiny little punches, but he saw how hard she was concentrating and felt really proud of her. When she stopped, she was breathless.

Then she smiled.

"Oh, my *God!* That was amazing! My arms feel like spaghetti, but wow! What a rush!"

Nodding, he agreed. "Okay, my turn again."

"Do you need me to yell at you again?" she asked with a sly grin as she walked over to the wall.

"Um...maybe. Just...not so insulting this time, okay?"

"Deal."

For an hour, they took turns and Elliott had to admit that he definitely felt good by the time they called it quits. It wasn't a permanent fix, but a step in the right direction.

Together they walked up to his kitchen and he grabbed two bottles of water. It took several minutes for either of them to talk.

"Thank you," he said.

"For what?"

"For coming over and helping me. I think I still need to talk through some stuff, but...this definitely helped."

"I'm glad, Elliott. And for what it's worth, I think you're going to be fine."

"I know, but I did come to several conclusions."

"Oh? Like what?"

"Like...I guess I don't really need an embargo because... I'm done."

"Done?"

He nodded. "Yeah. I'm done with all of it. Clearly I'm

not cut out to be in a relationship and the thought of going there again and getting hurt is just beyond unappealing."

"O-kay," she said slowly. "But you mean just for the... you know...year, right?"

Now he shook his head. "Nope. As in forever. I can't do it anymore and I don't really want to."

"Now you're just lashing out. Once you calm down..."

"Oh, I'm calm. We all have our strengths and weaknesses," he explained, "and relationships are definitely not a strength for me so...I'm done."

"Um..."

"This is a good thing. Really."

"But you said you still need to talk through some stuff. I thought you meant..."

"I mean, I guess I still want to know why I was clinging to this illusion of having to fall in love and get married for so long." Then he shrugged. "But I'm seeing that it's not in the cards for me. I should take after my sister and just be okay with being alone."

"Josie's not alone. Not really."

"She doesn't get serious in any of her relationships. She's very practical and doesn't get emotionally involved. So that's what I'm going to do."

"I don't think it's that easy to just change your entire way of thinking, Elliott."

"That's what my focus is going to be."

"Then I can't..."

"No, I get it. I'm not asking you to help me with that. If anything, I just like hanging out and talking with you because...you get me. And even you have to admit my life's been a bit of a shit show for a while."

"I wouldn't say that. Not exactly."

"On a personal level, it has and everyone knows it." He

paused and finished his water. "So how about this–we still meet up once a week but to do things like this where we talk, hang out, and either do some more kickboxing..."

"We never did get to the kicking..."

"Or find some other activities to get out some aggression."

She studied him for a minute. "Elliott, don't take this the wrong way, but...don't you have some...you know...guy friends you can do this with?"

"I do, but...they're all still being a little weird with me and that's getting old. Everyone thinks if I go out and get laid that everything will be alright and while it's not the worst idea, it's not the solution to everything."

All she did was nod.

"So, what do you say? You up to helping me out for a couple of weeks?" And then he held his breath and hoped she'd say yes because he really needed a friend he could relax with right now.

"I guess we can try..."

He never let her finish. Hugging her close, he thanked her and already couldn't wait to find something for them to do next week.

CHAPTER 5

You can lead a heart to love, but you can't make it fall in.

UNKNOWN

"You want me to what?"

"You throw it."

"Are you crazy?" Skye cried, several weeks later. "Elliott, you have witnessed how freaking uncoordinated I am! Why would you suggest we throw axes?"

He shrugged. "I don't know. It seemed like a great way to get out a little more..."

"Aggression. Yes, I know. You keep saying that."

"Then why did you ask?"

Rolling her eyes, Skye questioned her own sanity. Not only was it crazy to keep hanging out with Elliott like this because, if anything, she was getting *more* attracted to him, but the activities he picked were just way out of her comfort zone.

"Maybe next week I can pick where we go, huh?" And before he could answer, she said, "Or maybe we can go and sit in your living room, order a pizza, and have a normal conversation about how you're doing."

"You said you didn't want to go that route with the whole therapist thing," he reminded her.

"I know, but I also know that I can't keep up with things like this. Are you sure you're not ready to do this with the guys yet?"

"I've seen them, but it's still all about them encouraging me to hook up with someone as a way of moving on." He shrugged. "I'm just not interested. I've said it before and I'll keep on saying it; I'm done. My family was right and I wish they had all spoken up sooner because I'm finding that I'm much happier being single."

"Oh, well...that's good," she murmured, staring at the axe again. "Great, actually. Good for you."

He nodded. "I think so too. It's just all so freeing! I'm finally doing stuff for myself and I realized just how much energy it took to be in a relationship! It's like a giant weight has been lifted off of my shoulders!"

"Yeah, great."

"So come on. Let's do this!" He stood on the allotted spot and stared at the target. "You ready?"

"How about I just watch you? I've had a very mellow week and have no absolutely no aggression to get out. I think all of our activities cured me."

With a patient smile, he faced her. "You've done great these past few weeks! Come on, admit it. You enjoyed the shooting range last week."

It had been fun to shoot the targets once she stopped

jumping at the sound of the gun firing. Elliott even took a picture of her in the classic Charlie's Angels pose.

"And the batting range was fun, too."

"Um...no, and I still have the bruises to prove it."

"You wouldn't have those bruises if you kept your eyes open," he teased.

"A baseball was flying at my face at ninety miles an hour, Elliott!"

"Okay, okay, okay. You've been a real trooper; I'll admit it. But I really want you to try this. Please! For me..."

"Oh, knock it off," she huffed. "We both know I'm never going to get anywhere near that target and with my luck, I'm going to end up going to the emergency room because I've hit myself with the axe."

"That's why I'm going to help you," he said, stepping behind her.

Like...really close behind her.

Skye felt like Elliott was pressed against her back from shoulder to toe. He gently gripped the hand that was holding the axe. "Okay, you need to relax," he began.

Yeah, that was *not* going to happen...

One large hand rested on her hip while the other guided her through the motions of how to throw the axe. His breath was warm on her cheek as he talked her through what he expected her to do, and it took everything she had not to fall into a puddle at his feet.

"You got this, Skylar," he said softly, and it always made her feel good when he used her full name. It was a silly thing, but for some reason, she loved it.

Her eyes squeezed shut as she raised her arm over her head. With her heart pounding, she said a silent prayer that she wasn't going to hurt anyone and could just...get this over with.

"Open those eyes, brave girl, and think about something that's really pissing you off," he coaxed. "Something or someone that's got you so frustrated and angry that you just want to hit it with something."

It was as if Elliott's face appeared on the target, and Skye heaved the axe with all her might.

And surprisingly, she hit the target.

"Oh, my God! I did it! I really did it!" And before she could truly process it, Elliott had her in his arms spinning her around.

"I knew you could do it!" he said, hugging her tight. "Good for you!"

She was getting dizzy both from the spinning and being in his arms, but she never let it show. When he placed her back on her feet, he was smiling down at her with pride.

"I can't believe I really did it," she said giddily. "Now it's your turn. If I can hit the target, anyone can."

With a nod, Elliott turned and picked his axe back up and got into position. He raised his arm slowly and grinned at her. "Bet I can do it with my eyes closed," he said, oozing confidence.

"I bet you can too!"

Elliott closed his eyes and threw the axe.

And completely missed the target.

And the wall it was mounted on.

"What?!" he cried. "That's not possible!" Angrily, he grabbed another axe, got back into position, and threw it.

Missing it again.

A string of curses were out of his mouth and Skye had to stifle a laugh.

For his third throw, he seemed to calm down, and this time he barely nicked the target. "That's it! This is stupid!

I'm not doing it again!" He stormed away and Skye had to chase him down.

"Elliott, come on! Don't be like that."

He turned on her. "How is it that you were able to get it and I can't?"

"Um...for starters...wow," she said with a hint of annoyance. "And maybe because I'm not as arrogant as you, I was able to actually focus."

Staring down at her, she could tell he was still really angry and all she could do was smile up at him.

"And really, can't you just give me this one? You totally kicked my butt at every other activity."

That seemed to do the trick because he raked a hand through his hair and seemed to relax. "Yeah, okay."

"How about this—we go and sit over in the concession area and talk for a little while and then we'll go and try again. Okay?"

He nodded and she led him over to the snack bar where they each ordered a salted pretzel and a drink. Skye waited until they were seated at a table in the corner before she started talking.

"So," she began cautiously. "How are you doing?"

"Right now, I'm pissed."

"That's not what I meant and you know it. I'm talking about overall. Are you still thinking all relationships are bad and embracing the embargo?"

He let out a small snort. "Every time I hear that word, it gets to me. And honestly, it's the best thing my family could have done for me. So yeah, I'm embracing it and feeling really good about my future."

That was...a little shocking. "You're thinking about the future?"

"Absolutely," he said around another bite of pretzel.

"The way I see it–and I know it's a cliché–but the world truly is my oyster! I'm going to travel where I want, probably sell my house and move into something a little smaller, and I'll probably do the same with my car and get something sportier. I've been so damn practical and boring for years that I'm really looking forward to embracing bachelor life."

"How is that possible?" she blurted out before she could stop herself. "A month ago, you were the poster boy for wanting to get married and have kids and a dog! You're the guy who proposed to four different women in your quest to achieve your goal of having the American dream! And now you're telling me it's as easy as flipping a switch?!"

And yeah, Skye realized her voice was getting louder and she was sounding a bit like a crazy person, but...she couldn't seem to help it.

For years, she had to sit back and watch Elliott fall in love over and over and over and never with her. And she compared every guy she dated during that time to Elliott, because she wanted everything Elliott did! And now she was left wondering if he ever truly wanted to get married or he thought he was supposed to want it because of his family!

"Geez, lighten up," he said, frowning. "I don't know why you sound so upset about it. I would think you'd be happy that I'm moving on."

It was on the tip of her tongue to argue that she wished he didn't keep going to such extremes because not all women were like Tracy.

Or the other three.

Hell, she wanted to yell that she wasn't like them and demand that he *see* her!

But she didn't.

"I...I am," she said, focusing on ripping off a piece of her pretzel. "I just want you to be sure about how you feel and that you're not just...reacting. I get that you've been burned, but...there is a woman out there who isn't going to do that to you." She couldn't meet his eyes as she said it, so she had no idea how he was reacting until he snorted and then laughed.

"Somehow, I greatly doubt that."

And we're getting nowhere...

They ate in companionable silence for several minutes before Skye stood up. "Come on. Let's go throw some axes." And this time, she didn't need his encouragement. Right now she was frustrated enough to throw the damn things completely on her own.

For the better part of the week, Skye's words played over and over in his mind.

"How is that possible? A month ago, you were the poster boy for wanting to get married and have kids and a dog! You're the guy that has proposed to four different women in your quest to achieve your goal of having the American dream! And now you're telling me it's as easy as flipping a switch?!"

And the thing was...he couldn't explain it. For him, it really was like flipping a switch. The day after his failed wedding, he woke up and felt...fine. Sure, he was embarrassed that all his friends and family witnessed the most humiliating moment of his life, but...he wasn't upset about Tracy leaving him. For years he'd thought there was something wrong with him because he was so anxious to get married, but now he feared there was something wrong with him because he felt nothing about *not* getting married.

"I guess I seriously do need therapy," he murmured.

The outings he had talked Skye into taking with him were helping. It was nice to talk with someone who wasn't directly hounding him about his feelings and he could tell that she wasn't judging him–not really. Tyler and his other friends were all still tippy toeing around him and it was getting old, but he had Skye to hang out with and he was enjoying it.

He just wasn't telling anyone about it and apparently, neither was she.

Elliott knew eventually she'd tell him she didn't have the time to hang out or she was just done playing amateur psychologist with him, but for now he was going to simply take what she was willing to give him.

His doorbell rang promptly at seven and he smiled when he opened the door and found her standing there.

And not just because she was holding a pizza.

He was genuinely enjoying her company.

Although...tonight they agreed to do away with the physical activities and sit down and talk about how he was doing. It wasn't something he was particularly looking forward to, but if he was going to talk to anyone about how he was feeling, it was Skye.

It was weird how it took him hitting rock bottom to realize just how awesome she was. His sister was always going on about Skylar, but this was the first time he was finding out for himself.

"Hey," she said, smiling as he took the pizza box from her hands. "I'm just warning you now that the last thing I ate today was half a granola bar at around ten, so I may eat more than you tonight."

That just made him laugh. "Okay. We'll see how that goes." They walked to the kitchen where he already had the table set for them and within minutes, they were eating. "Any crazy clients today?"

"I don't even want to talk about it," she said around a mouthful of pizza. "What about you? How's your week been?"

His week was pretty tame, but he wanted to get right to the deep conversation so they could move on because, honestly, the topic of his failed relationships was bringing him down. If he could just ignore it and move on, he'd be so much happier. But over the last several weeks, Skye had been telling him that he needed to deal with it *before* he could move on.

So...here they were.

After finishing his first slice of pizza, he jumped right in.

"You know how you've been telling me that I need to really think about all the failed crap and why I did what I did?"

She paused mid-chew and stared at him. "Really? You want to do this now?"

"No time like the present," he said with a grin.

"Fine. But I'm just going to keep eating." And to prove her point, she took another bite of her dinner.

"Should I, like...stand up or something?"

"Why? Are you planning on doing this like a book report?"

Elliott knew she was teasing, but he had no idea how he was supposed to do this. "No, but...I don't know! If I were at a therapist's office, I'd be lying down on a couch or some-thing, right? So since we're in the kitchen, I just thought..."

"Elliott?" she interrupted patiently. "Just...talk."

With a curt nod, he did.

"Okay, so proposing to my high school girlfriend at

seventeen had seemed wildly romantic," he began. "We were young and we thought we were in love. We always talked about going to college together, adopting a handful of rescue dogs, and finding the perfect little home with the white picket fence...you know, goofy stuff like that."

Grabbing a second slice of pizza, she nodded.

"But the wild-eyed look on Wendy's face at graduation when I got down on one knee? I don't know why I didn't just shut up and stop before I made such a grand–and public–declaration."

Nodding, she gave him a small smile. "That's not terrible, Elliott. You were young. It happens."

He agreed. "That's why I didn't even *think* about proposing to my college girlfriend until our junior year."

"Three years later is a completely decent amount of time to wait between these things."

"Exactly. And I really believed she was the *one*. I went a different route this time and proposed on Valentine's Day."

"A little clichéd, but romantic. So what happened there?"

"I was completely oblivious. Again," he grumbled. "On paper, we were completely compatible. We both loved sushi, reading, board games, and binge-watching rom-coms. We would stay up all night talking about all the ways the world could use a little more love and compassion."

"O-kay..."

"But it turned out she had given her love, compassion– and my chocolates–to someone else. Actually, multiple someones."

Skye groaned and refused to look at him.

Rather than stop, Elliott plowed onward. "Proposal number three was really the case of a rebound relationship, and I should have known better. But we were in Vegas and a little drunk and...you know, I threw it out there and she said yes."

"Does this *she* have a name?"

"Kate," he replied and toyed with a piece of pizza crust. "Anyway, there was this Elvis impersonator who seemed just a wee bit too flirty, but hey, it was Vegas, right? Next thing I know, I'm filling out paperwork and Kate is making out with Mr. Blue Suede Shoes!"

A small snort of laughter was out before Skye seemed to realize it, and she gave him a smirk. "I guess that means you spent the night at the Heartbreak Hotel?"

"Ha, ha. Very funny. Needless to say, I was more than happy to let what happened in Vegas, stay in Vegas."

Beside him, she seemed to get her laughter under control before murmuring an apology.

"And then there was Tracy and...you know the deal there."

Taking her third slice of pizza, Skye put it on her plate and let out a long breath. "I'm going to say some things now," she began slowly. "And you may not like them but... you definitely need to hear them."

All he could do was nod.

"I don't think you've done anything wrong."

Elliott stared at her for a solid minute in disbelief.

Nodding, Skye explained. "First proposal? You were a kid and too young to really be held accountable. Proposal number two? That stung, but...still a little too young to really be at fault. The third? That was just stupidity. And Tracy? For what it's worth, that was all on her, not you. So if you're going to beat yourself up, it's pointless."

"Yeah, but..."

"I'm not saying that this embargo thing should be lifted or anything because it seems like you're doing fine with it. I think you're being overly cautious and overreacting by saying you'll never get involved with anyone again, but..." She stopped and shrugged.

"You think that's a mistake?"

She nodded again. "Definitely."

Interesting...

Maybe it was time to turn the tables...

"What is so wrong with not wanting to fall in love and get married? Especially after everything I've been through?"

"There's nothing wrong with it," she said fiercely, leaning forward in her seat. "It's actually understandable. But I also believe this is a knee-jerk reaction. I've known you for a long time and I can't believe you're just completely okay with giving up everything you said you wanted. It seems crazy to me to say you're never going to fall in love again."

"But how do any of us really know we're in love?" he countered. "I mean, think about it. People confuse love and lust all the time. Obviously, I have, and it sucks being wrong."

"Elliott, no one is saying it's wrong. You can fall hard and fast and believe in love at first sight. Those are great things. The issue is how you immediately began planning a future with these women before you truly knew them–or yourself. What would be the harm in being in a longer-lasting relationship before putting a ring on someone's finger? You can still be happy and in love, can't you?"

"Trust me, I speak from experience and it's not that simple." Shaking his head, he reached for another slice of pizza and tossed it on his plate. "I'd just rather not go there again. Not now. Not a year from now or whenever the hell this embargo thing ends, just...not interested. End of story."

The look on her face told him he was trying her

patience, but he didn't care. She had no idea how fed up he was with the whole situation. He could finally breathe freely because he took the pressure off himself to try to emulate what his parents and grandparents had.

"You're angry and you're hurting right now. I get it and I'm sorry you feel that way. Just promise me that you'll also try to be a little more open-minded about your future."

"I am being open-minded, Skye. There's a world of possibilities out there waiting for me. Just because marriage isn't one of them anymore doesn't make my life any less fulfilling. Plenty of people go through their entire lives without committing to another person."

She frowned. "You're right. They do. But that doesn't mean they're all okay with that decision. We're all individuals, Elliott. Why does it all have to be black or white?"

Raking a hand through his hair, he sighed. "I...I don't know. It just feels better to take that pressure off of myself."

Apparently she must have felt like the conversation was over because she quickly changed it. "The wedding we're doing this weekend has a guest list of three hundred! Can you believe it? And the reception is being held at this massive historical home in Winston-Salem. It's going to be a nightmare."

Message received and Elliott was kind of relieved himself. It did help to say everything out loud, but she wasn't going to change his mind. The old saying of "Once bitten, twice shy" certainly came to mind along with the old "Fool me once" one.

And he was definitely done being a fool.

It was only eight-thirty when Skye slowly got to her feet. "I think our weekly therapy sessions are done."

"Why?"

"Because you're fine, Elliott," she said with a hint of

annoyance. "There's nothing else for us to talk about and really, from this point forward, I think Tyler and your other friends would be of more help than I would."

He didn't fully agree, but it was clear nothing was going to get settled tonight. Standing up, he slid his hands into his pockets and offered her a small smile. "Thanks, Skye. For what it's worth, I've enjoyed our time together."

She didn't respond, and as they walked to the front door together, Elliott felt mildly disappointed that she was leaving already.

"You don't have to rush out, you know," he said casually. "I realize we don't have to talk about me and my situation, but that doesn't mean you have to jump up and leave."

Skye looked extremely perplexed by his statement.

Stepping in front of her, Elliott stopped her from going any farther. "Okay, there is something on my mind and if I don't ask, it's going to drive me crazy."

Her eyes went wide. "Um...o-kay..."

"Did I do something wrong?"

Now she frowned. "When?"

"I don't know...tonight? Ever?"

"Elliott, what are you talking about?"

"I want to know why you're rushing out of here," he quickly stated. "We've known each other for years and I thought we were having fun hanging out together these past few weeks, but now you can't wait to get out of here! So... what's the deal?"

Maybe he just didn't want to be alone and was taking it out on her, but he didn't think that was it. Whatever was going on, it had to do more with Skylar than it did with him. He truly couldn't imagine what he possibly could have done to offend her. They always got along and they never had any issues before, so he was truly stumped.

"I'm not *rushing*," she murmured, but she also wouldn't look him directly in the eye.

Feeling bold, Elliott gently grasped her by the shoulders and she flinched. "Skye, come on. Is it because we're sneaking around behind Josie's back?"

Her eyes went almost comically large. "*What?!* I mean... we're not sneaking around, Elliott! God, you make it sound like we're having an illicit affair or something!"

"Okay, so poor choice of words," he admitted. "But you know what I'm saying. Is that what's bothering you?"

"If I say yes, can I go?" It was followed by a nervous laugh and he knew he couldn't let her leave until he got a straight answer from her.

"Skye, come on. I'm already dealing with all kinds of rejection issues, so can you please just spare me the chase and tell me what I did so we can move on?"

Her shoulders sagged and she let out a long breath. "Fine. It's not you; it's me. You and I never hang out alone and knowing what your family said to you about the whole dating embargo thing just makes me feel guilty. I mean, I know we're not dating or anything, but..."

"Yeah, you don't have to worry about that," he said with a small laugh, rubbing his hand along the back of his neck. "Because...well...that's crazy. No one would think twice about you and I hanging out together." He let out another laugh and quickly noticed that she wasn't laughing with him. If anything, she looked hurt.

And then she looked pissed.

"What? I just meant that we've been friends for so long and you're practically family, so..."

Holding up a hand to stop him, Skye quickly stepped around him. "No, you're right. I guess I'm just overthinking things."

Her words made sense, but her tone told him she was definitely *not* happy. "Skye..."

"No. It's fine. Really. Not a big deal."

It wasn't until her hand was on the doorknob that Elliott decided enough was enough. "Obviously it's not fine!" he snapped. His patience was shot and his loud tone was enough to shock them both into silence. "Look, maybe I'm overreacting here, but I'm telling you, the way you're acting just seems off. And for you to be worried about anyone thinking we're dating is just..."

"It's what?" she asked tightly.

"Um..."

"It's weird because I'm Josie's friend? Or unthinkable because everyone thinks we're like family?" Her tone was sharp and her expression fierce, and clearly he had touched a nerve. "Or...or...maybe I'm *so* unattractive compared to all the other women you've dated that it just wouldn't be believable for you to want to date someone like me?"

Say what now?

"Skye, that's not...no one ever said you weren't attractive," he quickly corrected. "You're beautiful–probably one of the most beautiful women I know."

"Oh, really?" And yeah, the sarcastic tone was strong.

"Yeah, really."

She snorted with disbelief.

Elliott moved a little closer and gently grasped her shoulders. "Skye, I don't know where any of this is coming from and I want you to know that I think the world of you. You're a good friend and you've been very gracious to me during this whole wedding drama and I hate that you have some sort of issue with me–like you're mad at me for something that I don't know anything about."

He felt her relax a bit under his hands and he almost let out a sigh of relief.

Instead, he stepped in closer and hugged her. She stiffened, but just for a moment, and then she relaxed against him.

Hell, she even put her arms around him and hugged him back.

And it felt good.

Really good.

She smelled like sunshine and the beach, he realized as he inhaled a little deeper. Maybe it was creepy, but he turned his head slightly and sniffed her hair and sensed a hint of coconut. He'd never cared much for that scent, but right now it was almost intoxicating.

Had he ever noticed a woman's scent like this before?

And the answer was a big no. He had no idea what Tracy's favorite shampoo was or what scents she preferred, but he had a feeling this was a favorite of Skye's. He took another deep breath before he forced himself to put some distance between them because...well...this was highly inappropriate–especially after the conversation they just had.

Only...Skye didn't release him and Elliott's arms were still loosely around her.

This is new...

Skye licked her lips and he found himself fascinated by that small action. When his gaze met hers, it was like he was seeing her for the first time. It wasn't his sister's best friend standing there, but a very desirable woman.

Or maybe it's been a few months since I've been near a woman and I'm romanticizing it–which is what I'm trying to learn to stop doing!

Okay, there was that, but...it didn't feel like he was romanticizing it.

It felt real.

Genuine.

And before he could question it, Elliott closed the distance between them once again and carefully pressed his lips to hers. She was probably going to slap him or, at the very least, push him away, but...she didn't. In an instant, Skylar melted against him and let out the sexiest little sound.

His kiss was tentative, but that one little sound from her was all the encouragement he needed to take it a little deeper.

But Skye beat him to it.

Her tongue teased at his bottom lip and his gasp of surprise was all it took for them to take the kiss to the next level. It wasn't wild or frantic, but more of a lazy and languid exploration and it was sexy as hell.

Skye was sexy as hell.

Why had he never noticed it before?

Next, he felt her hands rake up into his hair. Her nails gently scratched along his scalp as she pressed closer to him. She was all soft curves and warm skin, and damn if he didn't want more.

For several minutes he simply enjoyed the gentle tangle of tongues, hearing her soft sighs, and the feel of her body against his. When he broke the kiss to catch his breath, he whispered her name and went to kiss her neck when she gasped loudly and took a step back.

"Ohmygod!" she panted before a look of sheer panic crossed her face.

And before Elliott could process what was happening, she was moving around him and out the door.

CHAPTER 6

The saddest thing about falling in love is that sooner or later something will go wrong.

UNKNOWN

"I DIDN'T THINK this was ever going to end," Josie said wearily as she sat down at one of the now-empty reception tables.

"Me either," Skye agreed as she kicked off her shoes. It was two in the morning and one of the longest days of her life.

"Here," Leanna said as she sat and joined them. "I think we all deserve some cake."

"I know I do," Josie told them as she reached for her plate.

Skye took a bite of the decadent chocolate cake with Boston cream filling. It was exactly what she needed after the wedding from hell was finally over. After a second forkful, she put the plate down and sighed happily. "I think we are going to have to come up with a way to cut some of these difficult clients loose. We all knew Brittnee with two Es was going to be a nightmare after our initial consultation. We're doing much better now and the business is stronger than it's ever been that I think we can afford to turn down some of them."

"I fully agree," Josie said around a mouthful of cake. "I honestly thought she'd relax a bit today and ease up on some of her complaining but...geez, she never did."

"Good luck to her new husband," Leanna chimed in. "You know that guy's going to have his hands full for a long time." Then she shook her head. "He must really love her."

"Or he's a glutton for punishment." Putting her plate down, Josie leaned back in her chair and sighed. "Personally, I think a relationship like that can't be a love-match. It's got to be like a business deal or..."

"Or someone lost a bet," Skye offered with a snicker. "Why would anyone willingly tie themselves to someone who is just so mean?"

"And why would anyone get married as part of a business deal in this day and age?" Leanna asked. "That just seems a little archaic, don't you think?"

"I don't know," Josie said after a minute. "I think there could be certain perks to it."

"Like what?" Skye couldn't help her incredulous tone because it seemed like such a bizarre thing for her friend to say.

"You know, like a marriage of convenience. You need or want companionship and you're helping someone out who needs to get married."

"No one needs to get married anymore," Leanna said with her own hint of disbelief at this conversation. "People should get married because they're in love and want to spend the rest of their lives together. End of story."

"I disagree. Look at my brother," Josie went on. "I think he loved the idea of being married so much he was willing to settle to make it happen."

Leanna nodded. "How's he doing? It's been...what...a little over two months since the whole left at the altar thing. Is he getting better?"

Skye picked up her plate and focused on counting crumbs rather than speaking up. There wasn't anything wrong with Elliott that he needed to "get better" from. She hated when people talked about him like he was sick or something because he wasn't.

What he *was* was one hell of a kisser.

And that one kiss was playing on a constant loop in her head for days.

Yeah, she'd basically run from his house and sped away in her car and refused to look back.

Coward.

Yup. That was her—a big, fat coward.

Okay, maybe that was a little dramatic, but...kissing Elliott was a mistake. Although...technically, he kissed her first.

It was the way she reacted that was the mistake, and obviously he must have felt the same way because he hadn't come after her.

Ugh...why did he finally have to notice her when he was banned from getting involved with anyone? And why did he have to be such a good kisser? No wonder women were always drawn to him! If Elliott had gotten down on one knee right then and there, Skye would have agreed to marry him too!

"...yeah, so I think it's a good thing for him," Josie was

saying, and Skye realized she had seriously zoned out. "You can ask him yourself when he's at the office on Monday."

"Um...why exactly is Elliott coming to the office?" Skye asked as she once again put her cake plate down.

"He's taking me to lunch," Josie explained with a big smile. "I was shocked when he called and asked, and I totally jumped at the chance. We've seen each other a lot since the breakup, but we're usually with my folks. It will be nice for it to be just the two of us."

"How sweet!" Leanna said. "Aww...I love it! That's so nice that he's reaching out like that."

"I thought so too. Plus, he almost never takes time off of work; he usually eats lunch at his desk, so this is huge for him. I think this embargo thing is really working!"

Great...

"Good for him! Oh, I can't wait to see him," Leanna went on. "If Elliott can be happy being single, I guess I can too, huh?"

"There's nothing wrong with being single," Josie said wearily. "No one needs a significant other to complete them or make them happy. You should be happy with yourself."

"How are you even a wedding planner?" Leanna asked, shaking her head. "You talk to people about the importance of love and happily-ever-after, and yet you're the most jaded person I know!"

"I'm not jaded. I just don't think we need someone us to make us whole. Plus, after watching Elliott's journey over the last twelve years, I certainly don't want to deal with any of that. No thank you."

That made Skye speak up. "So you're saying all the things that used to speak to your brother–things like how your parents and grandparents all have these amazing relationships–hold no appeal to you?"

Josie was quiet for a moment. "You know, I guess I just don't look at it the same way he does. Sure, they've all been married for a long time, but those relationships aren't perfect. My parents fight, my grandparents fight..." She sighed. "Elliott just never realized that there's nothing overly special about our family. Lots of people have long marriages. There's no magic to it and you certainly can't force magic where there is none."

"So sad," Leanna murmured as she finished her cake.

"Oh! But that does remind me," Josie said as she sat up straighter. "My nana and pop-pop–my dad's parents–are going to be celebrating their sixty-fifth anniversary and they want us to help plan the party! They want to renew their vows and Nana swears she's going to wear her original wedding gown! How cool is that?"

"So romantic!" Leanna said with a sigh, and yet all Skye could think was how at one time, this was on the long list of things Elliott wanted for himself.

Not anymore...

Rather than voice that opinion, she opted to lick the remainder of the frosting off of her fork.

It was safer that way.

"You're awfully quiet tonight, Skye," Leanna observed. "You doing okay?"

"Just tired," she lied.

"I think we all are," Josie agreed as she stood up. "Let's get things in motion so we can possibly crawl into bed as the sun comes up."

Sadly, that was exactly the way it went. After the entire venue was cleaned up, their supplies were taken back to the Meet Me at the Altar offices, and the staff was paid, it was nearing five in the morning. Skye dragged herself to bed and said a quick prayer of thanks that it was Sunday and she had nothing else to do but sleep.

The next time she woke up it was after lunch and she enjoyed being lazy and doing nothing but laundry and having her dinner delivered.

It was glorious.

On Monday morning, she hit the ground running. The week always started off with a staff meeting–which was really just Skye, Josie, and Leanna sitting around their consultation table with coffee and bagels as they talked about the upcoming schedule for the week. Most of the time they stayed on task, but sometimes–like today–things went off the rails.

"She called me at six thirty this morning wanting to know if we could accommodate an additional thirty guests and still stay on budget!" Josie explained, her Starbucks coffee precariously close to spilling.

"What did you tell her? I mean, if they want to stay on budget, then something else has to go!"

"That's what I told her and she demanded a meeting today at eleven."

Both Skye and Leanna groaned. "Oh, come on, Jos," Skye whined. "Why? Why would you agree to that on a Monday morning?"

"What was I supposed to do? This is going to be one of our biggest events in the history of Meet Me at the Altar! We need to quickly come up with some options on how we can add thirty people without breaking fire codes and the budget. And if we can make that happen, do you have any idea how much business we could gain from this?"

"I hate when you're right," she grumbled.

"Okay, let's start with me because I can say with great certainty that adding extra dessert won't cost them anything extra. I can easily add an extra tier to the cake or we can even work on going with slightly smaller slices if she doesn't want to change the overall design of the cake," Leanna offered. "I believe we can also get by without having to add too much to the cocktail hour menu. It's the main course that's going to blow the food budget. Thirty extra people will more than likely add another five to seven thousand dollars to the overall cost. In the grand scheme of things, that's not too terrible when you consider how much they're already spending."

Skye nodded in agreement. "I say we lay that out from the get-go–give her the dollar amount it's going to cost for the additional people and then mention how we're throwing in the extra dessert for free. Think that will work?"

"No idea," Josie replied. "But we have to start somewhere, right?"

Once that was agreed upon, Skye went to work up new paperwork so everything would be ready just in case. Leanna went and put together a tray of mini-cakes and cookies to offer, and Josie got on the phone with the venue they were going to be using to see if they could accommodate the extra guests. By the time eleven o'clock rolled around, they were all completely prepared and ready to go.

Unfortunately, the Buchanans weren't easily convinced and clearly wanted a discount of some sort. Skye let Josie do the bulk of the talking and it took almost ninety minutes to come to an agreement. While Josie wrapped things up, Skye wished them a good day and practically sprinted back to her office.

And ran right into Elliott.

"Oh!" she cried before he reached out to steady her.

"Sorry," he said, smiling down at her. "You looked like you were anxious to get back here. Is everything okay?"

"Fine," she said breathlessly. "Everything's fine."

Except I want to grab your face and kiss you.

Bad Skylar!

"So...how are you?" he asked softly.

The sound of his voice and his nearness mesmerized her. She bit her bottom lip as her gaze met his. "I'm good," she replied, her voice equally soft.

He nodded. "I'm here to take Josie to lunch, but...I had hoped to see you and talk to you. You ran from the house after we had dinner together and..." He paused and shook his head. "I should have gone after you. I hate that you left that way."

So did she, but she wasn't going to admit that to him. Swallowing hard, she said, "It was for the best. We never should have done that."

"I disagree."

And when his hands were still holding her and he was still smiling down at her, Skye felt herself melting and wondered what harm there could be in one more kiss.

Clearly, Elliott must have been feeling the same way because they were each moving a little closer. And when she could feel his warm breath on her cheek, she practically sighed with relief.

Just another few inches...

"Oh, Elliott! I forgot to text you!" Josie said as she breezed into the office and walked over to her desk. "I'm in crisis mode with a client and won't be able to do lunch today."

Luckily, she wasn't looking at either of them, but Skye still all but jumped out of Elliott's grasp. She made her way over to her own desk and began shuffling papers just to keep busy.

"I made reservations at Winston's, Jos," Elliott was saying. "And I took some extra time off this afternoon."

Josie turned and looked at him. "I really am sorry. We just finished our presentation with a very important client and I'm having lunch brought in while we finish up."

"Why?" Skye asked. "I thought everything was good. I never would have left you alone in there if I thought they were still upset."

But Josie just waved her off. "It's all going to be fine. I'm just smoothing things out so they leave here in a good mood and hopefully that will lead to them sending people our way. Leanna's even making up some chocolate mousse because Mr. Buchanan mentioned it was his favorite dessert."

"Do you want me to go back in there with you? Maybe if all three of us are there…"

"No," Josie told her as she scooped up a file. "I think they'll feel like we're ganging up on them. Leanna's just going to make the mousse and bring it in and go. It's no big deal."

"If you're sure…"

"Um, hello!" Elliott interrupted. "Remember me? The guy you were supposed to have lunch with?"

"Elliott," Josie whined. "Don't make me feel bad about doing my job. I would never do that to you."

"You're right," he said. "I'm sorry. I was just really looking forward to hanging out with you and you know how Winston's is one of my favorite places."

"I know and again, I'm sorry." She paused and glanced over at Skye. "Take Skye with you."

"What?" they cried in unison.

Nodding, Josie explained, "Yeah, the two of you should go.

Elliott, I know you hate to eat out alone and I sort of sprung this whole crazy client situation on Skye this morning. She deserves a good lunch. So, you two go and I'll talk to you both later." And before either could comment, she walked out of the office.

———————

Elliott was totally fine with the change of plans, but when he caught the look of sheer panic on Skylar's face, he realized he was the only one.

"So," he said with more enthusiasm than he felt, "you ready?"

If anything, her eyes went wider. "You're not serious, right?"

"Why wouldn't I be?"

"Elliott, think about it! You're not supposed to go out with anyone–even if it is just me," she argued lightly. "I know Josie said it was okay, but...I don't think it's a good idea."

There was a part of him that completely agreed with her–going out for lunch together was going to confirm what he already knew.

He should have paid more attention to Skye while they were growing up.

The few times they spent time together–alone–made him realize just how much they had in common and how amazing she was.

Unfortunately, with his reputation and the whole no dating for a year thing, he really was courting disaster by pushing the whole lunch thing.

And yet...he couldn't stop himself.

"Come on, Skye," he pled with just a hint of groveling. "Don't make me go to lunch alone. You know Sullivan's has the best menu and I happen to know you are a fan of their lobster salad."

"How...how do you know that?"

She was sitting behind her desk again and Elliott placed both hands on it and leaned in a little close. "We talked about favorite restaurants and meals the day you drove me home and I remembered."

"Oh."

It was adorable how flustered she was and he knew he had to do something to get her to agree to go out with him.

Now he sat down on the corner of her desk. "You know my sister is going to wonder why you didn't go with me. How are you going to explain that to her?"

"I would tell her that I already had lunch plans," she countered.

"And do you? Have lunch plans?"

"Well, no. But Josie doesn't know that."

"Hmm...and you're okay with lying to her?" And before she could respond, he was going on. "You'll probably end up grabbing a salad or something from one of the local fast-food places because you can't go and sit someplace nearby to eat. Everyone around here knows you and Josie and Leanna and there's always the chance that it will come up that you didn't actually eat wherever it is that you'll tell my sister you ate."

"I don't really think that's going to happen," she said, but she didn't sound overly confident.

"Of course, you could possibly get away with it, but I have a feeling you'll feel guilty because my sister is the queen of throwing a guilt trip and are you sure you really want to subject yourself to it?'

"Oh, alright!" She pushed away from her desk and stood up. "Geez! Josie is good at throwing guilt around, but she's got nothing on you! Good grief!" Reaching down, she grabbed her purse before walking around to him. "And just for the record, I don't appreciate being badgered."

Elliott went to comment but she was already walking out of the office and he had no choice but to follow.

Out in the parking lot, Skye insisted on taking her own car but he wore her down on that too and once he had her in his car and they were on their way, he let himself relax.

"So, what's the deal with the difficult client?" he asked.

Skye explained the whole situation to him and it seemed a little crazy for anyone to expect to add thirty extra people without having to pay for them.

"You didn't cave, did you?"

"I wouldn't say we caved, but we're certainly jumping through hoops to keep the cost down for them. They're still paying, just not as much as they should."

He shook his head. "I wouldn't have given in to them. I mean, everyone's always looking for a deal, but this was way more than asking for an additional dessert or maybe an upgrade on the menu."

"Believe me, I agree, but Josie is convinced that if we give them their perfect day that it will lead to more high-paying clients. I'm not sure I believe her, but I'm going to have to trust her on this."

"And if it doesn't?"

She shrugged. "It's not like I'm going to do an I-told-you-so dance or anything, but the next time something like this comes up, I'll probably remind her that it didn't work out."

"That seems fair." He glanced over at her. "I know you don't like to make waves."

With a small frown, she sighed. "Yup. That's me. Boring, unwilling to rock the boat, Skylar."

"What?"

"Never mind. It's nothing." Then she straightened and pasted a smile on her face that didn't quite meet her eyes. "So, what was the special event that had you taking time off to go to lunch with Josie?"

Before he replied, he made a mental note to come back to the whole unwilling-to-rock-the-boat thing because he felt like there was a story there.

"You know my sister and I are very close and even though we see each other for Sunday dinners with our folks whenever she's not at an event, there are times when it's nice for it to just be the two of us." He shrugged. "I get the feeling she's not comfortable talking about anything deep or personal when we're with them, so I wanted to check on her and make sure she's okay." Then he paused. "Do you think anything's going on with her?"

"Elliott, even if I knew something, I wouldn't tell you. Josie's one of my best friends and if she didn't want to tell you something, then I wouldn't betray a confidence."

And that brought them right back to her not making waves.

The rest of the drive was made in relative silence except for the random comment about the weather and traffic.

Normally, it would make Elliott crazy – the lack of conversation–but it wasn't like that with Skylar. He was comfortable with her and didn't feel the need to always be 'on' or entertaining her.

It was kind of freeing...

At the restaurant, they were seated and heard the lunch specials and even though he was fairly certain she was going to order the lobster salad and he was going to order the beef tenderloin with truffle fries, they went through the motion of looking through the menu.

And five minutes later, they ordered exactly what he thought and they were finally forced to talk.

"Other than dealing with difficult clients, how's business been?" he asked, hoping to break the ice and get Skye to talk.

"Well...we had an event this past weekend that we didn't think was ever going to end," she began, and talking about her job seemed to put her at ease. Within minutes she had visibly relaxed and returned to her usual animated self. Elliott realized he enjoyed listening to her talk and really liked hearing her laugh.

Something she did a lot of when talking about the crazy things she'd witnessed at recent weddings.

"I don't know how you do it," he said when she was done with her story. "I'm not the kind of person who can multitask like that while dealing with so many different personalities."

"You get used to it," she explained. "In the beginning, we were all a little too nervous to stand up to a difficult bride or her parents, but we've done so many weddings and parties now that we have more confidence and it shows. It's just mentally exhausting. The weekends where we have back-to-back events are the hardest. Sometimes we trade off and Josie will do one and I'll handle the other, but poor Leanna ends up at both because she's very particular about who handles her cakes and desserts."

"I can understand that. But, to be fair, she's not handling things on the same level as you and Josie, right? She's not as hands-on with the entire event."

"That's true, but she puts a lot of pressure on herself over the cakes because they are one of the main attractions of a reception or any party, really."

"She's definitely got a gift. We're hoping she'll do the cake for my grandparents' anniversary party."

"Josie mentioned that to us." She paused and then gave him a sympathetic smile. "Are you going to be okay with that?"

He looked at her oddly. "About Leanna doing the cake? Um...yeah."

Rolling her eyes, she gave him a more meaningful look. "I mean about the party. From what Josie told us, it sounds so...you know...wildly romantic. Sixty-five years of marriage and she's wearing her original wedding gown? Come on, those are some serious relationship goals and I know how you are about things like that."

Elliott let out a long breath and leaned back in his chair and frowned. "Used to be. I used to be like that, but..." He held up his hands and shrugged. "I'm fine with it and I'm happy for them. They're my grandparents and I love them so of course I'm going to be there and celebrate with them."

"Oh, I knew you were going to go to the party; I guess I was just curious about how you were feeling about it."

"I'll admit that I'm a little self-conscious about seeing everyone again and not being able to bring a date, but... that's against the rules." He let out a mirthless laugh. "It's crazy, right? I'm a grown man and my parents are telling me I can't date. Like I'm supposed to be celibate for a year because they think it will teach me a lesson or something."

"Wow, I didn't know they were demanding celibacy too..."

"They're not, but it's kind of implied."

Wasn't it?

"I guess they figure you'd only sleep with someone you were dating. But I'd bet good money that no one was thinking about...you know...sex when the whole embargo thing came up."

That got him thinking...

"I would hope not, but now that it's out there...I can't help but wonder."

"Oh God, Elliott. I'm sorry. We can change the subject. We really don't need to sit here and talk about your sex life."

"More like lack of a sex life," he murmured.

"Either way, let's talk about something else." Then she looked around frantically. "I wonder where the waitress is with our bread and butter."

He was hungry too, but he couldn't get his mind off of the fact that his entire family had essentially cock-blocked him.

"Can I ask you something?" he asked when Skye finally faced him again.

"Of course."

"Would you agree to go for a year without sex?"

Her cheeks turned red and she immediately averted her gaze. "Elliott...that's a very personal question!"

"I know but..."

Then she seemed to compose herself. Clearing her throat, she primly folded her hands on the table. "Okay, personally, I would not agree to go for a year without sex. Sex is a personal thing and no one–especially not your parents and the rest of your family–have the right to impose that sort of restriction on you. I want to believe that they weren't thinking of that when they came up with the idea of you taking a break from dating." Then she paused. "But the bigger question here is how do you feel about casual sex?"

Elliott knew he wanted to talk about this, but now that they were doing it so bluntly, he was feeling more than a little awkward.

"Um..."

She studied him while he tried to find the right words. "You never used to strike me as the casual sex kind of guy. But with your newfound attitude toward relationships, who's to say? However, everyone makes it sound like you've had a ton of failed relationships when, in fact, it's only been four. And that's in twelve years, so..." She held up her hands. "Did you only ever have sex with those four women?"

"Skylar!" he hissed, hoping no one around was listening. "Weren't you the one who was just telling me my questions were too personal?"

Her soft laugh was her first response. "Fair enough. Sorry."

Luckily, their waitress arrived with their bread and drinks and that was the perfect distraction.

"Mmm..." Skye hummed. "I love when the bread is crusty on the outside and soft on the inside. And warm like this so the butter melts. It's perfect."

He took a bite of his own piece and the taste didn't even register because his mind was racing with just how many women he'd slept with in his life and how many were there that he wasn't seriously involved with.

The number depressed him.

"We are definitely going to need more bread," Skye was saying as she reached for another piece. "I love dunking it in the salad dressing. So yummy."

"I've had sex with more than four women," he blurted out and watched as she stopped chewing. It seemed like the entire restaurant had gotten quiet, but he chose to ignore that and kept his focus on Skye. "I don't need to be in a serious relationship to sleep with a woman so...I don't have to be celibate."

She took another large bite of bread and nodded. "Okay, good for you."

"Damn right it's good for me," he said firmly. "I can have sex any time I want and no one can tell me I have to have an embargo on that too!"

"Exactly." But she wasn't looking at him. She was studying her bread plate and playing with the silverware.

Clearly I've made things awkward...

They sat in silence until their lunch arrived and then the conversation was primarily about their food.

It was incredibly boring and as much as he hated to keep harping on the subject, he couldn't seem to let it go.

"What about you?"

"What about me?" she repeated.

"Where do you stand on casual sex?"

She blushed again but seemed to consider her response. After a moment, she told him, "I'm not really a fan of it. Back in college I was in a friends-with-benefits kind of situation, but other than that, I prefer to be in a committed relationship."

That's what he figured.

Although...if she had said she was okay with something casual, Elliott knew he would have introduced the topic of potentially getting together. After all, they were friends and therefore, safe for something casual.

Unfortunately, now he knew that wasn't her thing and he didn't want to even suggest it and bring her into a relationship–even a casual one–when she clearly deserved better.

For some reason, it bothered him to think of Skylar in a casual relationship with a guy who didn't realize how special she was.

While they finished their lunch, she asked about his job and seemed more than happy to move off the topic of sex.

He drove her back to the Meet Me at the Altar office, and he knew he couldn't let her leave without addressing the one thing they seemed to be avoiding.

The kiss.

"Thank you for lunch, Elliott," she said when he parked the car. "You didn't have to pay, but I appreciate it. Everything was delicious."

Nodding, he agreed. "Before you go back inside, I need to ask you something."

"O-kay..."

"Why did you kiss me at my house that day?"

As usual, her eyes went wide before she answered.

Then her shoulders sagged and she let out a long breath as if resigning herself to responding.

"It was just an impulse," she said quietly. "I don't know. I guess I got caught up in the moment and...there was a time when I was attracted to you and I guess..."

"When? When were you attracted to me?"

Looking at him, she frowned. "Does it matter? It was just a kiss, Elliott. Can we just let it go?"

"I would, but we almost kissed again just a few hours ago in your office," he reminded her.

"But we didn't."

"Only because Josie interrupted us. If we had been alone, I definitely would have kissed you again."

Her lips parted and her expression softened. "Really?"

He nodded. "Yeah, really."

"Well...it really doesn't matter because it's not going to happen again."

"Why?"

She studied him hard. "What are you saying?"

"I'm saying I'm attracted to you, Skylar. That I want to kiss you again and not have you run away."

"Elliott, you're just saying that because...well, the whole conversation we had over lunch. For all your talk about embracing being alone, we both know that sort of thing didn't change overnight and I'm convenient," she said lowly.

Was that all this was? Was he that shallow that he was thinking of her like this?

No!

"Jeez, Skye, I'm sorry. I don't want you to feel that way, and I certainly don't think of you like that. You're a good friend and maybe you're right and all the sex talk got to me." He paused. "Although...I don't think that's really it."

She looked at him with wide-eyed disbelief. "So... what...you want us to be friends with benefits while you're forced to be single?"

"What?! No! I would never ask that of you! I'd never put you in that kind of position and I would certainly never use you like that!"

But secretly, he really wished he could because... suddenly, she was all that he wanted.

"Oh. Okay," she said solemnly as she reached for the door handle. "I need to go. Thanks again for lunch."

It wasn't until the door was open and she was about to climb out that he spoke. "If I were going to ask anyone, Skylar, it would be you. But I don't want to jeopardize our friendship. But...I just wanted you to know that I've been thinking about you and if things were different..."

"I know," she whispered, and then she was gone.

CHAPTER 7

Love is like falling down...in the end you're left hurt, scarred, and with a memory of it forever.

UNKNOWN

"Stupid, stupid, stupid..." Skye murmured to herself as she walked back to her office. Humiliation washed over her and she prayed Josie and Leanna were busy so she wouldn't have to face them.

What the hell was I thinking?

It was one thing to confide in a friend about her stupid crush, but it was another to admit it to his face!

Groaning, she tossed her purse under her desk and sank down onto her chair. Things were quiet, but that wasn't anything new. Chances were that Leanna was in the kitchen and Josie stepped out after having to deal with the impromptu client lunch. Closing her eyes, Skye leaned back and thought about her own lunch.

What on earth possessed me to ask him about the women he'd slept with? Who does that?

"Apparently, I do," she said quietly.

"What do you do?" Leanna asked as she breezed into the office in a flour-covered apron.

"I make bad casual conversation."

Leanna looked at her funny but made her way over to her desk and sat down. The three of them shared the massive office space and normally she loved it. Today, she would kill for a little privacy so she could continue to berate herself without any interruptions.

"That's ridiculous. I've never noticed that about you. Who did you have this bad conversation with?"

Before she could answer, Skye asked, "Where's Josie?"

"She pretty much ran screaming from the building after the Buchanans left. I'm surprised you didn't run into her outside. She left about fifteen minutes ago."

"I just got back less than five."

"Oh." Pausing, Leanna gave her a curious look. "You had lunch with Elliott, right?"

"Yup."

"And that was the bad casual conversation?"

"Yup."

"Hmm...and what were you talking about?"

"Sex."

Leanna gasped with surprise before her smile grew from ear to ear. "Really? Oh, my goodness, I love it! Finally!"

"What? No! Not finally!" Then she paused. "Wait... what do you mean finally?"

"I just take it you mean you and Elliott are finally going to...you know...get together. Hook up." When Skye didn't respond, Leanna let out a long sigh. "Sleep together! Have sex! Sheesh! Stop making me talk about it!"

"See? Talking about sex makes things incredibly bad and awkward!"

"It depends on who you're talking about it with, I guess. But now I have to ask how you and Elliott got on that subject."

Skye explained the conversation and how she was the one to initially bring it up. "Honestly, we were just sort of in this zone where my psychology brain kicked in and it seemed like a perfectly harmless question to ask. Then I realized how inappropriate it was and after the kiss it seemed even *more* inappropriate..."

"Wait, wait, wait...kiss? What kiss? When?" Leanna asked excitedly.

Ugh...me and my big mouth...

"You can*not* tell Josie about this."

Leanna made a zipping motion over her lips before doing a giant X over her heart.

With a weary sigh, Skye told her about the night she had gone to Elliott's for dinner and why she agreed to go and what eventually happened. When she was done, she rested her head on her desk. "This is bad, Lea. Really, really, bad."

"No, it's not," she countered. "This is great! Really, really great!"

Lifting her head, she looked at Leanna like she was crazy. "How can you even say that? He's on a dating embargo!"

"Actually, he's on an engagement one, but..." She waved that off. "Skye, this is what you've always wanted! Elliott's totally into you! Why aren't you with him right now?"

Standing, she began to pace. "Oh, let's see...how about

the fact that he's not supposed to be involved with a woman for another nine or ten months? Or maybe because he's Josie's brother? And finally–and this is a big one–maybe because he only feels this way because I'm convenient?"

"What?! That's crazy! Why would you even think such a thing?"

"Think about it," Skye went on, now pacing in front of Leanna's desk. "We all know that Elliott loves being involved with someone. Always has, always will, no matter what he says."

"O-kay..."

"Now his family tells him he can't do that for a year. Then I'm there and probably the only female companionship he's had in a while and, Elliott being Elliott, he's drawn to me." She stopped. "But not me, Skylar, just me as a woman. I bet it wouldn't matter who the woman was; if she were hanging out with him, he'd be attracted to her too."

"Now you really are crazy," Leanna said with a small head shake. "And shame on you."

"On me? Why?"

"Think about who you were dating when you were eighteen."

"Billy Slater."

"Are you telling me that you didn't think you were going to marry him at the time?"

She thought about it for a minute. "Well...yeah. We talked about it, but he never proposed."

Nodding, Leanna stood and walked around to the front of her desk. "The two of you broke up when he went away to school. Now, college. Who were you serious with in college?"

"I don't see what this has to do with..."

"Humor me."

"Fine. I dated Patrick Davies throughout my sophomore and junior years."

"Did you picture yourself marrying him?"

Rather than say anything, she just nodded.

"Any other guys you envisioned yourself marrying?"

"It's still not the same, Lea!"

"Yes, it is! Elliott was eighteen when he proposed to that first girl! They were both too young and immature. We've all been there." She paced a few feet and then turned. "The college girlfriend was a more stable relationship, he was older, and felt like he was ready to settle down."

"We all know this..."

"When that crashed and burned, he did something impulsive in Vegas! Tons of people do the same thing, but he was fortunate and escaped before they took the walk down the aisle."

"Lea..."

Stopping in front of Skye, Leanna gave her a weak smile. "He's not impulsive, and he's not a serial dater. There have been plenty of times over the years when he was single and not doing anything over the top about it. He's just a man who loves with his whole heart. It's not a crime."

"So...what are you saying?"

"I'm saying that if Elliott is attracted to you, it's because of you and not just because you're a woman. I strongly disagree with the premise that any female would do. And if I were you, I'd go and talk to him and see where this could go."

"That's just it! It can't go anywhere! His family would have a fit, and I certainly don't want to be the reason he gets any grief from them."

Leanna seemed to consider that for a long moment. Crossing her arms, she sighed. "I still think you need to talk to him. You may not be able to do anything right now, but...he's not going to be off-limits forever. Think about it."

Skye was about to comment when the business phone rang. Leanna went and answered it, leaving Skye alone with her thoughts.

And there were enough of them to make her head feel like it was ready to explode.

The timing was all wrong; that was a given. But then again, how could she possibly have known Elliott would return her feelings?

Whoa...don't get ahead of yourself. He's attracted to you. He could just be...you know...horny.

Ugh...that would be her luck.

Then something occurred to her; was that really such a bad thing? After all, this could be a very simple and sexy solution to getting over him.

And why do I want to get over him? After all these years?

For starters, after knowing each other for so damn long, if he hadn't been interested in dating her before–or even in getting to know her better–why would he suddenly want that now? She's been right there under his nose for almost twenty years.

Refusing to dwell on that, Skye went back to their conversation earlier and how he seemed to mildly fixate on the friends-with-benefits thing. And the more she thought about it, the more she fixated on it.

It was a practical solution.

Elliott said he'd never use her like that, but...what if she was the one using him? They'd both be getting something out of it, and maybe during that time, Skye would realize she'd built him up in her head all these years and that he wasn't so great. She'd see that he was too clingy or too needy or...or...too into Hallmark movies and rom-coms for her liking!

Oh, who am I kidding? I love a good Hallmark movie too!

Okay, maybe he had some gross habits or something else that would turn her off.

She could only hope.

Now she just had to come up with a way to let him know she had given their conversation some thought, and she was more than willing to help him pass the next several months until he was free to go out and fall in love again.

Because she knew he eventually would.

No matter how much he tried to deny it.

It was after ten and Elliott tossed the remote aside because there was nothing holding his interest on TV. Hell, nothing held his interest all day since he dropped Skylar back off at her office. He'd gotten nothing done at work, his dinner was completely tasteless, and everything on television just wasn't for him.

So where did that leave him?

Standing, he walked to the kitchen and grabbed himself a bottle of water and realized it was too early to go to sleep and that meant he was going to have to force himself to find something to read. Normally he was all for reading before going to bed, but he had a feeling tonight it would all just be a blur of words that didn't sink in.

Maybe I've got some melatonin around here someplace to help me fall asleep.

With nothing else to do, he walked down the hall to his bedroom and then went straight to the master bath to look in the medicine cabinet for something to help him sleep. He scanned shelves and then looked in the linen closet and eventually found himself back in the kitchen, searching through the cabinets there.

"Well, shit." The next step was getting in the car and driving up to the twenty-four-hour pharmacy, and he was already searching for his keys when there was a knock on his door. He froze in place because no one ever came by at this time of night and certainly not without calling first. Grabbing his phone, he checked his doorbell camera and couldn't believe what he saw.

Skylar.

A slow smile crossed his lips.

She knocked again–louder this time–and Elliott quickly went to open it. "Skye," he said breathlessly. "What are you doing here?"

Looking up at him as she wrung her hands, her expression was incredibly serious.

"Skylar?"

"Here's the thing," she began. "I thought about everything you said earlier and I know you said you would never ask it of me–you'd never use me–but I don't care. If given the chance, I'd say yes to it all. Friends with benefits, casual sex, I don't care. I've thought about you–about us–for so many damn years that I'm sick of it."

He was pretty sure he was having a heart attack because he couldn't believe she was actually here and saying what she was saying. "Skye, I..."

She stepped into his house before turning to face him again. "Do you want me?"

"You know I do." And his hands began to twitch with the need to touch her and make sure she was real–that he wasn't dreaming this. "But..."

Reaching out, Skye placed a finger over his lips. "No buts. I don't care if it's just tonight. I just know that I'm going to continue to kick myself if I don't do anything about this. About us."

Elliott gently wrapped his hand around her wrist before kissing her palm. She was being honest with him, so he owed it to her to do the same. "Before we do this—before we do anything—you need to know that I haven't changed my mind. I know it's a shitty thing for me to be saying right now, but...

"Elliott...I..."

"There's a part of me that feels like I should tell you to go. To leave and just forget about this. You deserve so much more than someone who has sworn off relationships."

"But...?"

"But..." he said huskily, "I really don't want you to go."

She blushed. "I don't want to go either."

He stepped in closer and shut the door behind him. "So...what happens now?"

A shy smile crossed her face. "I was hoping we could save the Q & A for after."

"After?"

She nodded, biting her bottom lip. "Yeah. After." Then, because she was definitely the bolder of the two of them, she moved in close and kissed him.

It was all the encouragement he needed.

His hands reached up to anchor in her hair, but first he pulled out the clip holding it back. Then, her gloriously long hair cascaded down over his skin and it felt as good as he imagined it would. Skye pressed closer and wrapped her arms around him and it seemed crazy that they were doing this.

While still standing in his entryway.

As much as he hated to stop kissing her, he hated the thought of standing here even more. "Can we...I mean... would you mind if we...?"

"Took this inside?" she breathlessly finished for him. "Um...yes, please."

Taking Skye's hand in his, he walked to the living room and then stopped because...was this inside or did she mean...

"Keep walking," she whispered huskily, and so he did.

In his bedroom, he let go of her hand and turned to look at her. His first thought was, "Yes! Finally!" while another was asking, "Why is Skylar in my bedroom?"

He told that second one to shut up as he stepped in close and wrapped his arms around her waist. Then he simply let his gaze devour her. How had he gone for so long without realizing how stunning she was? The girl he'd known all these years had turned into a beautiful woman. There was a small smattering of freckles across the bridge of her nose and a few on her cheeks. She had a beauty mark next to her right eye that he knew she was a little self-conscious about, but he always thought it was cute. And her body? Yeah, Skye was always on the trim side without a lot of curves, but holding her close now, he knew the curves she did have were perfect.

Stop thinking like that! You're not supposed to be getting all romantic and attached!

As much as his mind told him he shouldn't, his heart seemed to have other ideas.

"You've gotten quiet," Skye said, interrupting his thoughts. "Are you having second thoughts?"

Shaking his head, he leaned in and placed a soft kiss on the tip of her nose. "Never. I was just thinking that this is...

new. Different. I'm afraid to do something wrong and ruin it."

She let out a soft sigh and moved out of his arms and Elliott feared he did exactly that.

"I was hoping we could wait to talk about all of this, but I guess it's smarter to do it first," she said before sitting on the corner of his bed. "This is about...maybe satisfying some curiosity and helping you while you're on this whole year-long ban on dating. This isn't about anything serious."

He knew what she was saying made sense, but it still felt all kinds of wrong to him.

"There's no chance of us falling in love because...well, you're done with that," she said firmly, and it was on the tip of his tongue to disagree, but he kept it to himself for now. "I think since we've both expressed an...interest, we owe it to ourselves to explore this."

Okay, that he agreed with, but...

"Is this a one-time thing, Skye?" he asked and, unable to help himself, he sat down beside her, caressing her cheek.

"I...I'm not sure. That's why I had thought we'd wait until...after to talk about it. But if you're not comfortable with this..."

He pulled her to her feet and cut off her words with a kiss. Both hands gently cupped her face as he deepened the kiss, desperate to keep her from talking either of them out of this.

For years he had talked himself out of acting on his attraction to her because he thought it was wrong and she'd never shown any interest in him other than as a friend. But knowing she was hiding her feelings just like he was?

Game changer.

For now.

This was different.

Skye was different.

They had a history together which meant this wasn't just a casual hookup. It couldn't be. And over the past few months, he felt like they really got to know each other and that made this feel a whole lot more...intimate.

Which should have scared the crap out of him and made him say "thanks but no thanks," but he didn't. He couldn't.

For all he knew, they were going to find that they weren't the least bit compatible and this was a one-time thing and his curiosity would be settled.

But if this kiss was anything to go by, they were not only going to be compatible, but combustible.

Lifting her in his arms, he turned and guided them both down onto the bed. He stretched out on top of her and heard her hum of approval. Her arms tightened around him as her legs did the same.

Their kiss turned wild, carnal, and it seemed crazy that they were doing this to each other after so many years of...*not* doing this to each other. But again, he wasn't going to complain.

Skye arched her back beneath him and gave him a nudge that sent them rolling and changing positions. She lifted her head as she sat up and smiled down at him. Her long hair was in sexy disarray, her lips were wet and slightly swollen, and she looked ready for more.

And he desperately wanted to give that to her.

His hands rested on her hips and gently squeezed, causing her to smile. "You're really good at this," she said, licking her lips.

"Oh, yeah?"

She nodded. "Yeah. Kissing. Really, really good at it." She licked her lips again before reaching in front of her and pulling her sweater up and over her head. The plain white satin and lace bra certainly wasn't designed for seduction, and yet on her, it looked sexy as hell. Skye glanced down at herself and frowned.

"What? What's the matter?"

"I should have planned better," she murmured as her hands came up to cover herself.

Elliott was quick to slowly guide her hands away. "I like that you didn't plan. In my head, I like to think that you wanted me so badly that you couldn't wait and came as you were."

"I did," she whispered. "I really did."

He lifted up slightly and cupped a hand around her nape and guided her back down for another kiss.

And it didn't seem possible for it to be hotter than the one before, but it was.

They rolled all over the bed–each of them taking a moment to be the dominant one–and Elliott swore he was going insane with need. Skye's skin was so warm and soft and he wanted to touch and taste more of her. When he couldn't take anymore, he rolled her beneath him again and sat up and mimicked her earlier move of whipping his shirt up and off, tossing it to the floor. This time when he leaned back down, he kissed along her throat, her collar bone, and then the sweet valley between her breasts. He heard her soft hiss of pleasure before reaching up to lower the flimsy bra straps off her shoulders and down her arms so he could reach more of her.

The first swipe of his tongue over her nipple had her humming with pleasure. Her hands raked up into his hair and held on. The longer he teased her, the louder she got. When he switched to the other side, she was panting his name and begging for more.

"Elliott...please. I need...I want..." She was writhing beneath him and he knew exactly what she meant because he definitely needed and wanted more too.

It would have been easy to go forward with this mindless passion. To simply strip them both and claim her. He knew it would be amazing and beyond satisfying, but there was something he had to say first.

Lifting his head, he looked down at her. Her eyes were closed and she was still a little breathless and squirming.

"Skye," he whispered, and when she slowly looked up at him, the sight of her took his breath away. She was so beautiful and he felt humbled that she was here with him like this.

She quietly said his name as her hand stroked his jaw before slowly skimming down over his shoulders before resting on his chest.

Right over his heart.

For a moment he reconsidered. Maybe speaking up would ruin the moment and then all of this would just go away. But there was still a twinge of reason swirling in his head and he knew better than to ignore it.

"I just wanted to make sure you were still okay," he said gruffly. "That we're not going too fast or...or that you're not having second thoughts."

Her expression softened and she looked up at him in a way most people only dreamed of. "Elliott Sullivan, I am 100% sure that this is what I want. No second thoughts."

Carefully, he lifted her hand from his chest and kissed it. "I really wanted to be sure. I thought that..."

"Elliott?"

"Hmm?"

"Stop talking," she said with a sexy grin. "We've been

talking for almost twenty years. Now I'd really like…" She paused, glancing away, and he could see her blush.

"Tell me," he urged. "Tell me what you want."

When her gaze slowly met his again, she said, "I'd really like for you to…show me how much you want me."

A primal side of him that he didn't recognize sparked at her words. He wanted to tell her how much he wanted her– to describe everything he wanted to do with her–but instead, he claimed her lips with his and did his best to prove it.

The next time Elliott had a clear thought, the bedside clock read two a.m. Skye was curled up beside him with her head on his shoulder, their legs tangled together, and her hand on his chest.

It was damn near perfect.

"I should go," she sleepily murmured. "It's late."

He held her tighter. "And that's why you're not going anywhere. It's too late and you're too tired to be out driving."

"But…"

"No buts," he insisted before placing a soft kiss on the top of her head. "Besides, I like holding you."

"Elliott…" Maybe she was going to say more, but she yawned and seemed to drift off to sleep.

It bothered him that she wanted to go, and there wasn't a doubt in his mind that if she were more awake, she would have argued with him as she got dressed.

That's what people do in casual relationships. They don't spend the night…

And while he knew that was a thing, it felt wrong where Skye was concerned.

He agreed to her offer, her terms, but she fell asleep before they could talk more about it. And that meant only one thing...

They were going to have to do this again.

And for the first time in months, Elliott fell asleep with a smile on his face.

CHAPTER 8

If you're afraid of getting hurt and feeling severe pain, then avoid falling in love.

UNKNOWN

SNEAKING out of a man's bed before the sun comes up was not something Skye enjoyed.

Yet that's exactly what she did.

Going into work later that morning had her feeling a bit paranoid and she did everything she could to avoid Josie, but as the week went on, it got harder and harder to do. They had three events planned for the weekend and on Thursday afternoon, Josie cornered Skye in the office.

"What's going on with you?" she demanded.

"I...don't know what you mean." *Liar, liar, liar!*

"Skye, come on. We've hardly spoken at all this week and that's been pretty damn annoying since we have all these weddings this weekend that we need to be communicating about!"

"We have," Skye argued. "I sent you emails and texts and..."

Slamming her hands down on Skye's desk, her friend glared at her. "We need to actually talk! There are too many details to manage by text!" She paused and straightened. "This is about Elliott, isn't it?"

Skye felt herself pale. "Um..."

"Dammit, I knew it." She shook her head.

"Josie, listen. Let me explain..."

"No, no, I get it. I never should have pushed you to go to lunch with him," Josie said wearily, walking over to her own desk and sitting down. "And that was after I forced you to go and see him the day of the wedding." She groaned. "It's just...there are times when I can't be there for him and I want to be, so I automatically think of you because you're like a sister to him too!"

Yeah, not so much anymore...

"I get it. Really. It's just that..."

"Honestly, I don't know how to act around him anymore," Josie was saying. "Like I really feel bad about the way we all ganged up on him after Tracy ran off and things are safe when we're around my parents because no one wants to bring it up. I know if we're hanging out alone–just the two of us–that it's going to be a topic I can't avoid." She gave Skye a sad smile. "I'm sorry I keep throwing you under the bus with him."

"It's okay," she said, feeling incredibly grateful that Josie had no idea about how she really felt about her brother.

"No, it's not. I'm going to have to sit down and hang out one-on-one with him, eventually." Pausing, she shook her head. "Oh, and while we're on the subject of my family, they're all coming in on Monday to start planning my grandparents' anniversary party."

"Don't take this the wrong way, but...why?"

"Because we have to plan the party."

Skye fought the urge to roll her eyes. "Yeah, I got that. What I'm saying is...why do they need to come in? It seems to me you can do all of that from the comfort of your parents' home over Sunday dinner and then just fill me and Leanna in on what you need us to do."

"You're not going to believe this, but Nana is insisting on being treated like any other client. She wanted to make the appointment and come in and see our presentation." She shook her head again. "Personally, I think she's adorable and Pop-pop told me to indulge her and let her pick whatever she wants for the party."

"We're giving them a discount though, right?"

"Well, I didn't want to just assume," Josie replied. "We're just going to have to wait and see what it is that they want to do and then figure out all the costs. Oh, and get this, they booked the event space at the arboretum for it because that's where Pop-Pop proposed all those years ago. How cute is that?"

Unable to help herself, Skye sighed dreamily. "That is incredibly romantic."

Josie shrugged as if she didn't agree.

"You don't think it's romantic? They've been married sixty-five years, they're renewing their vows, and doing it in the spot where he proposed! Hallmark would make a movie out of this if they heard about it!"

But Josie just waved her off. "Of course I think it's great and I'm happy for them. But it's more sentimental than romantic. Plus, it's probably the only place they have a connection to from way back then. Everything else has been either torn down or changed into something different."

All Skye could do was stare.

"What? Now what?"

"Seriously, who hurt you as a child that you are this jaded?"

"Ugh...not this again. I'm not jaded; I'm just practical."

"No, you're jaded, and it's hard to see how you and Elliott are related."

"Another thing we're not doing again," Josie argued and then let out a long sigh. "Can we please just focus on the weekend events now–face-to-face–and then work on a plan for my grandparents?"

"Of course."

They had a lot to cover and Leanna came in and joined them a few minutes later. They called in a dinner order to be delivered and worked until after nine. By the time she walked through her front door, Skye was exhausted. Tossing her purse down, she padded into the kitchen and grabbed a bottle of water before heading into the bedroom to change into pajamas.

Whipping her bra off felt like a religious experience, and she was down to just her panties when there was a knock on her front door. Grabbing her robe, she slid it on and tried to think of who would be showing up at this time of night. Maybe it was one of the girls because she had forgotten something at the office. Or maybe it was her neighbor Mrs. Gayle; she always picked up any packages that got left on Skye's porch while she was at work. Or perhaps...

"Skye? Are you in there?"

Elliott.

She hung her head and let out a long breath because she knew they were going to see each other again.

But secretly she had hoped to be the one to initiate it when she'd be wearing more than her robe and panties.

There was no way to avoid him so she walked over and opened the door. "Hey," she said with a small smile.

"Hey. Mind if I come in?" He looked slightly disheveled–his hair was its usual scruffy self and his glasses were slightly askew. It must have been a long day if he'd already taken out his contacts.

Skye stepped back and once he was inside, she shut the door and leaned against it.

"You just getting home from work?" he asked, walking around her living room. Her condo was definitely smaller than his place, and right now, she felt a little self-conscious about it.

Pushing away from the door, she replied, "Yes. We've got multiple events this weekend so we had to go over all the specifics, and then we worked on some plans for your grand-parents' party. They're coming in Monday afternoon to talk about it."

He nodded and walked over to the fireplace and studied the pictures she had on the mantle. "I heard they booked the arboretum. They used to take me and Josie there when we were kids. My grandfather can tell you every kind of plant and flower there. I always thought that was amazing."

"It is," she agreed and then waited to see if he was going to call her out on sneaking out the other morning.

Looking at her over his shoulder, he smiled. "Mean-while, I couldn't name even one flower or plant and that's why I got poison ivy seven times."

That made her laugh softly. "I remember you having it a few times. I had no idea it was that many."

He nodded. "Yup. And every time after it cleared up, he would take me back out and point it out to me and explain how to recognize it and then..." He held up his hands. "I can do coding for multiple computer programs at the same time and remember all kinds of crazy tech stuff, but I could never remember to look at the kind of grass I was walking through."

"That's because it wasn't important to you. There's nothing wrong with that."

"Tell that to thirteen-year-old me who cried from all the itching."

She laughed softly at that and wrapped her arms around her middle. "What are you doing here, Elliott?" she asked, her voice barely a whisper.

Walking over to her, his expression was unreadable. "Why'd you leave without waking me up?"

Dammit.

Unable to look at him, she shrugged. "I shouldn't have even stayed the night. That's not part of what we agreed to do."

Now he moved in even closer but didn't touch her. "Actually, we didn't get to agreeing on much of anything. We said we'd talk, but then we didn't."

Skye felt her cheeks heat with remembrance. "It was late and I couldn't seem to keep my eyes open."

"No one's blaming you," he said softly. "I was just disappointed to wake up and find you gone."

The sigh was out before she could stop it and she looked back up at him. "This is the kind of thing you're supposed to be avoiding, Elliott."

He took her by the hand and led her over to the sofa so

they could sit. "Okay, I think you and I are not quite on the same page with some of this, so why don't you lay it out for me—what you think it is we're supposed to be doing."

Ugh...

When she sat back on the sofa with a little more force than intended, her robe gaped open at the top and at the bottom—essentially exposing a whole lot more of herself than she intended. With a small gasp, Skye did her best to cover herself, but when she looked up at Elliott and saw his heated gaze, she was lost.

There was no way of knowing who moved first, but the next thing she knew, they were kissing and Elliott was gently tugging at the tie around her waist. His mouth slanted over hers over and over as his hands seemed to be touching her everywhere. It was madness and such a turn-on to know he was just as needy for her as she was for him.

Because she was totally needy.

All week long she had thought about what would happen when they saw each other again and while the practical part of her brain tried to reason that nothing would have to change, the woman who still harbored a fairly large crush had hoped for this particular scenario that was being played out right now.

She wanted to remind him how he was the one who wanted to talk, but...

Later.

There would be plenty of time later.

Breathless, Elliott stared up at Skye's bedroom ceiling. Beside him, she was also trying to catch her breath and just thinking about why they were both breathing hard made him smile.

Round one had been out on her sofa.

Round two had been in her kitchen.

Round three brought them to the bedroom, and he was fairly certain that he couldn't get up and walk, even if someone put a gun to his head.

But what a way to go...

Yeah, she completely rocked his world–again–and he had a feeling they weren't going to have their talk tonight either.

Not that it mattered. He wasn't interested in having a list of rules–didn't feel like they needed them. They weren't strangers; they were friends, and as such, they should be able to sort of go with the flow until one of them didn't. Rules would complicate things, and Elliott knew that Skye tended to thrive on things being organized and well-planned, but that wasn't going to fly where sex was concerned.

Turning his head, he looked at her and smiled. Her eyes were closed, her skin was flushed, and he couldn't resist rolling toward her and lazily touching her.

At the first touch of his hand on her shoulder, she jumped slightly. "You scared me," she whispered.

"Sorry." And yeah, he couldn't help but laugh softly. "You were maybe expecting someone else?"

"No, but I just wasn't expecting you to...you know...touch me."

Frowning, he stared at her. "Why not?"

Now it was her turn to turn and stare. "What do you mean, why not?"

"Why wouldn't I touch you again?"

Rolling onto her side, she faced him and shrugged. "I just thought we were...you know...done."

Ah...now they were getting someplace.

Rather than answer, he took his time letting his hand caress her from shoulder to shoulder and down to her breasts. He kept his touch light as he circled her nipple and he loved the sound of the slight catch in her breath.

When she didn't stop him, he skimmed lower–over her stomach, up and over her hip, and down her thigh. She was soft everywhere and he couldn't make himself stop. It wasn't until his hand rested on her bottom and squeezed that she let out a little moan of pleasure.

"Elliott..."

He might not be able to walk, but he could certainly roll them both over and kiss her while he continued touching and pleasuring her. And once he had Skye beneath him, he rested his forehead against hers. "I'm not leaving tonight," he told her, his hand now moving on to other spots on her body that he knew drove her wild. "I'm staying and I'm not sneaking out in the morning."

Her head thrashed from side to side as she began to pant from his touch, and he had to admit it was an extremely satisfying sight.

"Are you okay with that?' he asked gruffly.

"Yes," she said frantically, arching beneath him, seeking more of him.

"Good." And with that, he kissed her and it was wet and wild and he swore they shouldn't be like this again so soon.

And yet...they were.

Who was he to argue?

Early the next morning, Skylar's alarm went off and Elliott had to wonder what time it was. It had been some time after one when they finally crashed.

She was in his arms and groaned sleepily as she rolled over to turn off the alarm.

"What time is it?"

"Six."

That was when he normally got up, but it felt much earlier.

Neither of them moved for several minutes and when the alarm went off again, Skye turned it off and slowly climbed from the bed without a word. He watched as she padded to the bathroom and shut the door, and then promised himself he'd just close his eyes for a minute.

"Elliott?"

"Hmm?"

"You need to wake up," she said, shaking him slightly. "It's getting late."

Late? It had only been a minute, maybe two...

Then he turned and focused on the clock and saw it was after seven. That had him sitting straight up and when he looked at Skye, he saw that she showered, put on makeup, did her hair, and got dressed. "Why did you let me sleep?" he asked, scrambling from the bed.

"I didn't *let* you sleep," she replied tartly, "I was getting ready for work! I thought you would get up on your own!"

Well...shit. She had him there. He totally should have.

He walked naked from her bedroom and out to the living room to get his clothes and heard Skye in the kitchen. When he joined her, he was dressed and doing his best to wake up a bit more. Without a word, she handed him a travel mug of coffee.

"Thanks." Stepping around her, he added milk and sugar and took a sip. "So, what time do you have to be in?"

"Eight," she said as she continued to move around the kitchen, cleaning things up from their escapades in there the night before. When he tried to help her, she told him it wasn't necessary. "You probably need to go home and shower and change, right?"

It didn't take a genius to figure out she was pushing him out the door.

"Yeah," he murmured before taking another sip of his coffee. "Can I see you this weekend?"

She stopped and looked at him oddly. "Um..."

"I know you mentioned you had a couple of events, but I have no idea what that means in terms of your time, so..."

Combing her hair behind her ear, she seemed flustered. "It's going to be a pretty hectic weekend, Elliott. I'm not going to have any free time. I'm sorry."

It was probably for the best because he didn't want to push too much where she was concerned. Besides, this was probably a good time for him to start going out with the guys again.

It was time.

With nothing left to do or say—not really—he leaned in and kissed her on the cheek. "Not a problem. Don't work too hard and tell my sister I said hello."

Skye's eyes went a little wide—like she was expecting him to argue a little more about the weekend or...

"I can't tell Josie you said hello! Then she'll want to know where I saw you and why I saw you and..."

"Okay, okay, okay," he said calmly, trying to soothe her. Without thinking, he wrapped her in his arms and placed a soft kiss on her forehead. "I wasn't thinking."

She nodded and when he let her go a minute later and

walked out the door, he felt a little out of sorts–like leaving her like that felt wrong.

But this was who he was now. He wasn't looking to get involved or committed or date or whatever you wanted to call it. Even if there wasn't an embargo, he wasn't that guy anymore.

But as he pulled out of Skye's driveway, he wondered if he was only fooling himself.

CHAPTER 9

Sometimes you have to forget what you feel and remember what you deserve.

UNKNOWN

MONDAY MORNING, Skye finished her second cup of coffee and was already pouring her third when Leanna peeked into the office. "They're here," she said cheerily before walking away.

This was the meeting with Josie's grandparents and as much as she knew it was going to be a very sweet meeting, she was still battling some exhaustion from the weekend. Three events that all ran long meant she had very little sleep and add that to her night with Elliott and...yeah...she needed a few days off to get caught up.

With her coffee in one hand and her tablet in the other, she made her way to their consultation suite and froze.

Josie's entire family was there.

Including Elliott.

He caught her eye and raised his coffee mug to her with a smile, and she knew she had to just smile in return and take a seat or someone would accuse her of acting weird.

Which...she was.

So, with a smile, she walked into the room and took her seat–on the opposite side of the table from Elliot–and then said her hellos to everyone. Josie sat at the head of the table and began the meeting.

"Okay," she said, smiling from ear to ear. "Nana and Pop-Pop, tell us what you envision for your party."

"Whatever my Millie wants, we're going to do," her grandfather said, holding his wife's hand. "She's given me the best years of my life and I want her to have the perfect day."

Skye found herself getting a little teary by that sweet declaration and carefully dabbed at her eyes without being too obvious.

Except when she looked up, Elliott was watching her and gave her a smile that told her he had seen it.

Refusing to focus on that, she turned her attention back to his grandmother and what she was describing for her day–lots of her favorite foods, all their friends and family, some of Leanna's most famous cakes, and music so everyone could dance. She wasn't overly specific and that's where Josie chimed in with suggestions before Leanna gave them a list of dessert selections. Honestly, Skye wasn't particularly needed here, but it would look strange for her to excuse herself so...she sat and listened and made notes to refer back to later.

Before she knew it, Josie was wrapping things up. "I hope none of you have plans for lunch, because I have food being brought in and Leanna has a selection of cupcakes for us! So just give me a few minutes and we'll have everything set up in the tasting room!"

This was Skye's chance to leave, but she got caught up talking to Mr. and Mrs. Sullivan, then Leanna asked her to help set up the dessert, and the next thing she knew, she was sitting in the tasting room and had a plate full of food in front of her–compliments of Elliott.

Dammit.

"You looked ready to bolt so...I brought food," he said with an easy grin as he sat beside her.

"If you knew I wanted to leave, why make me the plate?" she asked quietly–and possibly with a little more snark than needed.

His laugh was low and throaty and shouldn't have been even the least bit sexy, but...it was.

"Because everyone would wonder why you left and I figured you wouldn't want to answer those questions."

"Maybe I have someplace I need to be," she quipped, even as she took a bite of potato salad.

That seemed to bring him up short. "Oh, um...I didn't think of that. I just thought you were maybe trying to avoid me or something because...well...you know."

Seriously, was he trying to draw attention to them? "Elliott," she hissed, leaning in close even as she felt her face heat up. "Can you just not say stuff like that?"

"What? I technically didn't say anything. I was just implying or hinting at..."

"Just stop doing that!" she cried, and everyone stopped and stared at them.

Awesome.

Beside her, Elliott was trying hard not to laugh. "Sorry," he called out to his family. "I was just goofing around while Skye was trying to eat. Don't mind us."

Fortunately, everyone went back to their own meals and conversations as Skye glared at him. "Thanks. Like that wasn't incredibly awkward."

He shrugged and took a bite of his sandwich. "It's not that big of a deal." They ate in companionable silence for a few minutes. "So how are you? How was your weekend?"

"I'm good," she replied, feeling a little more at ease. "The weekend was its usual form of chaos and I have tomorrow off so I am going to try to get caught up on some sleep. What about you? How was your weekend?"

Rather than answer right away, he took a drink of his Coke and then ate a few chips. Skye was about to prompt him to respond when he finally did.

"It was...good," he said, not looking at her. His focus was on his plate and it just seemed...odd.

"O-kay..."

"I went out with Tyler and Alex Saturday night. We went to Flanagan's downtown, played some darts and...you know...hung out."

"They have the best wings there," she commented, since for whatever reason, he was being awkward with the conversation. "I haven't been there in a long time, but before we opened Meet Me at the Altar, me, Josie, and Lea would go there a lot on the weekends. It's a great place to meet..."

Oh.

Oh...

Well...crap.

"Yeah," he murmured. "So there was that."

At first, all Skye could do was nod because...really... what was she supposed to say? They weren't dating; there had been no talk of being exclusive in this stupid casual relationship thing they were doing. And that was definitely her fault because she kept putting off having that conversation.

Lesson learned.

Clearing her throat quietly, she focused on her own plate, even though her appetite was gone. "So what do you think of the party plans? I love the way your grandfather let your grandmother take the lead. Super cute."

"Yeah," he said with very little enthusiasm. "Listen, Skye, I want you to know that…"

There was no way she wanted to talk about this here and immediately cut him off. "It's okay, Elliott. Really. You don't owe me any explanation and you are free to do whatever you want with…you know…whomever you want." Now she did look up at him and saw his expression go from frowning to being almost furious.

"Really? That's how you feel?"

The lump in her throat prevented her from saying the words, but she forced herself to nod.

Pushing his plate aside, he leaned in close. "I cannot believe you," he said, his voice a mere whisper. Angry, but still a whisper. "I guess this is part of the rules we never got around to talking about."

For the life of her, Skye had no idea why he was so angry. He was basically getting to have his cake and eat it too! What more did he want?

"This really isn't the time or place to be having this discussion, so…"

"Skye?" Leanna said, leaning over her shoulder and giving her a gentle squeeze. "Can you give me a hand in the kitchen? I've got that cupcake order to prepare and I'm a little behind." Then she smiled at Elliott. "Good to see you, Elliott!"

There was no cupcake delivery that Skye was aware of, but she wasn't about to turn down a lifeline.

"Sure. No problem." Then she pasted a smile on her face as she looked back at Elliott. "Good to see you again. Take care." And before she could say more, Leanna took her by the hand and practically dragged her from the room and didn't stop until they were in the far corner of the kitchen. "What in the world, Lea?"

Her friend maneuvered them around until she gently pushed Skye onto a stool. Leanna wasn't the least bit intimidating, but she was certainly going for that look right now. "If you could see what I was seeing, you'd know why I dragged you out of there."

"Um...what?"

Nodding, she explained, "The two of you were looking way too intense–angry intense–and in another minute, everyone else was going to notice it too." She paused and pulled up a stool for herself. "So what's going on?"

Groaning, she leaned back and hit her head against the wall. "Ouch..."

"Nice stall tactic. Spill it."

"I really don't want to here."

"Well, too bad. I didn't want to have to make a scene and force you out of there and yet...here we are."

Not wanting to argue, Skye told her about her two nights with Elliott and then what he just shared with her. "I mean, I know we didn't talk about any rules or whatever, but...it just stung that he went out to meet someone within hours of leaving my bed!"

Without a word, Leanna got up and walked over to her refrigerator. Skye had no idea what she was doing, but when she came back, she handed Skye a container of icing.

It would be rude to decline so...

"Eat your icing and hear me out," Leanna said as she got situated on her stool again. "First, I am so excited for you! You finally got to be with your dream man!"

"For all the good it's doing me…"

"Oh, hush. Yes, the two of you never talked about any rules, but honestly…he didn't really admit that he hooked up with anyone."

"He was out with the guys at Flanagan's and you know there's only one reason single people go there." She took a heaping spoonful of chocolate icing and moaned with pure pleasure. "We used to go there all the time whenever we were looking to meet guys."

"Okay, yes. That's true, but…he went out with his friends and he's a single guy. Where else did you think they were going to go?"

She stuck another spoonful into her mouth and refused to speculate.

"Skye, he's doing what everyone wants him to do, but that doesn't mean it's what *he* wants to do."

"But it is!" she countered around a mouthful of sugary sweetness. "He's done with relationships and wanting to get married and…and…everything he's been chasing for years! Now all he wants is casual and no commitments and a good time! And like an idiot, I threw myself at him and thought I could handle it. Two dates later and I'm crying in a bowl of frosting!" She licked the spoon and then paused. "How did you know I was going to need this?"

"Oh, please. Once a week I put a fresh bowl in there for you." Laughing, Leanna shook her head. "There's always a chocolate one for you and I try to have either butterscotch or strawberry in there for Josie."

"I had no idea." Tears stung her eyes. "You are seriously an awesome friend."

"Hey, it's just what I do," she said with a slight blush. "So what's going to happen now?"

With a shrug, Skye let out a long breath. "I guess it's over. I thought I could do casual, but it turns out, I can't. There's no way I'd be okay with him coming around and knowing he slept with someone else the night before or something. I could handle knowing this wasn't going to be permanent or even long-term, but I can't be one of many." She shuddered. "Serious ick factor for me."

"Yeah, that would be a huge deal breaker for me too." Reaching out, she squeezed Skye's free hand. "I'm really sorry. I wanted things to work out for the two of you."

She took another spoonful of icing before replying. "The timing was just off. I should have known better than to get involved with him so soon after his breakup. That's totally on me. I got so caught up in the fantasy of it all that I wasn't being particularly smart."

"Love doesn't always make you smart," Leanna said wistfully.

"This isn't love," she said miserably. "This was me and my stupid crush that I should have gotten over years ago. It was all much better when it was in my head. The reality sucks."

Leanna looked around for a moment before leaning in close. "Was the sex bad? Is that why it sucked?"

"What?!" Choking on the icing, Skye coughed hard for several seconds until she could catch her breath. "No! No, that's not what I meant! I meant the current situation and the whole casual aspect of it all." Then she sighed. "The sex was so freaking good that I think I'm ruined for other men."

"Wow...what's that like?"

"Um..."

"No, seriously, what's it like to have great sex?"

"Lea, surely you've had great sex," Skye said, placing the icing down. "What about Nathan...oh, what was his last name? You guys dated in college."

"The sex was fine, but I definitely would never say he ruined me for other men. I want some of that."

"Don't we all," Skye muttered and sighed again. "I'm glad I'm off tomorrow because I think I'm going to have a total pity party of a day and just lick my wounds." She paused. "And possibly burn my sheets, I don't know."

Leanna hopped off of her stool and hugged her. "I'm really sorry, Skye. I truly believed this was going to be wildly romantic and everything you dreamed it would be."

"Sadly, so did I."

When the weekend rolled around again, Elliott didn't have a reasonable excuse for not going out with his friends again. This was something they always did when he wasn't in a relationship, and maybe if he just put in a little effort, he'd enjoy himself.

Or he could continue to think about Skylar and the look on her face when they talked on Monday.

Climbing into his car, he let his head fall back as he let out a huff of annoyance. This was what he said he wanted—his freedom, to be single and uninvolved. So why wasn't he enjoying it? Sleeping with Skye was supposed to be safe. They were friends and that was it.

Friends who had amazing sex, but...still friends.

She wasn't making any demands on his time and seemed perfectly fine with keeping things casual...

Then why did she look hurt when she thought he hooked up with someone last weekend?

"This is bullshit," he murmured. All week long he had made himself crazy thinking about that look and he wasn't going to be able to go out and do a damn thing until he got an answer. "Or I'm using it as an excuse so I don't have to go to Flanagan's again."

Okay, there was that, but as he continued to sit in his driveway and think, he knew what the true motivation was.

He wanted to see her.

The only problem was that it was Friday night and he knew from conversations they'd had and also from his sister that it was usually a work night for them. She could be at a wedding or a rehearsal or some other kind of event.

"So now what?" he wondered. Did he drive over to her place and take the chance or did he do a little research first?

The solution was a no-brainer. He pulled his phone out and pulled up Josie's number and hit send. It rang several times before she answered.

"Hey, El!" his sister said when she answered. "What's up?"

"Nothing much. I was wondering if you were free tonight to hang out?"

It was pretty much the last thing he wanted to do, but... it was the first scenario to come to mind.

"Ooh...what did you have in mind?" she asked excitedly, and Elliott wanted to kick himself.

"I was planning on going downtown to Flanagan's with everyone," he explained, and did his best not to oversell it. "You know, no big deal. It's just going to be me, Ty, Alex, and Jared. No biggie. But since we haven't hung out much and you know everyone..."

"You picked a great night, big brother! We don't have any events until tomorrow night and it's an engagement party, so it's very low-key, so...yay! We get to hang out!"

Me and my big mouth...

"We don't have to go to Flanagan's, you know. We can go and grab some dinner or something if you'd prefer."

"Why wouldn't I want to go? Flanagan's has the best selection of craft beers and some seriously addictive wings. Besides, I've been meaning to catch up with Ty for a while now, so..."

"Wait, wait, wait...why do you need to see Tyler?"

She let out a little huff that told him how much she hated when he questioned her on anything, but that didn't deter him.

"You know he's really gunning to make partner at the law firm and he's in charge of organizing some big fundraiser thing. I told him I'd help him and we just haven't had any time to get together and talk about it. So if he's going to be there, maybe we can get the ball rolling and then get something down on the calendar. It's no biggie."

And for some reason, relief washed over him. "Oh, okay. Good."

She laughed. "You are such a dork! Like I'd ever go out with any of your friends. Please! Give me a little credit. That would just be weird."

And I've clearly stepped in it again...

"Fine. Whatever. Forget I said anything," he grumbled.

Yes, please forget I said anything!

"I usually do," she teased. "And besides, Ty and I are just friends. He's seriously like another brother to me–just less annoying than you."

That made him laugh and relax. "Good, can we let this go now?"

"I wasn't the one who got weird about it in the first place. But...speaking of friends...would you mind if I invited Skye and Leanna to join us? We haven't been out for a girls' night in a while and even though we're technically crashing your guys' night, I think it could be a lot of fun. Are you okay with that?"

Don't sound anxious...don't sound anxious...

"Um...yeah. Sure. I don't see that as a problem. Do you want me to come pick you up?"

"No, I'm good. Plus, I'll bet you're already walking out the door and I'm definitely going to need to put a little effort in before I can be seen in public. Figure I'll be there in maybe an hour. Ninety minutes, tops."

They hung up and suddenly Elliott was filled with nervous energy and wasn't so sure he should head out just yet, but...there wasn't anything else to do and the guys were probably already there holding a table, so...

Muttering a curse, he pulled out of his driveway and made his way downtown and tried not to think about whether or not Skylar was going to show. If she didn't, he at least knew she wasn't working and could possibly be at home. He could fake...something...and leave and go to her place to talk to her if he had to.

Feeling better now that he had a plan, he cranked up the radio and finished his drive to Flanagan's.

As he expected, Tyler and Alex were there already and had snagged a corner booth–which was fortunate considering they were going to be adding more people.

"Hey," he said, sliding into the booth. "Um...slight change of plans. Josie, Skye, and Leanna are joining us. I mean...Josie definitely is, but..."

Tyler chuckled. "If your sister's coming, her posse will be here."

Elliott couldn't help but laugh too because it was true. "Well, when I talked to Josie a little while ago she hadn't talked to them yet, so..."

Taking a pull of his beer, Tyler nodded. "Did she invite herself or did you?"

"I called her and mentioned we were going to be here, and then she told me she had been trying to get together with you about some fundraiser thing. What's that about?" He slid farther into the booth when Jared showed up and joined them.

"The last guy who made partner planned this big-ass fundraiser for one of the big guy's favorite charities. It's a major suck-up move, but...it certainly did the trick. So I want to have a plan worked out with Josie's help before I present it to the team. I can't make it look like I'm totally copying what Ted did, but..."

"But you're totally copying what Ted did," Alex said with a laugh. "You are going to have to come up with something extremely creative to make it seem completely unrelated to what that guy did."

"That's why I need Josie's help," Tyler murmured before taking another drink.

"My sister can plan a hell of a party, but I'm not so sure she can be that devious and help you manufacture a reason to organize a fundraiser. I'm not sure that's in her wheelhouse."

Tyler leveled him with a stare. "Dude, your sister is brilliant–like an evil genius. Trust me. She was the one who started throwing out ideas, but I've just been too busy with work to sit down and strategize with her."

"Josie's an evil genius?" he repeated. "Seriously?"

"Oh, definitely," Tyler replied, and Alex and Jared nodded in agreement.

He racked his brain for memories of his sister being devious and other than the usual brother-sister stuff where they got each other in trouble, he never saw her that way.

But obviously, everyone else had.

Weird.

Their waitress came over and took their drink order a few minutes later and they decided on several appetizers–including some wings–to hold them over until Josie and the girls arrived.

If they arrive…

"I can't believe you invited your sister," Jared said a few minutes later. "And her friends."

"Why? What's wrong with that?"

"No woman is going to come over here when they see a table with four guys and three girls," he reasoned. "It looks like a couples' outing and one poor schmuck who couldn't get a date."

"I don't think it will be like that," he countered. "We're not going to just be sitting here in the booth all night. We'll get up and play darts or pool or…you know, there's a whole game room back there plus the bar, so…"

"No, I agree with Jared," Alex chimed in. "Did you do this so we'd lay off pushing you into finding someone to take home with you?"

"I didn't…"

"I know we pushed you a little hard last week," Tyler interrupted. "But we're just looking out for you. It's time for you to move on after the whole…you know…Tracy fiasco, and considering your folks are hell-bent on you not dating, there's no harm with a little recreational sex." He grinned. "Hell, you certainly had your pick last weekend. I can't believe you didn't take one of them home!"

"I can't believe you didn't take *more* than one of them home," Jared said with a snicker. "That redhead and her friend seemed more than willing to take care of you."

Ugh…he didn't need the reminder.

It had taken two showers to get the smell of her perfume off of him.

So yeah...he didn't hook up with anyone last weekend, and if Skye had just given him a chance to explain, she would know that.

"Look," Alex said, pointing at him. "He's frowning. Probably regretting letting them get away!" There was a round of laughter, but Elliott didn't join in.

"We're not going to let you get away with that crap tonight," Jared said with a huge grin. "You are definitely going home with someone tonight. This whole carrying the torch for Tracy ends now."

"I'm not holding a torch for anyone," he murmured and was relieved when their first few appetizers arrived. They each grabbed what they wanted and Elliott hoped they'd move on from the topic of his sex life.

"If you're not holding a torch," Tyler questioned, "then what was the deal last weekend? I can't remember the last time you showed such a lack of interest in women."

How the hell could he explain that he had plenty of interest in women—it just so happened that his interest was heavily focused on one particular woman? There was no way he was going to tell any of them he slept with Skye because they wouldn't be able to keep it to themselves.

Although...

He let out a dramatic sigh. "Okay, look...I wasn't inter-ested because...I've sort of been hooking up with someone already and it's completely casual and not a big deal so..."

Three pairs of eyes stared at him until he started to squirm.

"Um..."

"Why wouldn't you say anything?" Tyler asked. "Who is she?" And he seemed genuinely giddy with curiosity.

Without missing a beat, he said, "Someone from work." He shrugged. "Like I said, super casual...super secret..."

"Good for you!" Jared said, saluting him with his beer.

"But if it's casual, that means you can still..."

This time he held up a hand to stop him. "Nuh-uh. That is not my style–even when it's casual. She's not looking for anything serious and obviously I'm not, but that doesn't mean I'm looking for anything with anyone else so... back off."

Before anyone could comment, Josie strolled up to the table with a big smile, and Elliott couldn't help but glance behind her to see if Skye was with her.

She wasn't.

"Well, well, well...it looks like you guys couldn't wait a little longer to order, huh?" she said as she slid into the booth. "I hope we're getting more wings."

Immediately, conversation started around him–his sister had that effect on people–and Elliott found himself to be mildly disappointed that she showed up alone.

"Leanna and Skye not coming?" he asked casually.

"They are," Josie replied, snagging a wing. "Leanna had to pick Skye up so they should be here any minute."

A slow smile played at his lips, but he hid it behind his drink.

But when he spotted Skye walking toward the table a few minutes later, he knew he was grinning like an idiot and did his best to tone it down.

Turns out, it wasn't that hard because she shot him a hard glare before turning and smiling at everyone but him.

CHAPTER 10

Sometimes you don't know how much something means to you until it's taken away.

UNKNOWN

"I DON'T KNOW why I let you talk me into this," Skye said to Leanna for the tenth time. Now they were practically at the table and her nerves were getting the best of her.

"It's for your own good. You tried something, it failed, and it's over. Unfortunately, Elliott is Josie's brother and, therefore, always going to be in your life. You need to get used to hanging out with him again as just friends."

It all sounded perfectly logical, but her stupid heart still hadn't gotten the memo.

Everyone moved to make room for them, and somehow Skye ended up wedged between Elliott and Jared. She'd met him a few times before and he was an IT guy or something. "Hey, Jared. How are you?"

"Good," he said with a warm smile. "Glad you ladies decided to join us tonight."

Somehow she doubted that, but she smiled nonetheless. "I haven't been here in years, but I seriously used to love playing Skee-ball. Do they still have them back in the game room?"

"They do and you're on!" he told her, playfully nudging her shoulder, which caused her to bump Elliott's arm. "I happen to be the king of Skee-ball!"

She heard Elliott's snort but refused to turn and acknowledge it.

Their waitress came by and brought more plates and took all of their orders for more food and drinks. It was a great distraction and as soon as she was gone, conversations started up all around.

Unfortunately, they all started up with other people, leaving Skye and Elliott to talk to each other.

Awesome.

"So," he began after a few awkward moments. "How was your week?"

She shrugged. "It was a little quiet, thankfully. This is an off week for us and as much as I hate to feel good about it, sometimes we need it to sort of refresh and regroup."

He nodded. "I get that."

Her stomach growled and she reached for a mozzarella stick and nibbled on it because she had no idea what else to say.

Then she felt Elliott's arm move to rest behind her along the top of the booth. He then leaned in close so he was practically whispering in her ear.

"I'm really glad you came out tonight. I wanted to talk to you, but I wasn't sure you would want to talk with me."

Sadly, neither did she, even though they were sitting

ridiculously close and talking right now. If she turned her head, they would practically be kissing, so she focused on her mozzarella stick while he continued to talk.

"We got interrupted on Monday and I think you jumped to the wrong conclusions," he explained. "I did come here last weekend and the guys definitely were encouraging me to...you know...get back on the bike, for lack of a better phrase, but...nothing happened."

Now she did turn her head and they bumped noses.

Skye jumped back a little and banged into Jared, and he took that to mean that she wanted to talk to him.

Ugh...

For five minutes she listened to him talk about the rec basketball league he was on and she seriously had to fight the urge to yawn. When she couldn't take it any longer, she put her hand on his arm and gave him her most endearing smile.

"Hey, I hate to be a bother, but I need to go to the ladies' room," she said sweetly. "I hate making you move, but...this is the downside to booths, right?"

"No worries," he said, sliding out of the way for her, and after thanking him, she quickly made her way through the crowd and outside to the party deck for some air. Right now, she just needed a minute to herself without being sandwiched next to Elliott and listening to uninspiring conversation.

She felt someone move in close behind her. "Can I buy you a drink?"

Turning, she put a smile on and...froze.

"Elliott, what are you doing out here?" she asked as her eyes went wide. Looking beyond him, she frowned. "Don't you think it looks a little suspicious for us both to get up to use the bathroom?"

"I told them I was going to see about getting pitchers of beer for the table," he said, leaning in close and giving her a playful tap on her nose. "And if we're being technical, you're not in the bathroom."

Taking a small step back, she groaned. "I just...needed some air." Maybe it was rude of her, but she walked away and found a quiet corner because she still felt a little claustrophobic. Of course he followed, and she knew they couldn't stay out here forever. Eventually she was going to have to go back to the table, and so did he.

But as he moved in close to her once again, all Skye could think about was how she didn't want to go back to the table. Hell, she didn't even want to go back inside. Elliott effectively kept her moving until she was literally backed into a corner, and it was the least claustrophobic she had felt all night.

Swallowing hard, her eyes slowly traveled up the length of him–from his dark khakis to the black polo shirt, up over his strong stubbled jaw, kissable lips, and eyes that were equally devouring her. "We should probably..."

She never got to finish.

One strong hand wrapped around her nape and hauled her in close before his lips crashed down on hers. And dammit, it was a sexy as hell move and she loved every second of it. Skye gripped the front of his shirt to keep him close even though she didn't think he needed the help.

She loved the way he kissed–loved how soft his lips were and how hard and muscular everything else was on him. Right now, she wanted to climb him like a tree and wrap her legs around him and then hold on for the ride! One kiss blended into the next and they were wet and needy and full of so much promise that she didn't know how she was going to survive the rest of the night.

As if reading her thoughts, Elliott abruptly ended the kiss and stared down at her. "Tell everyone you're not feeling well and let's get out of here," he was breathless and his voice was gruff and deep and sexy and made her knees weak.

"I...I don't know if they'll believe me..."

He looked around and took her by the hand before leading her back inside. By the front entrance he said, "Stay here," and then he stalked back toward their table. There was no way for her to know what he was saying or to guarantee Josie or Leanna weren't going to come running to her aid, but a minute later, he was back. Once again he took her hand in his and led her out the door and she practically had to run to keep up.

"Elliott, slow down," she said with a laugh, and they were in his car a minute later. He hadn't said a word to her and she was curious about what he'd told everyone. They drove for almost ten minutes in total silence and she couldn't take it anymore. "What did you say in there?"

"I told them you got sick in the ladies' room and I was taking you home," he said firmly, his eyes never leaving the road. "Leanna got up and wanted to make sure you were okay, but my sister whined a little about being left alone and since I had it under control..."

"Wow. Nice to know Josie was concerned," she muttered.

"She definitely was but I sort of left no room for argument and she said something about how you saved my ass last time so now it was my turn...or something like that."

Now that made her feel better.

Her phone dinged with an incoming text and when Skye pulled it out of her purse, she saw it was from Leanna.

. . .

Leanna: I hope you're really not sick and you and Elliott were just making a hasty escape to make up! :)

Leanna: But if you really are sick, I hope you feel better and call me if you need anything!

Skye: Not sick at all. Everything's good and I promise to call you tomorrow!

Smiling, she slid her phone back into her purse.

"Everything okay?"

"Yeah, that was just Lea making sure I'm okay and asking me to call her if I need anything." There was no way she was admitting that Leanna knew what they were doing–not only tonight, but in general. "She's a worrier and sort of like the mom of our little group, so I knew she was going to check up on me. If I hadn't responded, she probably would have shown up at the house at some point tonight to make sure I wasn't feverish or hadn't fallen down and hit my head." She laughed softly. "She's good like that."

He nodded. "What about my sister? What does she do in a situation like this? You know, if you were really sick?"

"That's easy–she'd tell me to stay the hell away from her because she didn't want to get sick and then she'd call in an order from any one of my favorite restaurants and have food delivered. She's nurturing in her own way."

"I'm finding out all kinds of things about Josie tonight and it's starting to freak me out."

That was...odd. "Like what?"

But he was already shaking his head and before she could push him on it, she noticed they were pulling into her driveway. He parked and shut off the car but made no move to get out.

"Elliott..."

He had a white-knuckled grip on the steering wheel and was staring down at it. "We are going to talk tonight, Skylar. I don't want there to be any misunderstandings like what we had on Monday."

Well drat. She was really looking forward to them picking right up where they left off on the party deck, but it looked like that wasn't going to happen.

Talk about a mood killer.

Then he released the wheel and turned his head to look at her. It was dark in the car and the only light came from her front porch so he was completely in shadows. "We're going to talk but...not right now." Reaching out, he caressed her cheek. "Right now, I want to get you inside and carry you right up to your bedroom. It's probably not the smartest thing to do considering we still have so much to discuss, but...I don't even know how I haven't pounced on you right here in the driveway. I'm holding on by a thread here."

Her breath came out as part laugh, part relief. "Thank God! I thought I was the only one feeling like that."

"Let's go inside then," he said, and before the words were fully out of his mouth, they were climbing from the car and running for the front door. It was the first time all week that she felt light and happy and full of anticipation.

And it was only the beginning.

Skye swore she'd never felt as clumsy as she did trying to open her own front door, but when she finally managed to stumble through, it was all worth it. Elliott kicked the door shut and pressed her up against it as he kissed her again–slow and deep and oh-so-wet. If all he did was kiss her tonight, it would almost be worth it.

Almost.

He had her caged in against the door like he had back at Flanagan's and now she could climb up him exactly as she wanted to. Looping her arms around his shoulders, she gave a little hop and Elliott immediately reached down and cupped her bottom and lifted her. After that, they were obscenely close and all Skye could imagine was how awesome it would be if they were naked like this.

Maybe...

They were on the move before she could even attempt to tell him what she wanted, but it was all good because a minute later they were in her bedroom, on her bed, and Elliott's hands were sliding under her top to take it off.

They could try the whole door thing another time.

It was fast and frantic and over way too soon, but Elliott was more than okay with it because the sight of Skylar naked never failed to make him wild.

And tonight was no exception.

It was risky to leave their friends the way they had, and normally he was too cautious to do anything like that, but kissing her out on the deck was like hitting the launch button. There was no way he was going to get through several hours with their friends when all he wanted was to get her alone and into bed.

She was breathless beneath him and there was a primitive side to him that really enjoyed knowing he was the one that did that to her. Her skin was flushed and he saw several spots where he had been a little too enthusiastic and bit or sucked too hard, but other than that, she was perfect.

Carefully, he rolled off of her but made sure he pulled her in close while they both cooled down.

He'd meant what he said earlier–tonight they were going to talk–and he knew it needed to be sooner rather than later.

One hand gently skimmed up and down her arm as he placed a kiss on the top of her head. Somewhere in the back of his mind, Elliott knew that when the person you were sleeping with was just someone casual you didn't cuddle like this, but he pushed that thought aside.

"So," he began quietly.

"So," she repeated. Her own hand was softly scratching his chest and it felt good to the point of being distracting, but he knew he had to ignore it for at least a little while.

"Okay, I think we both need to acknowledge that this new part of our relationship is not over yet."

Skye nodded but didn't comment.

"And I know this is casual and neither of us are looking for anything deeper or anything like that, but I'm sure you'll agree that we need to keep this exclusive."

Another nod.

"Of course, if you were to meet someone who you...you know...wanted a more committed relationship with, I wouldn't stop you," he went on, hating the words even as they came out of his mouth. "But at that point we'd agree that this was over. Right?"

When she nodded a third time, Elliott reached down and tipped her head up so he could see her face. "Feel free to jump in with some words of your own, Skye," he teased lightly.

Beside him, she shifted slightly before tangling her legs with his and snuggling closer.

He seriously loved when she did that.

"Everything you're saying is what I want too," she said, but...she didn't sound all that happy about it.

"Are you sure? Because..."

Lifting her head, Skye met his gaze. "Elliott, we both said we wanted casual–no strings, no commitments, no... future. I don't think we need to overanalyze it. We're sleeping together and we're exclusive. End of story." Then she collapsed back down beside him and resumed her previous position pressed up against him.

It took him a minute to decide whether he should add anything and knew there were a few details they should probably address. He gently cleared his throat and held her a little closer. "We're not telling anyone about this–about us–that's a given, but do we make some kind of schedule or just call when one of us wants..."

"A booty call?" she asked with a snicker.

"For lack of a better word, sure. A booty call." He hated that phrase, but...whatever. "How do you want to handle this?"

"Hmm..." She paused, and he knew she was trying to think it all through. "I'd say it would be safer to text each other if we want to...you know..."

He nodded.

"I know I always have my phone with me and sometimes it's easier for me to deal with a text than an actual call..."

"Same." It was all making sense and falling into place and he couldn't believe it was this easy. "Would you prefer we met here or my place?"

She shrugged. "I guess it would depend on what was

going on, so if you're okay going with the flow on that one, then I think we're good there."

Nodding again, he said, "Yeah. I guess we are." Then another thought hit him. "I'm assuming we're both okay with spending the night?"

"What?"

"You know, we're not kicking each other out of bed in the middle of the night because we don't want this to start feeling too intimate or anything. I know that first night you were going to leave, but...I think we can handle doing the sleepover thing, don't you?"

"Sure."

"Okay, then," he said, smiling. "We're good."

"Good," she said.

"Good."

They both seemed lost in their own thoughts for several minutes and it all seemed oddly anticlimactic. For all his worrying about them needing to talk, there really wasn't much to discuss. And for the first time since this whole thing started, he felt good—like he could finally relax and truly enjoy what they were doing.

Well...he'd been totally enjoying it the entire time, but now there was nothing hanging over their heads. They were free to get together and have sex as much as they wanted and then go on their merry way. It was completely ideal.

Why haven't I done more of this? He wondered. Why was I always pushing to settle down?

Refusing to let that thought take hold, Elliott slowly rolled them over until Skylar was underneath him again. Her eyes went a little wide at the change in positions and he smiled down at her. "I think we should celebrate."

One perfectly arched brow rose. "Oh, really? And what are we celebrating?"

"Finally having the talk so we can...you know...go right to the good stuff from now on." He waggled his eyebrows at her lecherously before they both laughed. "Come on, you've got to admit that wasn't nearly as scary as we thought it was going to be."

She made a noncommittal sound before reaching up and raking her hand through his hair. "Since the talk is done, how about you stop talking and show me how we're supposed to celebrate," she said saucily and damn if she wasn't the cutest thing.

"My pleasure."

For a little more than a month, things were perfect.

Beyond perfect.

And not just between him and Skye.

He'd gotten a promotion at work, he sold his SUV and was now the proud owner of a brand-new Ford Mustang, and for the first time in months, he had his confidence back. Yeah, that one was the biggest achievement of them all because he felt like he had finally put the whole Tracy thing behind him. No one was talking about it anymore and he hadn't gotten any pitying looks in the longest time so he'd clearly turned a corner there and it was great.

He'd shared that last bit with Skye and she said she was happy for him–had actually congratulated him on it–and they celebrated by spending an entire Sunday in bed.

Perfect.

The next big thing was putting his house up for sale. It was just one more reminder of the life he was trying to put behind him, but he had no idea where he wanted to move so...he hadn't pulled the trigger there yet. Skye was off next weekend and he considered taking her with him to look at houses, but wasn't sure if that would be weird or not. It wasn't like he wanted her input because they were moving in together or anything, but he genuinely wanted her input because she was an intelligent woman with good taste. Maybe he'd bring it up with her the next time they got together.

Which reminded him...

Pulling out his phone, he decided to send her a quick text and see if she had plans for tonight.

Elliott: Hey, any plans tonight?

The little "sent" message was there and he hoped she was somewhere that she could respond right away. After a minute, he figured she was busy and put his phone down on his desk. It took an hour for her to respond.

Skye: Hey, sorry. I was on the phone with a client. My head is pounding.

Elliott: Sorry to hear that. I have a great cure for headaches...wink, wink...

Skye: As tempting as that sounds, I think I'm just going to go home and soak in the tub and rest. I've had back-to-back appointments all

day and I am mentally and physically exhausted. Sorry.

Well, damn. This was the first time she turned him down and it was more than a little disappointing.

They'd been the epitome of casual–their time together was all about sex.

Okay, maybe not *just* sex. They had some great conversations mixed in but there wasn't the pressure of having to plan any dates or decide where to go to eat or what movie to see and...for the first time since this all began, he kind of wished he could just go over and hang out with her.

Elliott: What time are you out of there?

Skye: Another hour. Why?

Elliott: I'm going to pick up some Chinese food while you take a hot bath. Then I'm going to feed you, rub your feet–or your head, your choice–and then tuck you into bed.

Skye: Elliott...that's really not necessary

Elliott: Are you kidding? What are friends for?

. . .

She went silent for almost five solid minutes and he was afraid she was going to turn him down. But then...

Skye: Thank you. I appreciate it

Skye: And I'd really love some egg drop soup with wontons and a pint of beef with broccoli please 😊

Elliott: You got it

Two hours later, he pulled up to her house and grabbed the bag with their dinner in it. Skye had texted him that the door was unlocked and to let himself in, and he was going to lecture her on the dangers of doing that.

But not tonight.

Once he was inside, he set up their food in the living room, lit a fire in her gas fireplace, softened the lights, and pulled up Netflix on the TV. They both loved to watch *The Good Place,* so he figured it would be good for some background noise while they ate.

Walking into the kitchen, he grabbed a couple of bottles of water before getting plates, napkins, and silverware. By the time Skylar joined him a few minutes later, he had everything set up and ready.

Her hair was damp, she didn't have on any makeup, and she was dressed in a pair of pink plaid pajama pants and hot pink t-shirt. She looked exactly like she did when she used to sleepover with Josie when they were younger.

And he couldn't help but smile.

"Wow...look at this," she said softly as she padded over to him. Elliott could tell she was tired and he was glad he could do something like this to help her. "And I hate to admit that I love that you set us up in here instead of the kitchen."

"Yeah, well...I tend to eat in front of the TV when I'm home and I figured you might not mind it." They sat down and he used the remote to start the episode.

"Normally I'm at the kitchen table and have my phone or my laptop right there with me," she said as she poured some beef and broccoli onto her plate. "But every once in a while, I'll sit here and eat. And after the day I had, this is perfect." Balancing her plate in one hand, Skye got comfortable on the large sectional sofa and put her feet up. "Thank you for doing this, Elliott. I really appreciate it."

"Not a problem." After making up his own plate, he got comfortable and neither spoke during the first episode. "Want to watch another?"

She nodded and switched out her plate for the container of soup.

They ended up watching four episodes before Elliott noticed she was looking around for something. "Everything okay?"

Glancing at him, she gave him a small grin. "I was looking for some kind of dessert. Actually, I was hoping you had something hidden here in the takeout bags."

"Damn," he said, playfully smacking himself in the head. "I can't believe I didn't think of that."

Laughing, Skye shook her head. "Now I'm going to have to go and scrounge around in the kitchen for something."

Standing, she sighed dramatically. "I'm sure there's ice cream in there. Maybe some cookies…"

Elliott followed her and together they made a huge mess as they made themselves ice cream sundaes with crumbled Oreos on top. They weren't pretty, but they were definitely delicious. They changed up what they were watching and turned on some house hunting show that she loved. While they ate, they discussed pros and cons of the different houses and it was the perfect opening for what he wanted to ask her.

"So…listen," he began. "I really want to start looking at houses."

"You're really going to sell your place?"

Nodding, he replied, "Yeah. I want to start fresh. So far I've done a lot to make that happen and the house is the last thing to go."

"That's just a shame. Your house is awesome," she said around a spoonful of ice cream. "It could definitely use a major renovations, but other than that, it's kind of ideal."

It was?

"Why do you say that?"

"Elliott, please," she said with an eye roll. "You're in one of the best neighborhoods in Raleigh! It's close to everything, the backyard is so big that you could put a pool in and really make a great outdoor living space around it, and lastly, the houses aren't right on top of each other like in most newer neighborhoods. I'm sure you won't have any problem selling it, but it's just a shame you want to let it go."

If he were being honest, he did love the house, but if he wanted to move forward with this whole new mindset about being a bachelor, he had no use for a four-bedroom house. Which is what he told her.

"Yeah, I know," she said with a small sigh. "But let me

tell you, this place may be the perfect size for a single person, but I wouldn't mind having a little more space. Two bedrooms is technically more than enough, but I'd love to have an office here too." Then she studied him for a minute. "What if you converted one of your spare bedrooms into an office and another into a gym or something?"

He shrugged. "That could work, but...again...it's more about starting over than anything."

She mimicked his move. "Suit yourself. I still think it's a mistake. You can make that house into anything you want it to be even if you don't get married and have kids."

Kids were the main reason he had bought the house. There were enough bedrooms for a family to grow, the yard was big enough to build a jungle gym and play ball, and it was in a fantastic school district.

He had zero need for any of those things anymore.

"You're looking pretty fierce over there," she commented. "You okay?"

Twisting in his spot, he told her all his reasons for buying the house. "So now do you understand why I want to sell it?"

"Elliott, if you're truly okay with your decisions and moving forward as a perpetual bachelor, then it shouldn't matter." She finished the last of her sundae and shook her spoon at him. "You're the one who has to live there or wherever you want to move to. I don't have to agree with what you decide, and I'm certainly not going to stop you from selling the house. I was just offering my opinion, that's all. That's what friends do, right?"

He nodded and knew she was right. Tyler, Alex, and Jared all encouraged him to sell the house and move into one of those executive condo complexes where there would be other single people his age with tons of amenities and social activities. Personally, it didn't sound all that appealing to him, but then again, he'd never really looked into it so... who was he to say that it wasn't a viable option?

Skye put her empty bowl on the coffee table and got comfortable again. "Ooh...this one is about people finding houses at the beach and renovating them. You interested?"

Placing his bowl beside hers, he figured why not? It was definitely getting late, but he was comfortable and enjoying just hanging out and talking with her. "Yeah, sure. If these people can afford beach houses, they must have the money to do some major renovations."

"No, that's what makes this show so amazing–they're all looking for bargains because they don't have big budgets. It's kind of cool to see what you can do when you don't have a million-dollar budget."

"Renovations can really be a nightmare, can't they?"

"Shh...just watch. I think you'll be surprised."

An hour later, Elliott was hooked and was already asking if there were more episodes for them to watch.

CHAPTER 11

Sometimes we create our own heartbreaks through expectation.

UNKNOWN

SKYE WALKED into the office with a little spring in her step and found Josie already at her desk. "Good morning," she said cheerily, tossing her purse down before taking a seat.

Lifting her head, Josie smiled at her and then seemed to study her.

Hard.

"What?" Skye asked, feeling mildly self-conscious. When she left her house a little while ago, her hair looked good, her makeup was on point, and she was wearing a brand-new ensemble that she bought on sale. All in all, she felt pretty good about herself.

Plus, early morning sex certainly started the day off right.

Things with Elliott had been absolutely amazing. Last night was their three-month anniversary, but unfortunately, she was only allowed to think of it like that in her head. There was no way she was going to mention it and risk spooking him. Everything had been going so great since the night they sat and talked about their rules.

Stupid rules.

The funny thing was, Elliott may not want to acknowledge it, but they were in a relationship–and a pretty amazing one at that.

At first it was just about the sex. Then the night he came over with Chinese food and they did nothing but watch TV was a game changer.

To her, anyway.

Now they were getting together two to three times a week and hanging out, sharing dinner, and then toe-curling, off-the-chart sex.

Lots and lots of it.

She couldn't remember ever being so completely satisfied and if Elliott would just get over his own relationship embargo–because yeah, Skye had a feeling no one in his family was enforcing the one they'd put on him–things would be damn near perfect.

"Are you using a new moisturizer?" Josie asked, interrupting her thoughts.

"Um...no. Why?"

"Your skin is just all glowy and I figured you must have changed up your skin care routine or something." She paused. "Did you go to the spa for a facial?"

Shaking her head, Skye felt her cheeks heat and opted to look away and busy herself with getting her laptop booted up. "Nope. Just my usual stuff. Nothing new here."

"Hmph...I wish my skin looked like that. I've been

thinking about changing things up but have no idea what to try. I figured if you had something new, I'd try it too."

"Sorry, wish I could help, but..."

"My nana is coming in for a tasting today," Josie announced. "I was going to just bring some stuff over to her for dinner one night, but she wanted to come in and do it. She enjoyed coming in last time and wanted to do it again. She's adorable."

Skye had to agree. "Hard to believe she started planning so far in advance. We've got...what...another six weeks until their party, right?"

"Exactly," Josie confirmed. "I was hoping you wouldn't mind being there and sort of overseeing everything. I know I'm going to be there and could probably do it, but..."

"Oh, stop. You need to be there as a guest! I already planned on being the one to be on site. It's no big deal."

"Okay, whew!" Sinking down in her seat slightly, she smiled. "You are the best. Thank you."

Skye pulled up their schedule and saw that the weekend of the party was fairly quiet for them. There was a bridal shower the same day, but no one was needed to be there for that. Everything was being delivered the day before. "It would be nice if we kept that weekend free so you can truly enjoy yourself and not have to worry about anything the next day. I'm going to black it out, okay?"

"Awesome. Thank you. I can't believe I didn't think of that before." She sat up straighter again. "Honestly, where would I be without you?"

"Knock it off. You're being ridiculous."

Standing, Josie wandered over and sat on the corner of Skye's desk. "No, my brother is being ridiculous," she said, crossing her arms over her chest.

"Um...what?"

Nodding, her expression turned serious. "It's like he's going through a mid-life crisis and he's not even thirty!"

Skye's heart began to race and she was fairly certain that guilt was written all over her face. "What are you talking about?"

"Well, he got rid of his perfectly fine car and bought a Mustang." She shook her head. "Classic mid-life crisis move. Then he joined the same ridiculous basketball league that Jared is on."

"I don't think that's particularly ridiculous. It's a great way for him to socialize after work," she reasoned, but Josie wasn't really listening.

"And now he's going to put his house on the market and talking about moving into some executive condo community place! I mean...he's crazy! I told him that I thought it was a mistake and he got really pissy with me and said how he wished everyone would back off!" She stared hard at Skye. "That means his friends are giving him crap about it too, right?"

"Oh...I don't know..."

"Honestly, I don't know what we all expected him to do after everything happened. He moved on much faster than any of us expected and for the first time in years he seems... happy." She shrugged. "I mean, he's always been a fairly easygoing kind of person, but it's been a long time since I've seen him like this. I thought for sure we were going to have to have someone watching his place 24/7 to make sure he wasn't secretly dating, but...he's gotten involved in so many things with his friends that he doesn't have time to date or even think about it."

"Good for him," Skye murmured and pulled up her emails.

"I wonder if he'll go back to looking for his perfect

woman as soon as we give the all-clear," Josie mused. "He swears he's done with all of it and that he is perfectly content with being single forever, but I'm not quite sure I believe him." She paused. "But I've been encouraging him to keep thinking like that. It's really what's best for him. What do you think?"

It was almost as if her friend was goading her and unfortunately, Skye fell for it and snapped.

"What do I think?" she asked a little too loud and with a little too much heat. Pushing away from her desk, she glared at Josie. "I think you're terrible for encouraging him to stay single! I think it's terrible that on a day where he hit rock bottom that everyone ganged up on him and essentially banned him from having a life! Did any of you even think about what it was that Elliott wanted? Was there ever a conversation where someone said that maybe just loving him for who he is was enough?" Now she jumped to her feet because she had way too much pent-up energy to stay put. "And you, my friend, are an extremely jaded person and shame on you for pushing that same agenda on your brother! There was nothing wrong with him wanting to fall in love and get married! Isn't that something most of us want–to love and be loved in return?"

Muttering a curse, Skye stalked across the office to their Keurig and angrily tossed a pod into it. "One of the greatest things about your brother was how he wasn't like every other guy out there–he had a heart. Maybe he wore it on his sleeve and maybe he gave it away too easily, but he wasn't hurting anyone! Women are always bitching about how a good man is so hard to find, and you took one of the best men I've ever known and turned him into every jerk we try to avoid!"

When her coffee was ready, she stared down at it and

decided she didn't want it and simply walked back over to her desk. She was breathing hard, her heart was racing even faster, and she'd give anything to throw an axe right now to get some of this nervous energy out!

"Okay, wow," Josie murmured as she stood up. "Someone's got some strong opinions today."

Skye wanted to correct her and say how it wasn't just today, but she knew she'd already given way too much away with her little outburst.

"I just…," she began and sighed. "I've been friends with you for a really long time, Jos, and that means I've been friends with Elliott for just as long. I know your heart was in the right place, but…I hate the thought of Elliott being just another guy."

"Well, shit," Josie replied wearily as she sat back down at her desk. "Where were you when my family was trying to figure out how to handle the whole situation?"

"That's just it. I don't think it was anyone's situation to handle. It was Elliott's, and you all took that away from him."

"We thought it was for the best…"

"I know you did. You just should have talked to him about it more. And not on that particular day."

"Maybe I should invite him for dinner tonight and try to get a feel for what he's thinking. What do you think?"

"It's too late, Josie. It's been…what…almost five months since the wedding. Everything's in motion now for him to be working on this…new, stupid life."

"I wouldn't say it's stupid…"

"Oh, please," she snorted. "One day he's going to wake up and realize that he gave up on something he genuinely wanted, and by then it will be too late. He'll be alone." Just the thought of it was enough to depress her and when she felt her eyes start to sting, she knew she needed to reel it in or she'd really, really, *really* give herself away. "The damage is done. You need to let him figure things out on his own now."

Josie grew quiet before adding, "And I'm not jaded. I just don't feel like I need a man to complete me."

"Whatever."

Neither said a word, but Skye looked over and saw the frown on Josie's face as she stared at her computer and she was fairly certain her expression was about the same. The silence was awkward and she wasn't sure if she needed to say more or if she should just be thankful she hadn't blurted out all the ways this stupid embargo was ruining her potential happily-ever-after with Elliott.

"Jeez, who died in here?" Leanna asked as she walked through the door. She had a bag in one hand and a tray of drinks from Starbucks in the other that she placed on her desk before looking around in confusion. "Seriously, what's going on?"

"Nothing," Skye said quietly as she offered a small smile. "What's in the bag?"

"I stopped for bagels, but I'm not sharing unless someone tells me why you both look so ragey."

With a loud huff of annoyance, Josie responded. "We were talking about my brother and Skye pointed out all the ways my family and I did him wrong with the way we handled things after the wedding. And then she accused me of being jaded!"

"That's because you are," Leanna said cheerily, reaching into her bag and pulling out one wrapped bagel, then putting it on Josie's desk. "It's the olive oil and thyme one you like so much, with extra cream cheese."

"I'm not! Just because I'm not out trolling clubs looking

for a guy doesn't make me jaded! I've been focused on the business and that makes me happy!"

"Goody for you," Skye said with more than a hint of snark.

"Okay, everyone needs to calm down." Leanna was always the voice of reason. She pulled out a second bagel and placed it on Skye's desk. "Egg everything bagel with cream cheese and extra crispy bacon."

"Thanks, Lea."

She stood between their two desks and–with her hands on her hips–made a tsking sound. "I'm disappointed in both of you. We are friends first, and as such, we should be able to share when we think one of us is doing something that is wrong or unhealthy." Focusing on Josie, she went on. "No one's saying that you need to be out trolling for men. There's nothing wrong with enjoying your independence. It's a problem when you force that point of view on others who clearly don't share it."

"What are you...?"

"I heard you talking to your brother on the phone the other day. He clearly called to talk to you because he was struggling and instead of telling him that it's okay to feel the way he did, you made him feel stupid because he was questioning some of his rash decisions."

"Elliott called and told you he was struggling?" Skye cried with disbelief. When was this? Why hadn't he mentioned it to her? And did that mean that he was seeing their relationship as something special too?

"Ease up, Skye," Josie snapped. "I was having a private conversation with my brother!" She glared at Leanna. "And shame on you for eavesdropping!"

"You were in the kitchen scrounging for cake! And you were on speaker phone, for crying out loud! What was

I supposed to do? Unlike you, I needed to be in the kitchen because I was working on a cake for the Walters' party!"

The argument went round and round for several minutes. Josie was defending herself left and right, Skye continued to harp on the fact that Josie was the real reason Elliott was having second thoughts, and poor Leanna was trying to calm them all down.

A loud piercing whistle broke through all the yelling and they froze.

"Tyler!" Josie said as she stood and smoothed a hand down her skirt. "What are you doing here? I thought our appointment wasn't until ten."

He looked around warily and seemed hesitant to walk any farther into the room. "Um...yeah, I got here a little early and didn't think it was a big deal. Then I heard all the yelling and figured I better come in and make sure no one was getting hurt." He glanced at each of them. "Everybody okay now?"

The three of them each nodded their heads silently.

"Okay. Good." He slid his hands into his trouser pockets and smiled at Josie. "If now's not a good time..."

"No," she said quickly. "Now is actually the perfect time." She picked up her bagel and coffee. "Come on. I've got everything set up in the conference room."

She walked out but Tyler hung back and smiled again at Skye and Leanna. "Ladies, always a pleasure to see you." And then he was gone.

Walking over to the door, Leanna shut it before turning her attention to Skye. "For what it's worth, I get why you're frustrated, but you can't let it get to you like this. No matter what, Josie's your friend, and more importantly, she's Elliott's sister."

"Yeah, I know," she said, nodding. "I snapped. It won't happen again."

Nodding, Leanna walked over to her desk and sat down. "Are you going to be okay?"

Looking up, Skye knew she was on the verge of tears. "What if...what if he's really second-guessing his whole stance on relationships and she keeps talking him out of it?"

"Oh, sweetie...if he really wanted to go back to his old way of thinking, there isn't anything Josie or his parents could say to change that."

At one time she would have agreed.

But right now, she wasn't so sure.

His head was pounding, it was way too warm, and Elliott was fairly certain the leasing agent's voice was going to be the death of him.

"So what do you say, Mr. Sullivan? Are you ready to sign?"

She had just taken him on the hour-long tour of The Prescott—an executive condo community that felt more like an all-inclusive resort than a home. It had everything a person could ever want or need.

Except a soul.

Yeah, it was all sleek and shiny and new but it was all completely boring to him. Of course he could put his own stamp on his place, but...

"If it's okay with you, Maureen, I'd like to take a few days to think about it," he said as he got to his feet.

She stood and shook his hand. "Just don't take too long. There are only eight units left and we've had a lot of interest in them. I wouldn't be surprised if they were gone by the end of the week."

With a smile and nod, Elliott thanked her again and walked out. It wasn't until he was out by his car that he felt like he could breathe. Pulling at his collar, he shook it to try to fan himself a little before getting into the car and turning the air on full-blast. Then he simply sat for several minutes until he cooled down.

Glancing at the dashboard clock, he frowned. It was almost seven and he was supposed to meet the guys for basketball.

Why did I join that stupid league?

All he wanted was to go home, have something to eat, and watch some TV with Skylar.

Groaning, he closed his eyes because that was so not the way he needed to be thinking. He was coming to depend on her far too much. Their time together was always the high-light of his day–his week–and that wasn't part of the plan... or the rules. If anything, Skye seemed completely fine with the way things were between them and she never pushed for more time or more of anything from him. The reality was that he was the one who kept pushing the boundaries–calling her more often, texting her several times a week, and he was the one who usually initiated when they got together. It was everything he thought he wanted, but...he was definitely getting too attached.

Too comfortable.

And he'd definitely been thinking of Skye in terms that he had no right to think of her in–not just as a lover, but as someone he could seriously see himself being with in the long-term.

Like forever.

"And this is why I need to go and play basketball," he murmured, pulling out of The Prescott's parking lot.

But as he made his way across town, the urge to pull over and text Skye was ridiculously strong. He imagined stopping and picking up some barbecue from the place downtown that he knew she loved, showing up and kissing her until all the tension left his body, and then settling down on her large sectional while they ate and watching more of those renovation shows that he was now addicted to. After dinner, they'd clean up and he'd step in close behind her and rinse the dishes together before having a mini water fight that would force her to take off her top right there in the kitchen.

It was a favorite game of theirs.

Then they'd do that sexy little dance where they kissed and touched and laughed all the way to the bedroom. And once they were there…

Elliott let out a low growl because he loved what they did there. Skye was so damn sexy and they were beyond compatible in bed. Hell, if he closed his eyes right now, he could practically feel her pressed up against him when she…

The sound of a car horn blaring at him snapped him out of his reverie.

Gripping the steering wheel hard, he kept his eyes firmly on the road for the rest of the drive. As soon as he was parked outside of the gym, however, he let out a ragged breath because he was losing his mind and all this sneaking around was getting him nowhere.

Well, it almost got him into an accident, but…

It was only supposed to be about sex–friends with bene-fits…something to pass the time. At first it seemed weird that it was with Skye, but the longer it went on, the more it made sense. And for most of that time, Elliott was convinced that he was just fine with all of it and with his newfound belief that being a perpetual bachelor was a good thing.

Now he wasn't so sure.

That wouldn't be such a bad thing if he didn't already know how all of this was going to end. Even though it was Skylar—the girl he'd known for half of his life—odds were that it was going to end. And so would the next relationship, and the one after it. There was no way he wanted to be publicly humiliated in front of his entire family ever again.

Letting out another long breath, he knew that being with Skye was just putting off the inevitable. Eventually, he was going to be alone again. And the next time, it was going to have to be beyond casual and definitely not anyone he knew because...he was clearly incapable of not forming attachments.

That thought made him stop.

Was that all this was? Was he only feeling this way because he and Skye were friends? Was she just comfortable to be around and without any distractions of another relationship—or the possibility of having anyone around them—that he was feeling like this? Was it possible that he was making more of this than it really was?

"Or maybe I need to end this and seriously stop torturing myself and learn what it's like to truly be alone," he murmured.

Resting his head on the steering wheel, Elliott felt beyond exhausted and was seriously considering texting the guys and backing out of playing when there was a loud knock on the window.

Muttering a curse, he straightened and saw Tyler grinning down at him. "C'mon, El! What are you doing sitting out here moping?"

Now there was no getting out of it, so Elliott slowly climbed from the car and grabbed his gym bag from the backseat. "Sorry. Just...thinking."

"About...?" Tyler prompted, and for the first time, Elliott didn't give a damn about keeping things a secret. He needed to talk to someone about all of this and Ty was his best friend.

Leaning against his car, he raked a hand through his hair and sighed. "I need some advice."

With a frown, Tyler studied him. "Sounds serious. Everything okay?"

Shaking his head, he replied, "No. No, it's not." And then he told his friend everything–about Skye, his feelings, his doubts...all of it.

He had no idea how long they stood out there, but Tyler hadn't said a word and Jared and Alex had texted them numerous times already. Luckily there wasn't a real game night, just more rec time for them. Still, they couldn't stand out in the parking lot all night.

"Say something, Ty. Please."

"Damn, Elliott. I'm not even sure where to begin."

Well that didn't sound good.

"All these years, it seemed like Skye, Lea, and Josie were all off-limits and now you're telling me you've been sleeping with Skye for months? I mean..." He paused and raked a hand through his hair. "Do you have any idea how many times I wanted to ask her out?"

Um...what?

Before Elliott could respond, Tyler was speaking again. "I know that's not the point right now, but...damn."

"Yeah...well..."

"So you think you have feelings for her, but you're not sure if they're real. Do I have that right?"

He nodded.

"As much as I'd like to chalk this up to you just being you...I honestly don't know if that's the case. I'm almost certain that it is, but...what if it's not?" Then he muttered a curse. "Why would you do this to yourself again, man? You were supposed to be on an embargo!"

"I know! Don't you think I know that?" he demanded loudly. "It wasn't supposed to be like this! It was supposed to just be sex and nothing more!"

"Then you either have to get it in your head that that's all it is, or you have to end it!" Tyler snapped back. "And personally, I think you need to end it because it's obviously messing with you!"

He was about to comment when Jared came jogging over. "What the hell is going on out here? I thought we were shooting hoops and hanging out."

It was on the tip of his tongue to say he wasn't in the mood to play, but it was actually going to be a great distraction for him. Fortunately, Tyler let the subject drop and for the next several hours, they played basketball, trash-talked each other's skills, and then went to grab a pizza when they were done.

The next time Elliott was in his car, it was close to midnight. It was a Wednesday night, and he had work in the morning and he really needed to go home and get some sleep. But somehow, he found himself heading toward Skye's.

He didn't text to see if it was okay.

He didn't call to see if she was home.

It was completely against the rules and yet he didn't care.

Right now, he was determined to prove to himself that he didn't feel anything for her other than friendship and lust. He couldn't afford for it to be anything else and knew he could walk away any time he wanted to–could end this tomorrow if that's what needed to happen.

When he pulled into her driveway fifteen minutes later, he almost sagged with relief when he saw her car parked out front and a light still on inside.

There was a possibility that she would tell him to leave.

And there was a possibility she would be pissed off because he showed up unannounced.

Knocking on her front door, Elliott said a small prayer that she would do both of those things and make his decision easier–clearer.

But when she opened the door and he saw she was in her pajamas and her hair was tousled, he felt bad for waking her.

Then she gave him a sleepy, sexy smile as she reached out and grabbed the front of his shirt and pulled him inside, kissing him senseless.

And suddenly nothing was clear or made any sense, and there wasn't a damn thing he wanted to do to change it.

CHAPTER 12

Love is the only kind of fire which is never covered by insurance.

UNKNOWN

It was a rare Saturday morning that Skye didn't have an event to go to and she got to sleep in. And it was even rarer that she was waking up at a luxury hotel and waiting for room service to deliver her breakfast.

Elliott had surprised her yesterday when he texted for her to pack a bag because he wanted to get away for the weekend and...how could she possibly say no? If anything, this was one of her deepest fantasies come true! So, he picked her up after work last night and drove them up to the mountains for the weekend.

Stretching in bed, she smiled when he opened the curtains and showed her the gorgeous view outside. "Now that is quite the sight," she said as she sat up. The mountains had never been something that appealed to her before, but after seeing how beautiful they looked, she reconsidered.

Elliott knelt on the bed and crawled over her until she was lying down again. "No, this is quite the sight," he growled before kissing her again.

Unable to help herself, Skye wrapped her arms around him and held on tight. She had no idea what prompted this little getaway and she had to admit that she was more than a little apprehensive to ask. The drive last night took close to four hours and she had managed to stop herself from asking. Then they went to dinner at a fantastic little bistro and she told herself it didn't matter what Elliott's motives were; she was just so damn happy to be away with him.

When he lifted his head and smiled down at her, she swore her heart skipped a beat. She caressed his stubbled jaw and knew she was going to remember this moment forever. "How long until breakfast gets here?"

His grin turned a little bit wicked. "Sadly, too soon. But we have nothing pressing to do and nowhere to go so we can come back to this after we eat."

She pouted. "Okay, but I do want to go into town and walk around. I was doing a little research while we were driving yesterday and there's supposed to be a Christmas shop–and you know my obsession with anything Christmas–and a gourmet food and spice shop that I'd love to check out."

"I think we can do that and also have a lazy morning in bed," he told her before placing a soft kiss on the tip of her nose.

Skye gave him one last lingering kiss before climbing from the bed and going to brush her teeth. It seemed a little silly to be thinking of that at the moment, but she knew if she stayed tangled up in the bed with him, she'd end up being more than okay with their breakfast being left in the hallway.

No sooner was she done with her task than there was a knock on the door. Elliott took care of getting everything set up while she slid on her robe. When she stepped over to the small table set up in the corner, she realized there was only one chair. "Hmm..."

"Let's do this right," he said, motioning toward the bed. "I promised you breakfast in bed so...let's carefully get back in the bed."

It was a little awkward and time-consuming to get them both situated, but she had to admit, it felt pretty decadent. Her omelet was amazing, her toast was done to perfection, and the coffee was exactly the way she liked it. Beside her, Elliott was raving about his Belgian waffle and bacon, and she could tell he was equally satisfied.

"You know, I considered the beach for us," he began when he finished his meal, "but when I checked out the weather forecast it was supposed to rain. The temps are colder here, but I figured we could handle it."

Taking a sip of her coffee, she nodded. "I don't mind it being cooler. Sweater weather is my favorite."

He laughed softly. "Josie always says the same thing. She would usually bitch all summer long about the heat, and the first time the temperatures dropped below sixty degrees, she'd whip out all her winter clothes." He shook his head. "Like a weirdo."

"I'm not a huge fan of the summer weather. Never was. And now that we're doing so many events, I hate it even more because we're usually running around and I hate to look sweaty in front of clients."

"I get that." After taking a sip of his own coffee, he

asked, "But how often are you running around outside? Aren't most parties indoors?"

"I wish!" Leaning back against the pillows, she laughed at the shocked look on his face. "Summer weddings are a big thing, and outdoor ones even more so! We do tents and there are fans, but honestly, it's just never enough because we're always on the move. Guests get to sit down and relax, but me and Josie and Lea are almost always on the go. By the end of the night, I'm guaranteed to be sweaty and have excruciating pain in my feet. It's awful."

He studied her for a long moment. "Have the three of you talked about bringing more help on? You know, to sort of be the runners?"

"Not really. We've been so consumed with making the business a success, and this has been our biggest year to date. I'm sure it's something we'll get to eventually, but for now, it just makes more sense for us to be the ones doing it all." She shrugged. "Besides, now's the optimal time for us to be doing it. None of us are married or have kids so we might as well work like crazy now so that when we are in those situations, we'll feel better about letting someone else do the grunt work."

With a small snort, he shook his head. "I don't think you'll ever find my sister in that situation. Besides being a huge control freak, she's been extremely vocal about not getting married or having kids."

All Skye could do was nod because he was right.

"Lea's definitely going to be the one to get married and have kids," Elliott went on. "She's a total nurturer and I always figured she would have been well on her way to doing that long before now."

Again, all she could do was nod.

"What about you?" he asked, his tone a little more somber. "Do you ever think about all of that?"

This was a slippery slope and she hated to talk about it when they were just kicking off a fantastic romantic weekend. There was no way she couldn't answer, but she opted to keep it light.

"Well, yeah. I guess," she said with a small shrug. "But, like you, I really thought Lea would have had a couple of kids by now and we'd all get to sit back and watch her be awesome at it." Then she took a long sip of her coffee and prayed they were done.

"If Josie wasn't so anti-all of that, I always thought the three of you would have planned it out that you'd all get married and have kids at the same time," he said, staring down into his mug.

"There was a time when that was the plan, but we started the business and it keeps us all busy and we haven't talked or thought about it in a long time."

Liar. You think about it every time you think of Elliott...

Yeah, there was no way she was ever going to admit to that, so she opted to change the subject. "So, have you been up here before? Any cool places that you want to go and see today?"

Luckily, he took the topic change easily. "I was up here a few years ago for work and always wanted to come back. I was up in Asheville a little over a year ago, but coming here to Blowing Rock was always more my speed."

Skye remembered hearing about him taking Tracy up to Asheville for some luxury spa weekend and had to force her thoughts elsewhere, otherwise the little green monster in her would definitely come to the surface.

"I bet it's gorgeous up here when it snows," she comments, placing her coffee mug on the bedside table before carefully maneuvering her breakfast dishes off of the bed. "But I'm sure the roads are a nightmare."

"Yeah, I don't want to test that theory any time soon. I can't even remember the last time we had significant snowfall in Raleigh, so I have no idea how I'd do driving in it."

"Plus, your new sporty car probably wouldn't be the greatest in slick conditions," she mentioned, climbing from the bed.

"Maybe, but it's still better than a boring old SUV." He rose and worked with her to clean up their dishes and get them back on the tray for housekeeping.

Skye shrugged. "I don't think they're boring. Personally, I love mine and I think there are a lot of really cool ones out there."

"Sure, and they're great for couples or families, but I like driving around in something sleek and sporty now," he said, and she couldn't tell if he was trying to convince her or himself.

"Good for you," she said lightly, and before she could say another word, Elliott had her in his arms and was kissing her.

Excellent distraction, she thought.

And really, it was perfectly timed because she knew it was just another topic that was bound to make her crazy.

There were more and more of them lately and she wasn't an idiot. Something was going to have to give because they couldn't go on like this forever. It was like a sex bubble at first, but...her feelings were seriously more invested now and she knew agreeing to this kind of a relationship was only going to lead to her getting hurt.

And from the looks of it, sooner rather than later.

But as Elliott's hands skimmed down her arms–taking

the thin straps of her nightie with them—she knew this was a topic she was going to have to revisit.

Just not right now.

Or this weekend.

For now, she wanted to enjoy the extended bubble and the fact that they could go out in public together and not have to worry about running into anyone they knew.

Ugh... like a dirty little secret.

Again, she pushed that negative thought aside and did her best to focus on Elliott and his hands and his kiss and...

"Hey," he said softly, lifting his head. "You okay?"

Gently, Skye cleared her throat. "Yeah. Why?"

He gazed down at her like he didn't believe her. "You just seemed to... I don't know... like you weren't into it." Taking a step back, his eyes never left hers. "If you're not in the mood or if you'd rather get ready and head into town..."

"Elliott, I'm fine. I swear," she said, reaching out to take one of his hands in hers. "My mind wandered for a minute. It's not a big deal." Then she gave him what she hoped was a sexy smile as she stepped in close and pressed up against him. "And just for the record, I am into this. I do want to crawl back in bed with you and then I will want to go into town. In that order."

He still didn't look completely convinced, so she had to get a little persuasive.

Elliott was taller than Skye, so she leaned in and placed a kiss on his chest.

"As good as breakfast was, you taste even better," she whispered as she let her mouth and hands roam all over his body. She hummed as she placed another kiss on his chest. And then another. And another. "I love this chest." Her tongue ran slow circles around one nipple and then the other. She heard his soft hiss of breath and when she glanced up, his head had lolled back.

Then her hands ran up and down his arms, squeezing his biceps. "And I love these arms. These muscles…"

He let out a low groan.

And we're back on track…

She gave him a playful bite as her hands reached around and grabbed his butt. "And I really love this. You have the sexiest and most squeezable ass," she murmured, and by then, he seemed more than ready to pounce.

Yay!

Lifting her up, Skye wrapped her legs around his waist and kissed him even as he lay them both down on the bed. All thoughts of dirty secrets, sneaking around, and SUVs for them and their future kids were pushed from her mind.

And in their place were sexier, more pleasurable thoughts.

Because Elliott excelled at giving her pleasure.

So much so that she was panting his name as he kissed his way down her body. Her hands raked through his hair and gripped hard. "God, Elliott…what you do to me…"

He let out a sexy little growl in response and before she knew it, her head was thrashing on the pillow. His name a steady chant as she told him how good he was, how amazing she felt, and how much she loved…

Him.

"What would you think about trying the beach next month?" Skye asked Sunday afternoon when they were on their way back to Raleigh.

The weekend had been amazing and it felt good to be able to go out freely together and not worry about any of their friends or his family seeing them. They had walked through town shopping and tasting a variety of different foods. Skylar had insisted on getting him to try an assortment of gourmet fudge in the candy shop and then tasting different dips and breads in the spice shop. He also now had an assortment of new ornaments thanks to their spree in the Christmas shop.

And he loved every minute of it.

There had been a brief moment of panic yesterday morning when they'd made love after breakfast and Skye had said she loved him, but...she was in the middle of an orgasm so...she probably had no idea she even said it. Elliott hadn't brought it up and neither did she, so he knew they were good.

It had been so long since he'd done anything like this and he'd forgotten how much he loved being part of a couple and...

A sharp pain in his chest almost had him veering off the highway as the realization hit.

Beside him, Skye was talking about her favorite places at the beach and the places she wanted to take him to, and reality hit him like a ton of bricks. He was never going to see them.

He couldn't.

This whole thing was...wrong. He'd gone and done the one thing everyone feared he would do and he swore that he wouldn't.

"They're not the biggest rooms, but the hotel is right on the beach," she was saying, completely oblivious to the fact that he was on the verge of a major panic attack.

It was still another two hours until they were back home

and he swore he had no idea what to do or say–not now and not once they got there.

Luckily, he was saved from having to work at least half of it out when her phone rang. She smiled at him as she answered it. "Hey, Mom!"

Now he had some time to be in his own head to figure out how he was supposed to get out of this.

But is that what I really want?

Yes! He told himself over and over and over. Why? Because it was self-preservation! He'd been down this road so many damn times and other than what he and Skye were doing, he was enjoying his life for the first time in...well... years...maybe ever!

Or maybe you've finally learned how to balance having a life and having a relationship.

Okay, there was that, but...it was starting. This weekend was just the beginning of a pattern of behavior that everyone ridiculed him for. First, he was taking Skye away for a quick, laid-back weekend in the mountains but it was only a short step away from whisking her off to...to...Hawaii or...or...Hollywood because he knew how much she always wanted to do one of those quirky bus tours and see the different celebrity houses!

Yup, the tightness in his chest was getting worse and he rubbed his free hand over it and prayed Skye didn't notice it. If she did, he'd have to tell her he wasn't feeling good and then she'd undoubtedly want to take care of him and damn if he wouldn't love that. Next thing you know, they're making homemade chicken soup together and talking about taking a cooking class for couples!

"Oh, God..."

Skye put her hand over her phone and looked at him worriedly. "You okay?"

He nodded. "Uh...yeah. A little heartburn. I think I ate too many biscuits with gravy at breakfast."

"Do we need to stop and get you something?"

Shaking his head but keeping his eyes firmly on the road, he assured her that he was fine and to go back to her call.

"Sorry, Mom," she said, and Elliott could feel her eyes still on him. "No, I'm in the car with Leanna and she has a headache."

Great, now I've got her lying to her own mother...

Elliott shifted slightly in his seat and tried to focus on calming down. Maybe if she weren't sitting right there or they weren't locked in a car together for several hours it would be easier but...he could smell her perfume and her shampoo. He was sitting here listening to her sweet voice and her laughter as her mother must have been telling her a funny story. He was sure it was going to be a long time before he heard any of this again because no matter what they agreed to in the beginning, there was no way he was going to be comfortable hanging out with her as a friend.

Not for a long time.

If ever.

And how was he supposed to end it? No matter what, she was still one of his sister's best friends. There was no way he could be mean about it, and he certainly didn't want to ghost her and just walk away with no explanation.

He thought about all the amazing things they'd talked about–not just this weekend, but in the months since their affair began.

Yeah, think of it as an affair. That should ease your guilt...

He seriously wished his inner voice would shut the hell up.

Why couldn't he just keep things platonic? Why did he think for even a second that sex with a friend would be easier to deal with than sex with a stranger?

Um...because...ick. Yeah, hooking up with random strangers was so not his thing.

"I don't think I have anything going on Wednesday, Mom. But I'll have to check my calendar once we get off the phone," she was saying. "I can totally ask Lea if she'll bake some blueberry scones!" She paused. "Oh, you mean like right now?" Another pause. "Right, right...because she's sitting...beside me."

Elliott glanced over and saw her rolling her eyes and fighting the urge to laugh and couldn't help but smile. She was so damn amazing and sweet and beautiful and he had gone and messed with her when he had no right to.

With a wink, she asked, "Hey, Lea, my mom wants to know if you can make some scones for us on Wednesday. What do you think?" Then she placed her hand over the phone again as she silently laughed and shook her head.

"Um...maybe?" he said in his best girlie voice because he had a feeling he needed to say something so her mother could hear.

"What's that?" Skye asked her mother. "No, there's nothing wrong with Lea, why?" She paused. "Her voice?" Another round of silent laughter. "Her allergies are bothering her a bit." Her smile was infectious as she looked at him. "Listen, Mom, I need to go. We're pulling up to the mall. I'll check my calendar when I get home and let you know about lunch." She paused again. "Yes, and the scones. I promise. I love you! Bye." When she hung up, she doubled over and laughed out loud and Elliott found himself laughing with her.

"I wasn't sure if I was supposed to say anything," he began through his laughter.

"Oh my God! That was awesome! I had no idea what to do and that was just a riot!" She reached over and squeezed his thigh and it was all he could do not to react. "Seriously, thank you. I was just winging it."

He nodded as they both caught their breath and relaxed.

The rest of the drive was spent talking about everything they bought and then Skye pulled up her calendar and was sharing what her upcoming week was like. Normally they would compare notes and try to make plans for when they could get together, but...fortunately he was driving and couldn't pull his calendar up at the moment.

By the time they pulled into Skylar's driveway, Elliott's nerves were fraught. He put the car in park and knew he had to get out and help her with all her stuff, but it felt like he was simply biding his time until he faced the firing squad.

"Would you like to stay for dinner?" she asked, once everything was in the house. "Obviously I'm just planning on ordering something and having it delivered, so if you have any requests..."

Without a word, he walked over and sat down on her sofa. The look on his face must have spoken volumes because he saw the color leave her face. With little more than a nod, she sat down at the other end and let out a long breath.

"We both said we wanted casual–no strings, no commitments, no...future," he murmured, studying his hands instead of looking at her. It was the coward's way out, but he knew if he looked at her, he wouldn't get through this. Swallowing hard, he continued. "It occurred to me on the way home that…things have changed and they shouldn't have." When she didn't immediately respond, he forced himself to look up.

With her hands folded in her lap, she stared at him and Elliott saw the shine of unshed tears in her eyes. "Have I asked you for anything more than you were willing to give?"

He shook his head. "It's not you, Skye. It's me."

She let out a loud snort. "Seriously? That's what you're going with?"

"Yeah, I know, but it is what it is," he said flatly.

They sat in silence for several minutes before she spoke. "I don't understand how we went from a wonderful weekend to this, and I think you owe me an explanation."

Straightening, he met her gaze. "When we talked yesterday morning about you and Lea and Josie and about marriage and kids, you seemed hesitant to answer me. And you want to know what I think?"

She didn't respond.

"I think you do want those things, and being involved with me is…well…you're never going to get them. And you deserve them, Skye. You deserve to be happy and have everything you want." He swallowed hard again. "And that includes someone who doesn't cause you to lie to your family and friends. Not someone who takes you away for a weekend because he selfishly can't take you out here in your own town." Another pause. "Someone who wants all the same things that you do."

"Elliott…"

"Can you honestly say you don't want those things? Can you look me in the eye and tell me I'm wrong?"

Hanging her head, she shook it and he was pretty sure he heard her sniffle.

And he felt like the world's biggest jerk.

It took a minute, but she finally looked up at him. "You're right. I do want it all. I want the SUV, the four-bedroom house with a yard big enough for a jungle gym and for kids to play in. I want to fall in love and get married and fill that house with children," she said, her voice trembling. "And you know what? You talk a big game, but I know you, Elliott Sullivan. You still want all those things. You've always wanted them and it doesn't matter what you try to tell yourself or your family because all of that didn't just go away. It's not possible!"

"I hate to disappoint you," he said evenly, "but I don't want those things anymore. And if that's what you're thinking or hoping, then...you're just projecting that onto me. There was a time when it was true, but I'm done with all of it–relationships, marriage, kids...I mean, haven't you been paying attention? I'm selling the house! I sold my car! I...I..."

Jumping to her feet, Skye hovered over him. "I hate to break it to you, but we've been in a relationship for months, Elliott! Months!" she cried with frustration. "It may have started out as something casual and as just sex, but somewhere along the line, that changed! And you want to know when? It was when you came over to take care of me after I had a rough day! That wasn't me, pal; that was you!"

Now it was his turn to jump up. "It was just old habits, Skylar! Ask anyone we know; that's the kind of shit I always do and it didn't mean anything!" He hated the words even as they came out of his mouth, but there was no other way for him to make her understand. Raking a hand through his hair, he took several steps away from her and began to pace. For all his inner dialogue in the car about not wanting to fight or be mean, he honestly didn't see any other way for this to go.

"You keep telling yourself that, Elliott," she spat. "I've said it before and I'll say it again, you're just lying to yourself and you're going to be miserable for the rest of your life. And for what, huh? What do you think this is going to prove?"

"I'm not trying to prove anything!" he snapped. "Not to you, not to anyone! This is about me finally knowing what I want from my life and it's not this!" A growl of frustration was out before he could stop it. "And I don't know what you're fighting with me for! Now you can go after everything you want! A man who can make you happy and give you the future you deserve!"

"*You're* the man that I want, damn you! Don't you get it? Couldn't you tell?" Her growl wasn't nearly as fierce, but definitely showed her frustration. "I'm in love with you, Elliott! I've always been in love with you! Do you have any idea how hard it's been for me all these years? I've had to sit back and watch you fall in love over and over again with everyone but me!"

What? How was that possible? How had he missed the signs? She mentioned a crush when this all began, but...love?

Her tears fell in earnest and yet he refused to be moved by them. He couldn't. This is what needed to happen. It was for her own good.

Taking one step back and then another, Elliott slowly made his way toward the door. "I'm sorry, Skylar. I...I didn't know, but...it wouldn't matter. I don't...I don't feel the same," he said gruffly, and before she could respond, he turned and walked out the door, gently closing it behind him. If he looked back, if he dared to look in her eyes, he'd crumble.

It was all a lie.

Every word.

She was right about everything and...she loved him.

How could you just walk away from that? This is what you've wanted your whole damn life.

He was in the car and driving away before he could even fathom an answer. He felt numb and sick all at the same time and he had a feeling it was going to be like that for a long time.

Possibly forever.

Because as much as he talked a good talk about how okay he was, deep inside, he was a mess–even more so than he was after his failed wedding.

And why is that?

He cared about Tracy, but he knew now it wasn't love.

He loved Skylar.

And that's why he had to let her go.

CHAPTER 13

Sometimes you just need a good cry. Even if you don't know the reason why you're crying.

UNKNOWN

For the first time since Meet Me at the Altar began, Skye called in sick Monday morning. She had been alternating between crying and screaming with rage since Elliott walked out, and she had no idea when the pain was going to go away.

"It's my own fault," she told herself repeatedly. "I have no one to blame but myself." And yet no matter how much she said it, she knew if given a chance, she would do it all again.

When she called the office, luckily Leanna was the one to answer, so she didn't have to lie about why she wasn't coming in. Unfortunately, she *did* ask her friend to lie to Josie.

"I don't even want to think about how that went," she murmured from her spot on the couch. Leanna was an amazing person–always happy, always upbeat, and willing to do anything for a friend. But she was a lousy liar. Hopefully, Josie would just accept a blanket statement of Skye being sick and let it go at that.

Rolling onto her side, she closed her eyes. When Elliott left yesterday, she cried so hard that her shirt was wet and all her makeup was gone. After taking a shower, she threw on a pair of yoga pants and an oversized t-shirt before coming back out to the living room and collapsing on the couch.

And she'd been there ever since.

Sleep had been sporadic and for the life of her, she wished she had seen it all coming.

I should have seen it from the beginning...

Yeah, getting involved had been a risk, but she was more than willing to take it. On some level, she truly believed she was going to be the one to change his mind, the one to show him that relationships can work when you're with the right person. And now that she had spent so much time getting to know him on a level she never had before–and that wasn't including sexually–Skye knew without a doubt that Elliott was her right person.

But he didn't want her.

Didn't want a future with her.

And that made her start crying all over again.

Curled up in the fetal position, she didn't even try to stop crying. It was pointless to even try. At some point, the tears slowed and exhaustion overwhelmed her. Her entire body ached and her head was pounding, but the thought of getting up and doing anything about it was beyond overwhelming.

I guess I'll just lie here until I die.

Some time later–it could have been minutes, it could have been hours–there was a knock at her door. The immediate hope was that it was Elliott coming back to tell her he'd made a mistake, but she highly doubted it. Then she decided to just stay where she was because she didn't want anyone to see her like this.

So she ignored the knocking.

And the doorbell ringing.

And more knocking.

"Ugh...just go away," she moaned, pulling her fleece throw close around her.

There was a sound by the doorway and when she looked up, she saw Leanna walking in with a bag and several cups of coffee on a tray.

"Don't be mad," she said quickly with a sympathetic smile. "I used my emergency key. And from the look of things, this is definitely an emergency."

It was hard to be mad when she was in desperate need of coffee, so Skye forced herself to sit up. Pushing her hair out of her face, she said, "I'm not mad, but you really didn't have to do this."

Putting the coffee down on the coffee table, she smiled down at Skye. "Um, I really did. I thought your voice was the worst thing this morning, but now that I'm seeing you, I realize this was definitely the right thing for me to do." She held up a bag. "Bagels because...well...it's Monday." She fussed around getting things set up. "And again, please don't be mad, but..."

Skye took a sip of her coffee first. "Lea, I already told you I'm not mad. I'm actually really glad you're here."

"Uh...yeah. That's not what I was going to say. I want you to know that..."

"You were dating my brother!" Josie cried out as she strode into the house in a blur of energy. "How could you date Elliott? You know he was on an embargo!"

"You promised you were going to behave!" Lea said, stepping in before Josie could reach Skye. "We talked about this and you were supposed to wait for me to text you that it was okay for you to come in!"

"Well, too bad! Skye said she was just going to go and check on my brother, not sleep with him!" She moved around Lea until she was hovering over Skye. "Seriously, what were you thinking?"

"Everyone needs to calm down," Lea said, giving Josie a small shove that sent her sitting on the sofa. "No talk of this until we've all had something to eat. Personally, I think hunger causes more crankiness than anything."

"No, my best friend lying to me is the cause of my crankiness," Josie said firmly, but she grabbed the bag and pulled out her bagel. "I'm just eating this because I'm hungry. The two are *not* related."

The three of them ate in silence for several minutes before Lea was the one to speak.

"Okay, I want to just start out by saying that it's obvious Skye is devastated and yelling at her," she said pointedly at Josie, "is not going to help anything."

Fortunately, Josie nodded.

"This is a bit of an awkward situation, but more than anything, we're friends and as such, we should be supporting one another." Then she looked at Skye. "Seriously, sweetie, what can we do for you? What do you need?"

Tears stung her eyes again–damn them–and all she wanted to say was that she needed Elliott, but that certainly wasn't going to happen or help anything.

"Honestly, I...I don't know," she said quietly, staring hard at her coffee before looking up at Josie. "I have been in love with your brother since forever. When I went home with him the day of the wedding..."

"Oh, God! You didn't sleep with him that day, did you?"

"Are you crazy?" Skye demanded, her tears instantly drying. "And I can't even believe you would ask me something like that!"

"You're right. You're right," Josie said, shaking her head. "I'm sorry. I just...how did I not know this? Why didn't you ever say anything?"

Shrugging, she replied, "I don't know. It was weird. And I didn't want things to get strained between us, and it wasn't like Elliott ever showed any interest in me. It just seemed like the kind of thing to keep to myself."

Josie glanced at Lea. "Did you know about this?"

She nodded.

"All of it–the crush and now?"

She nodded again.

"Well, shit," Josie huffed, slouching back against the cushions. "I hate that you both kept this from me."

"Can you blame us?" Lea asked. "Look how you're reacting!"

"But you didn't know I would..."

"Oh, please. We all knew you would," Lea quickly interrupted. "And you know what, this isn't about you. This is about Skye. And if you can't see that, then you need to leave!"

Both Skye and Josie's eyes went wide because Leanna was never the forceful one–ever.

Then they looked at each other and burst out laughing.

"That was awesome!" Josie said, reaching over and

hugging Lea. "I knew there was a fierce mama bear in there somewhere!"

Skye slid over and made it a group hug. "And I'm so happy you were being fierce for me. Thank you."

They stayed like that for several minutes before breaking apart and sitting in silence as they ate and drank. Skye was more than happy to stay like that, but there was still so much to talk about. So she started at the beginning–the day of the wedding–and told Josie everything.

Within limits because...ew. Who wanted to hear about their brother's sex life?

When she was done, she was crying again and felt even more emotionally drained, but talking with her friends definitely helped.

They each came over–sitting on either side of her–and hugged her. It was the best medicine.

Well, that and the coffee.

"So what happens now?" Lea asked quietly.

"I don't know," Skye told her. "I'll get over it. Over him. I don't have a choice. It's just going to take some time." Straightening, she looked at Josie. "I'm sorry I kept this from you. In the beginning–well, the recent beginning–I really was just hanging out with him because I wanted to help him. I never expected things to turn into what they did."

"But maybe you secretly hoped?" Josie asked quietly.

Why deny it? "Yeah, I secretly hoped. I've always secretly hoped. And you know what? It was still the best relationship I've ever had. I love him." She wiped away some tears. "I know it's been less than twenty-four hours, but...I ache for him. I've never felt like this and I don't know how to move on, but I promise you that I will."

Her friends both nodded.

"And please promise me, Jos, that you're not going to let

this get awkward for us or for you and Elliott. I would hate if things were strained between the two of you. As it is, I hate that you're in the middle of it now."

"Yeah, um...sorry," Lea interjected.

"No, you were right to do this," Skye reassured her. "It was killing me to be sneaking around and not telling you. I just thought when you found out it was going to be because Elliott was going to tell your whole family that his embargo was over because we were in love." She wiped tears away again as she let out a mirthless laugh. "Pretty stupid of me, huh?"

"You're not stupid," Josie told her, hugging her close. "I'm so sorry he hurt you."

"I hurt myself," she admitted. "I knew the risks and I chose to ignore them, so...this is totally on me."

"What do we do now?" Leanna asked.

"The bagels and coffee were a good start," Skye said. "But any chance you brought some icing?"

Lea grinned as she grabbed her giant purse and reached inside. When she pulled out a container, she handed it to Skye. "As if I'd come unprepared."

The last thing Elliott expected when he pulled up to his house late Monday night was to see Josie's car in his driveway. He had specifically worked late because he needed the distraction and stared at codes on the screen until he couldn't see straight. Why would she show up like this?

His first reaction was that Skye must have told her about them, but...they pretty much swore not to tell anyone, so...

Muttering a curse, he pulled in beside her and prayed

there was nothing seriously wrong and this was just his sister coming to hang out.

Pasting a smile on his face, he climbed from the car at the same time Josie did. "Hey! What brings you by?"

"Oh, you know," she said, smiling, "I worked late and was on my way home and thought I'd swing by and say hello!"

It seemed plausible, so he went with it.

"As you can see, I worked late too." They walked to the front door and then into the house. "Have you eaten?"

"I had a yogurt and a cupcake," she said with a small laugh. "It's not an ideal dinner, but it was good."

He shook his head. "Do you ever sit down for a real meal?"

"Only if it's delivered."

"I was going to order a pizza," he lied. Honestly, he was going to come home and go to sleep because he hadn't slept at all the night before.

"Ooh…I would totally be down for that! Can we get pepperoni and mushrooms?"

"I hate mushrooms."

"So don't get them on your half," she countered with a grin before walking into the kitchen and helping herself to something to drink.

Within minutes he had their dinner ordered and accepted a bottle of water from her before collapsing on the couch.

"Any offers on the house?" she asked.

"Um…not yet."

"Really? That's odd. I would have thought this place would have sold the day it hit the market."

It probably would have if he had been more agreeable

with the real estate agent and actually let her bring people by to look at the place.

But he hadn't.

"Yeah, well...people are picky."

"How many couples have they brought through? Are you asking too much?"

He shook his head. "I think the price is fair."

"So what are people saying? What kind of feedback are you getting?"

Ugh...his sister was like a dog with a bone sometimes.

"I haven't really had any feedback because..." He groaned. "I haven't let them bring anyone through."

Josie's eyes went wide. "But...that's just stupid, El. Why would you list the house and then not let anyone see it?"

Good question.

"I've been working a lot and haven't had a chance to do all that...you know...staging stuff. It's not like I'm in a rush or anything."

"A month ago you seemed like you were. Having second thoughts?"

Second. Third. And fourth.

"No. Not really." Another lie. "Enough about me, what's going on with you? Everything set for Nana and Pops' anniversary party?"

Her whole face lit up as she got more comfortable. "This party is going to be amazing! We've got a videographer working on some of the old home movies and slides and making them into a video presentation. Mom and Dad suggested it, and I knew a guy, so I took care of that. Patricia finalized the menu and it's outstanding! She even got some of Nana's recipes and worked on them with her so we're going to be having her home-made ravioli and her meatballs. I am psyched about that!"

With a yawn, he nodded.

He could feel Josie's eyes on him and he couldn't bring himself to look directly at her.

"You must be working on a big project or something."

"Why do you say that?"

"Because you look like shit," she said bluntly. "You shouldn't work so hard. It's not good for you."

"Yeah, well…it's not like I've got anything else to do with my time." Now he did look up at her. "With the embargo and all."

"Oh, stop. You and I both know the embargo has nothing to do with this and it hasn't for a long time. It was just a little…creative encouragement to get you to explore some other aspects of your life. And you know, for the last few months, you were really thriving."

"Thriving?" he asked with a small snort. "That's a good one."

"It's true! You looked good! You were laughing and smiling and seemed genuinely happy!" She took a sip of her water and studied him. "Who knew joining a basketball league would be so invigorating, huh?"

He had a feeling she knew more than she was letting on, but he was afraid to comment on it.

"I'm working with Tyler on a fundraiser event for his company and he noticed how much happier you've been too," she went on. "Any other hobbies you've taken on?"

Shaking his head, he said, "Nope. Just getting out more with the guys."

"Hmm…I can understand that. I know I'm always in a better frame of mind when I get to hang out with the girls more. Especially when it's not work-related."

Elliott nodded.

"Actually, Lea, Skye, and I were just talking today about finding time for a girls' getaway–you know, checking the calendar and seeing when we're free. I'm thankful for how great business has been, but I would kill for a weekend away." She paused and took another sip of water. "When was the last time you got away for the weekend, El?"

Okay, that was too much of a coincidence and he knew he wasn't going to breathe easy until they put the cat-and-mouse conversation aside.

"Something you want to know, Josie?" he asked, his voice gruff.

Her expression was mildly amused. "Something you want to share, Elliott?"

God, she was such a pain in the ass.

They were at a standoff, and as much as he normally enjoyed this kind of banter with his sister, he just didn't have it in him tonight. Hell, if she weren't here, he'd be in bed asleep right now. So he yawned again and took another drink.

"What would you think of me going out with Tyler?" she asked casually.

"Considering you just told me you've been working with him on the fundraiser, I'm guessing you've already gone out with him."

Josie let out a low laugh before leaning forward slightly. "I meant on a date. Like a romantic date. Possibly having sex with him."

"Josie..."

"Like would you want to know? Obviously not the specific details or anything because that would be weird, but would you want to know that we were involved?"

Elliott hung his head and sighed.

"I always thought you and I were close, but...would it be totally weird to think of me being involved with like...your *best* friend?" She shook her head and took a sip of water. "Although, to be fair, he's kind of my friend too. Not a best friend, but...close enough. So maybe it wouldn't be weird since...you know...he's my friend too."

"Why are you like this?" he murmured.

Luckily, they were saved by the bell and neither had to answer or continue this ridiculous conversation for a few minutes while he got their dinner from the delivery guy and then set it up on the coffee table. Josie grabbed plates and napkins and when she sat back down, she was grinning from ear to ear.

"Want to watch some TV while we eat?" she asked.

"Yes. Please," he growled and tossed the remote at her.

"Touchy, touchy," she hummed and tsk-tsked. "I don't know why you're so grouchy."

And that was it. Tossing his pizza down, he jumped to his feet. "Obviously, you know exactly why I'm so grouchy, so can we please cut the crap already? You want to make me feel bad? Fine! I feel bad! I feel horrible!" he shouted as he stalked away from her.

Rather than respond right away, Josie took a bite of her pizza and then took her sweet time chewing.

And gently blotted her mouth with a napkin.

And then took another sip of water.

Elliott was pretty certain his head was going to explode.

"Tell me, Elliott, do you feel bad for keeping such a big secret from me? Or the fact that you lied to our entire family who essentially forbade you from getting involved with anyone?"

"You know what, Josie? Neither," he said firmly. "No

one had the right to forbid me to do anything. I'm a grown man, not a child. And as for keeping a secret from you, don't make me laugh. You've kept plenty of secrets from me and I never–never!–put the guilt trip on you like this!"

Her eyes went wide. "What secrets have I ever kept from you?" she demanded. "This I've got to hear." Then she crossed her arms over her chest and waited.

"There was the time when you snuck out to see Pearl Jam when we were in high school," he smugly reminded her. "And I was a fan of their music first!"

She rolled her eyes. "I would have told you, but you were such a goody-goody that I knew you would have ratted me out to Mom and Dad and I wouldn't have been able to go!"

"Still a secret..."

"Oh, please. Elliott, you cannot compare a concert to sneaking around for months with Skye! You just can't!"

If he weren't so damn tired, maybe he could argue it with her, but...he couldn't.

Hell, he shouldn't because she was right.

He hung his head in defeat. "I know," he said quietly before sitting back down.

"Well, shit," she replied, tossing her own pizza down. "I thought you'd be a little more...I don't know...defiant. I was really looking forward to fighting this out with you." She sighed. "Now it just feels like I'm kicking a puppy."

"I deserve to be kicked." Head back, arm thrown over his eyes, he let out a long breath. "Go ahead, kick me."

"I'm not going to kick you, Elliott. That's ridiculous."

"No, I'm serious. It's the least I deserve. Just do it."

"I'm not..."

"Just do it!"

"Elliott…"

"Oh, my God! Would you just…ow!" Sitting up straight, he looked up at Josie who was standing beside him. "You kicked me!"

"You told me to!"

Leaning forward, he rubbed his shin. "That really hurt." Then he looked at her feet. "Are you wearing steel-toed boots or something?"

"Nope. Just knew where to hit for maximum effect." She smiled proudly. "I took a couple of self-defense classes and learned that. Glad to see it really works."

"I'm probably going to have a bruise there."

"And you deserve it." Then she sat beside him, resting her head on his shoulder. "For what it's worth, I'm sorry about the whole embargo thing. We never should have done that to you. Especially that day."

He shrugged. "I understand why you did."

"Yeah, but…that really wasn't cool, and we put more pressure on you than you deserved so…I'm sorry."

Elliott rested his head against hers. "Thanks."

They sat like that in companionable silence for several minutes before Josie let out a soft sigh. "You going to be alright?"

"Eventually."

She straightened. "Elliot…"

"Hey," he said softly, taking one of her hands in his and squeezing it. "I got through being dumped at my high school graduation, being cheated on in college, finding my fling making out with an Elvis impersonator, and being left at the altar. I'll get over this too."

"And what is this?" she quietly asked.

He stared at her. "What do you mean?"

"Well, all of those events were easily summed up. How would you sum this one up?"

Good question.

It wasn't until much later when he was alone in bed that Elliott realized how he would describe what he and Skylar had.

Perfect.

CHAPTER 14

When you realize your self-worth you'll stop giving people discounts.

UNKNOWN

"AND YOU'RE sure you're okay with this?"

"I'm sure I'm okay with this."

"Because if it's too much, you know I'll go."

"I know you will, but it's completely unnecessary."

Skye let out a long breath and looked around the office. "I feel bad dumping this on you."

"You're not dumping anything on me," Leanna assured her. "We agreed a month ago that this was going to be the plan. Josie walked me through everything, you've walked me through everything, and honestly, I have handled some events on my own so I'm not completely clueless."

"No one thinks you're clueless, Lea. I just feel bad

because you have that huge cake order for Enchanted Bridal's expo."

But Lea waved her off. "It's not a big deal. I'm bringing all the cupcakes and display pieces over tonight and then tomorrow I'll bring the cakes and get them set up."

"It's three wedding cakes, Lea. How can you do all of that *and* Josie's grandparents' party? It's not possible!"

"I have my girls coming to assist me and we'll be fine." She gently grasped Skye by the shoulders and spun her around before giving her a playful shove toward the door. "Now go home and relax. We've got this under control."

It felt wrong to be leaving like this, but...

"Okay. But promise me you'll call if you need me."

"I will."

"I'm serious, Lea! I'm totally fine seeing Elliott. It's been a month and...I'm good. Better than good," she said with false bravado. "Let him see me and eat his heart out."

"Yes, I'm sure he would, but it will have to happen another time. Go and I'll call you on Sunday and tell you how everything went, okay?"

It took her almost another hour before she made it out the door, and once she did, Skye had no idea what to do with herself. They had blacked out this weekend for any other events and the Enchanted Bridal Expo was something they accepted simply because they loved the girls there and they were in a pinch.

Now, with nothing but a free weekend ahead of her, she had to try to muster up some enthusiasm to find something to do.

At home, Skye did laundry, made herself some chicken stir-fry for dinner, took a long hot bath, and read before crawling into bed. It was far from an exciting evening, but...

it had been the story of her life since her breakup with Elliott.

She meant what she told Leanna earlier–she could handle seeing him now. It wouldn't be easy, and she'd probably feel more than a little regret at the loss of their friendship more than anything–but she knew she could see him without bursting into tears and needing to lock herself away for days to recover. She never believed in the whole time heals all wounds thing, but she was finding that it was true.

Sucky, but true.

Josie kept asking if she was ready to date again, and Leanna kept asking if she was okay. Most days her answer to both was no, but lately Skye felt like maybe it was time to start dating again. It was probably the only thing that was going to get her to move on so...maybe one night next week she'd shock her friends and suggest they have a girls' night out.

The thought made her smile. It had been far too long since they'd done that–just the three of them, and with nothing else on the agenda except having some fun and seeing if some good-looking guys would buy them some drinks.

Rolling onto her side, she got comfortable and smiled. The look on Josie and Lea's faces would be comical, and she almost couldn't wait to spring it on them. Maybe they could try someplace new to be certain they wouldn't run into Elliott and Tyler.

"That is my goal for the weekend," she murmured around a yawn. "Research some new places to go." And it was with that last thought that she fell asleep.

The next morning, Skye got up and was looking forward to the day ahead. She was going to go online and look up some new and fabulous wine bars, and, she decided, she was going to go out for the day and hit the mall. The thought of hitting the bookstore made her giddy, and then she was definitely going to get herself one of those giant pretzels that she rarely treated herself to.

"Not my most exciting day, but I'm making the most of it," she told herself as she stepped into the shower. An hour later, dressed in her favorite jeans and hooded sweatshirt, she left for the mall.

It was loud and crowded, but as she wandered the aisles of Barnes and Noble, Skye found herself smiling. So many wonderful books to choose from and she landed on a rom-com that she'd heard good things about. Glancing at the back cover, she couldn't help but laugh at the warning label: *Warning — This sweet, sexy and laugh-out-loud funny romance is filled with all the most ridiculous road trip stories you can imagine and is sure to drive you crazy with all the feels!*

"That is exactly what I want," she murmured. "Something fun to read tonight."

Book in hand, she continued to shop around and she grabbed a few more books, a new planner, a travel mug, and a journal before venturing out into the mall. The pretzel place was right there, so Skye made that her second stop and moaned with pure delight after her first bite.

Oh yeah...that's the stuff...

She had barely finished chewing when her phone rang. Going over to the nearest bench, she put her stuff down and looked at the screen with a frown.

"Hey, Jos! What's up?"

"We have a situation."

"Um...what?"

"A situation, Skye! A code-red situation!"

"I have no idea what that means!"

There was a loud sigh on the other end of the phone before Josie explained. "So, Angie at Enchanted was under the impression that one of us was going to stay for the expo, and she specifically wants Leanna to do it because of the cakes!"

"I don't understand. I can totally go and do the expo. I know enough about what Lea does that it shouldn't be a big deal. And really, how did we not pay more attention to this? Even as a last-minute favor, someone should have remembered them asking for one of us to stay!" She took another bite of her pretzel. "I mean, for crying out loud, it's not like we had a lot on our plate that this should have slipped by us!"

"Are you eating something? Where are you?"

"I'm at the mall and having a pretzel," she explained before taking another bite.

"Oh, no...not the mall pretzel. Skye, those things are a carb nightmare! Throw it away! I know you've been depressed lately, but you don't want to spend the day dealing with mall carbs!"

"I have zero regrets about the mall carbs. If anything, I might grab a second one to go and have it for dinner."

"No, you won't because you're going to be here eating Patricia's version of my nana's ravioli and meatballs and whatever else you want off of the fabulous menu," Josie told her. "You'll need to be here by four, okay?"

"Um, no, it's not okay. I'm going to go to Enchanted and relieve Leanna and she'll be to your party at four."

"Did you not hear the part about them *only* wanting Lea there for the cakes?"

"You did, but it makes no sense! What difference does it make which one of us is there? As long as someone is there representing Meet Me at the Altar, they should be happy!"

"Look, I completely agree, but they are a good company to work with and we've always had a great relationship with the girls there. Why rock the boat?"

"They're the ones rocking!" Skye countered around another bite of pretzel. At this rate, she was going to need a second one now rather than later because she was stress eating her way through it.

"Skye, focus," Josie said calmly. "We've talked about this and you've been saying how you would be fine coming here if you needed to. Well...you need to. Please. I want to enjoy the party and visit with my relatives and basically, I'm not expecting any issues, but I won't be able to relax if you're not here."

She swallowed a ball of carbs and groaned. "Fine. I'll be there. But I'm not happy about it and we're going to talk about this on Monday, how no one paid attention to what was needed at the expo."

"Yes, we will. Now throw away the pretzel and go home and get ready. What are you going to wear?"

Unable to help it, she rolled her eyes. "Does it matter? I'll wear one of my event dresses–something plain and simple. No big deal."

"I'm just curious, that's all. You looked really good in that black dress with the open back. You should wear that. Make my brother regret letting you go."

Groaning, she fought the urge to throw something. "Why would you even bring that up right now? Just...why?"

"What? I thought it would be cool for you to wear a revenge dress–you know, like Princess Diana did. I'm just encouraging you. Plus, a good revenge dress would force you to get rid of the pretzel."

She took another bite. "I'm almost done with it because this conversation is stressing me out!"

"Fine, but don't come crying to me when you have a carb-filled belly bump later because I'll just have to say I told you so."

"I'll consider myself warned," she said wearily.

"Okay, then. I'll see you at four."

"Yup. Four." Sliding her phone back into her purse, Skye stood and considered her options. There was half a pretzel left and there was no way she was throwing it out.

But a revenge dress did sound appealing.

Pretzel. Dress. Pretzel. Dress. Decisions, decisions...

Grabbing her bags, she took another bite of her treat and walked over to Macy's to do a little dress shopping.

And an hour later walked back out without a dress.

"Damn mall carbs."

———

"Yikes."

Elliott didn't even bother to react to his sister's comment because she wasn't the first one today to make it.

Or any day for the last month.

"Seriously, bro, you could have cleaned up a bit for today," Josie said with a hint of disgust before reaching out and touching his face. "And you definitely should have shaved."

"Beards are trendy right now."

"Not that beard," she murmured, frowning. "What is going on with you?"

I made a huge mistake and miss Skylar more than I thought possible...

Instead of saying that, he shrugged. "Just putting in a lot of hours at work. I'm heading up a big project and it's taking more time than I thought it would."

It wasn't a total lie, but he had volunteered to head it up and only took on half the team he really needed because he wanted the extra work. Burying all his free time in coding was the perfect distraction so he wasn't thinking about his pathetic excuse of a life. It was what he should have done originally after the whole wedding thing instead of getting involved with Skye. Maybe if he had done that, he wouldn't be such a mess right now.

He wasn't sleeping; he was existing on pizza and coffee, and maybe if he stuck to the original time frame of the whole embargo thing, in three months he'd feel like he had his life back.

Or at least a better one than he was currently living.

Sliding his hands into his trouser pockets, he let out a long breath and decided to change the subject. "The place looks great. I was watching Nana and Pop walk around a little while ago and she was gushing over all the decorations. You really outdid yourself. And Leanna's cake is amazing."

"She had only one picture to work off of, but I think it looks exactly like their original wedding cake," Josie said, sounding pleased. "We really tried to recreate as much as we could and I think they finally got Nana to go and get changed into her gown." She looked around him into the room. "We should be ready to start in an hour." Then she paused. "Which reminds me, why are you here so early?"

He shrugged again. "I figured I'd come and see if you needed any help. I know your goal was to just be here as a guest, but I thought maybe Lea could use a hand or something."

Waving him off, Josie stepped around him. "Leanna's stuck at a wedding expo so she can talk cakes with potential clients. Skye's coming to oversee everything." She glanced down at her phone which was always in her hand. "She should be here any minute." Then she smiled at him. "I'm going to go and meet up with her and walk her through everything. I'll see you in a little while!"

Elliott watched as she walked away and felt like he was going to be sick.

And seriously regretted not shaving.

Looking around, he wondered what he was supposed to do with himself until the party started. He really did intend to come and lend a hand, but knowing that Skye was going to be in charge, he had a feeling she wasn't interested in any help from him.

And he couldn't blame her one bit.

So now what?

Spotting his parents walking around, he decided to join them. "Hey, Mom," he said softly, kissing her cheek. Then he turned and shook his father's hand. "Hey, Dad."

"Elliott," his mother said gently, taking his hand in hers. "You do realize this is a bit of a formal event, right?"

"Um..."

"Son, don't you think you should have...you know... cleaned up a bit for today?" his father suggested.

He looked down at himself and frowned before looking at them. "I'm dressed appropriately, I've showered and brushed my teeth. What exactly is wrong with how I look?"

"Sweetheart, when was the last time you got a haircut or...shaved?" His mother made a small disapproving sound as she shook her head. "Are you still upset about your wedding? Is this too much of a reminder? I'm sure Nana would understand if you..."

"I'm not upset about my wedding, Mom," he said wearily. "I grew a beard; it's not a big deal."

"Are you depressed?" his father asked. "You seem a little depressed. Is that why you grew the beard?"

"I'm not depressed," he responded through clenched teeth. "I've been very busy with work and for your information, beards are trendy right now. Ask anyone."

"Skylar!" his mother called out cheerily as she waved her over. "Look how beautiful you look!"

"Thanks, Mrs. Sullivan," Skye said as she hugged his mother, then his father, and completely ignored him.

"Skylar, settle an argument for us, please. Look at Elliott and tell him that beard isn't trendy. He looks depressed and a little like a...a...hobo."

It wasn't hard to miss the smirk on her face when she finally looked at him. Elliott forced a smile. "Hey, Skye."

"Elliott," she said softly before returning her attention to his mother. "Beards can be trendy but...not this time."

"And the hobo thing?"

This time she laughed a little before looking at him again. "I wouldn't exactly say hobo, but it's certainly not his best look. Sorry."

"See?" his mother said firmly to him. "No one likes it! You need to go shave right now!"

"Mom, I don't carry a razor around with me. I think for today everyone can handle this without it ruining the whole party."

"You'll ruin the pictures..."

"It's a beard! Why is everyone giving me so much grief about this?" he demanded.

"Elliott, maybe you need to see a counselor or something. You seem to have a lot of anger issues," his father chimed in.

"I'm angry because everyone is ganging up on me over something trivial," he reasoned. "And I certainly don't need you grabbing people to pile on!"

"It's not like we grabbed someone off the street, dear.

Skylar's practically family. And I'm sure if we flagged your sister down, she'd agree with all of us."

This was getting him nowhere, and he opted to simply give up. "I've already had this conversation with Josie and... I'm just going to go for a walk. Excuse me," he huffed before walking away.

Luckily, he made it out to the gardens without anyone else stopping him. There was a small sitting area set up for the party and he opted to go and sit out there to get some peace and quiet.

Running a hand over his jaw, he had to admit that it wasn't his best look, but...it hadn't really mattered. The only one he was spending time with was himself. He hadn't been to basketball or gone out with the guys since he ended things with Skye. Tyler had shown up at his house after a week and tried to find out what was wrong, but...Elliott kept it all to himself. Maybe if he had talked about it, he wouldn't feel so crappy right now.

The weather was beautiful and people were walking around setting up and he wished the damn party would just start so he could get it over with and go home.

"Mrs. Sullivan wants a few additional tables and chairs set up out here with an assortment of snacks," he heard Skylar saying as she walked his way. "Can we maybe station a server out here to oversee the area?"

"That shouldn't be a problem," whoever was with her was saying. When he looked up, he saw a man in a suit walking beside her and figured he worked with the arboretum events team. "We can even set up a small bar that offers water and non-alcoholic drinks if you'd like."

"That sounds wonderful. Thanks, Mark. I appreciate you being so flexible," she was telling him. They both stopped short when they spotted Elliott sitting on one of the benches. He thought she was going to turn and walk away, but Mark started directing his staff on what he needed them to do.

Unable to stop himself, he gave her a small wave. He noticed the slight flush of her cheeks when she waved back.

Then she slowly walked toward him. "Hey."

"Hey," he said, hating how awkward it all felt. She looked beautiful–her long hair pulled back in her standard sleek ponytail and the little black dress that hugged her curves perfectly. She was the epitome of the elegant professional. "How've you been?"

He caught her hesitation before she said, "Good. And you?"

He shrugged. "Other than being mistaken for a hobo? Good."

With a husky laugh, Skye clasped her hands in front of her. "Yeah, um...sorry about that."

"No worries. It's the unanimous opinion of the day, so..."

"Skye?" Mark called out. "Will these tables work?"

With an apologetic smile and another wave, she turned and walked away and Elliott's eyes went wide.

The backless dress left little to the imagination and he wanted to get up and cover her up. That was not what he was expecting from the damn front of the dress at all! He was about to go after her when he realized it wasn't his place.

Plus, she was working, not socializing. It wasn't like anyone was going to get up close and personal with her in the middle of his grandparents' anniversary party.

And what would you do if they did?

Nothing. He'd lost the right to.

Actually, he never *had* the right to. The entire time they

were together, no one knew about it, so even if they happened to be at the same place at the same time with their friends, he had no claim on her.

God, I'm an idiot.

It wasn't the first time he'd thought that about himself, and he was fairly certain it wasn't going to be the last.

Letting his head fall back, he let out a long breath as he closed his eyes.

A few minutes later, someone sat down beside him and he was almost afraid to open his eyes and see who it was.

"Your grandmother never let me have a beard."

Straightening, Elliott couldn't help but smile. "Hey, Pop. Shouldn't you be inside getting ready?"

With a small shrug, his grandfather grinned. "Already done. Your grandmother picked out this suit, this tie, my shoes, and socks." He chuckled. "I was ready in five minutes. Meanwhile, she's in there with a team of professionals and I don't understand why."

"I'm guessing she wants to look her best for you," he reasoned. "And this is a big day."

Waving him off, his grandfather shook his head. "She could have worn a housecoat and she'd be beautiful. I know she enjoys having a fuss made over her, but she doesn't need it. She's beautiful no matter what she wears."

"It's a female thing, Pop. They like the fuss."

"Maybe." He paused. "She's so excited about this party. The fact that she still fits in her gown has been a source of non-stop conversation. Personally, I'll be happy when we can talk about something else." He let out a soft chuckle and Elliott couldn't help but join him.

"So how does it feel, Pop? I mean, sixty-five years is a long time. How do the two of you make it work?"

His grandfather gave him a knowing grin. "You may

have everyone else fooled, Elliott, but not me. We're too alike."

"What do you mean?"

"I mean, you can tell your parents and your sister that you're okay with being a bachelor, but I hear the longing in your voice. I can see it in your face."

Damn. He hated being that transparent.

Still.

Then he looked at Elliott. "What about you? What's going on with you?"

"Not much. Working hard. I'm in the middle of a big project at work, and…"

"I wasn't talking about work, Elliott. What's going on with your personal life? Dating anyone?"

"I'm still dealing with the big embargo, remember?"

"Bah," he huffed. "Dumbest thing I ever heard of. I should have spoken up against it when your father brought it up, but I didn't want to add to the craziness of the day."

"Yeah, well…I haven't been a fan of it, but I understand why everyone thought it was a good idea."

"Nonsense!" his grandfather stated firmly. "You know what you and I have in common, Elliott? We follow our hearts. And there is nothing wrong with that."

"Four failed relationships would say otherwise."

"They weren't the right ones for you, and if you ask me, it's better you found out before you got married. Isn't it easier talking about a breakup rather than a divorce?"

"I guess…"

He pat Elliott's knee. "Let me tell you a story."

"O-kay…"

"You want to know why I went along with this whole party thing?"

"Um…because it's your anniversary?"

"I've had sixty-four anniversaries and we never went this wild before." He chuckled again. "I gave your grand-mother a hard time when we first met. I knew for certain I was in love with her, but I didn't tell her. I couldn't."

"Why not?"

"My parents–your great-grandparents–had a plan for me. My father owned his own construction company and he expected me to join him. The problem was...well...I was no good at building anything. I could do all the accounting and run the business end of it, but my father expected me to take over for him and do all the physical stuff."

All Elliott could do was nod.

"I didn't want to disappoint him, and the stress I was dealing with was killing me. Any time I went to go out with your grandmother, my parents would lecture me on the importance of having a good career so I could take care of a wife and kids. How now wasn't the time for dating; it was the time for learning my trade." He groaned. "The fights we would have! But I would sneak out and see your grand-mother and no one knew."

"You were a rebel, Pop!"

"No, I just needed to see my Millie," he said with a smile. "She knew what my parents wanted from me and she was patient for a time. And then she wasn't."

"Oh?"

Nodding, Pop continued. "She was the first one to say I love you. It was the most beautiful sentence I'd ever heard. Then she took my hands in hers and told me what she wanted for our future. I panicked–completely froze! There was no way I could tell my folks I wanted to get married and didn't care about construction." He sighed. "She listened to me go on and on about it and finally, you know what she asked me?"

"What?"

"She asked me what my heart wanted." He smiled. "Her. My heart wanted her."

"And what about your parents?"

He snorted. "My cousin Ed took over the building stuff and I took over running the office. And you want to know what my parents finally said to me after I got married?"

"What?" Elliott was literally on the edge of his seat.

"They said it took a strong man to follow his heart and that I better spend my life appreciating the gift I had in your grandmother." He shrugged. "Of course they didn't say that until after we had a couple of kids, but...they finally said it."

"Wow. I had no idea."

"What I'm trying to say, Elliott, is...don't let anyone tell you how you feel or try to tell you what you shouldn't feel. You know what happens when you let people do that? You have regret. Regret for all the things you never did because other people thought they knew better. Hell, it's our mistakes that make us who we are! If you had married that girl in high school, it never would have worked! You were too young! Every relationship teaches us something and I bet if you met a woman right now, you would know exactly what you want and have the confidence to go for it." He pat him on the knee again. "Any chance of us getting a beer before I have to go in there in this monkey suit?"

Laughing, Elliott stood. "Pop, I'll get you whatever you want." And when his grandfather stood, Elliott hugged him. "Thank you."

"For what?"

"For being the smartest man I know."

CHAPTER 15

Nobody is perfect until you fall in love with them.

UNKNOWN

"Ooh...you went with the backless one. Good call," Josie said midway through the party.

"Yeah, well, I was going to buy something new and even tried on a few at Macy's, but none of them looked right."

With a knowing grin, she said, "I blame the mall carbs."

"I blame the mall carbs too. But...this dress looks just fine so I'm good."

"I meant to tell you how pretty you looked when you got here but things were a little chaotic."

Skye looked around the room and was pleased. Everyone was having a good time, the room looked amazing, and all the food was delicious. "Well, it seems like it's all good now and your grandparents looked ridiculously happy. Good for them."

"Sixty-five years," Josie said with a hint of awe. "Can you imagine being with the same person for that long?"

Luckily, she was saved from having to answer that when Mr. Sullivan walked over and asked Josie to dance.

With a small smile and wave, she turned her attention to the staff that was clearing away the dinner dishes and getting ready for dessert. There wasn't much for her to do–everyone knew what they were doing–but she had no idea what to do with herself.

"Hey, Skye. Want to dance?"

Turning, she saw Tyler standing there smiling at her. "Um...I probably shouldn't. I'm working and..."

"Nonsense," he said, reaching for her hand and slowly leading her toward the dance floor. "I checked with Josie and she said it was fine."

"Oh, well..."

His arms went around her as the band switched to a slow ballad.

Damn them.

"You look really pretty today," he said as he held her close. She felt his hand on her back–skin on skin–and it took everything she had not to react. Had she known she was going to be dancing with anyone, this definitely wasn't the dress she would have chosen to wear.

"Thank you."

"It's great that you're here so Josie can relax. I swear she is always on the go. It's nice to see her enjoying herself."

She had to agree. "The two of you have been spending a lot of time together lately. Anything going on there?"

Laughing out loud, Tyler shook his head. "Definitely not. Trust me. But she and Katie get along great, so..."

"Wait, who's Katie?"

"My girlfriend. She really wants to help with this project, but she's never done anything like it before."

"Oh, so...how's the fundraiser planning going?"

He shrugged. "It's a lot more work than I anticipated. I'm considering putting it off for a bit, but Josie's convinced I can pull it off."

"When she's determined to make something work, she finds a way. Trust me." They swayed to the music for a minute when something came to mind. "So...how did you and Jared and Alex end up on the guest list? Josie never mentioned it to me and Lea about coming, so I just thought..."

Tyler laughed softly as he shook his head. "Basically, we're moral support for Elliott."

"Seriously? Why?"

"This is the first big event since his wedding, and he was having a lot of anxiety about being here with everyone. You know, afraid they were all going to want to talk to him about it. So we're here to make sure no one gives him a hard time."

It was weird because in all the conversations she and Elliott had about the party, he never once mentioned being freaked out about it. If anything, he was looking forward to it.

"Uh-oh, you're frowning," Tyler whispered dramatically. "No frowning at such a happy event!"

Skye couldn't help but roll her eyes. "Sorry. My mind wandered." She glanced around the room and saw most of the tables were cleared. "I should probably go and check on..."

"Mind if I cut in?"

She turned and saw Jared standing there looking hopeful. "Um...I was just about to..."

"Aw, c'mon, Skye," he said with a mock pout. "Just one dance. You already danced with Tyler."

She knew he was just being a goof, but she relented. "Okay. Just one dance and then I have to get back to work." Tyler gave her a playful spin right into Jared's waiting arms and again, as soon as his hand was on her back, she felt weird.

"Great party!" he said, grinning.

"It sure is," she replied, scanning the room.

"So how come you and I have never gone out?"

Her eyes went wide. "What?!"

He nodded. "Yeah, why haven't we ever hooked up and gone out alone without the whole group?"

"Jared, I...I..."

"I mean other than the fact that I never asked." He gave her a flirty wink and it was hard to tell if he was being serious or not. "Okay, here's the thing, Skye. After seeing everything Elliott's gone through, it got me thinking."

"O-kay..."

"I met a woman that I think is really amazing," he went on. "And we have a lot in common and...I think there's a vibe there, you know?"

Oh, God...

"So it occurred to me that..."

"Jared," she quickly interrupted. "I think you're a really nice guy, but I'm just not attracted to you in that way. I'm sorry. Really."

He looked at her like she was crazy as they continued to sway to the music. "Um...yeah. I wasn't talking about you," he said slowly. "I was going to ask you for advice because I think I've waited too long to make my move and..."

Unable to help herself, she let out a nervous laugh that was really full of relief before resting her head on his shoulder. "Okay. Whew!" She gave him a hug before pulling back slightly and smiling at him. "Tell me about the girl."

"Well, I met her at..."

"Hey, no hogging the prettiest girl here!"

Alex.

Because...of course.

"Dude, we were just in the middle of a conversation," Jared explained.

"Yeah, well, the song's over and I'd like to dance with Skye."

"Guys, I really need to get back to work. I'm not here as a guest," she told them, hoping this was her moment to sneak back to the kitchen and check on things.

"One song, Skye. Come on," Alex pled. "You danced with both Tyler and this guy."

Oh, for the love of it...

Pasting a serene smile on her face, she thanked Jared for the dance and promised to talk to him later before she turned to step into Alex's arms.

If only she got this much attention when she was out and actually *looking* for a date.

"So...what's new?" she asked him, thankful the band was playing another slow song.

"Not too much," he said with a shrug. "I'm going to be traveling a lot for work starting next week–going to Tokyo for six weeks and then Paris for a month."

"Wow! That sounds amazing! I'm a little jealous."

"It's not going to be nearly as glamorous as you think. I have a feeling I'm going to be locked in meetings all day without having a whole lot of time to sightsee." He shook his head. "My girlfriend is pissed because she wants to come with me and I just can't make it happen."

That...surprised her.

All of Elliott's friends had girlfriends?

"I had no idea you were dating anyone," she commented. "How long have you two been together?"

"A couple of months," he admitted with a shy smile. "Honestly? I don't like to talk about it in front of Elliott. With the whole embargo thing it felt...I don't know...like I would be bragging or something."

She nodded. "It's very considerate of you. You're a good friend."

He shrugged as his smile grew. "I try." He paused. "So what about you? What have you been up to?"

Sighing, she told him about all the jobs Meet Me at the Altar had booked and how it took up so much of her time. His hand skimmed up and down her spine and she wanted to swat it away, but it wouldn't be possible without making a scene.

"It's been really impressive to watch you and Josie and Lea build the business, Skye. Like seriously impressive. If things go as planned and I end up popping the question next year to Beth, we are definitely going to want to hire you for the engagement party and the wedding."

Her eyes went a little wide. "So this is serious, huh?"

He nodded. "Yeah. I know I can't take her on the trip with me, but if I could, I'd propose to her in Paris right in front of the Eiffel Tower." And with a shy smile, he added, "I know it's not terribly original, but...I just think it would be incredibly romantic."

She found herself sighing because it really was.

"I'm happy for you, Alex. And I can't wait to meet her. You guys need to stop tiptoeing around with your girl-friends. Elliott will be fine."

"For a while there I thought so, but...I don't know, this last month he's been all depressed again."

It was stupid how much that pleased her.

"There were several months that he was the happiest I've ever seen him—and I mean ever. Elliott and I have been friends since the sixth grade so I can say with complete confidence that he was in a good place." Then he shrugged. "Something happened and he won't tell us what it is, but he's in a funk again so...eventually the girls will come out with us. Just not yet."

"Again, you're a good friend, Alex."

When the song ended, Skye knew she had to act fast before anyone else swooped in and asked her to dance.

"Thank you so much for the dance, but I really need to go and check on things."

"No problem, Skye. And thanks." He leaned in and kissed her on the cheek before she made her way through the crowd and back to the kitchen.

"Shouldn't you be up and socializing?" Tyler asked.

All Elliott could do was grunt a response.

His so-called friends had all gone and danced with Skylar when he couldn't.

Or...shouldn't.

Or...wait. Could he?

Before he could think too much about it, his grandfather came strolling over and placed a hand on his shoulder. "Do me a favor, Elliott? Go ask your nana to dance. It would mean the world to her."

He wanted to kick himself for not thinking of it sooner, but he'd been so consumed watching Tyler, Jared, and Alex dancing with Skye that he hadn't been paying attention to anything else.

"Of course, Pop. Thanks."

When he reached his grandmother, she beamed up at him. "There's my sweet boy. Are you enjoying the party?"

Elliott held out his hand to her. "I am, but I'd enjoy it a lot more if I could dance with the beautiful bride."

He didn't think it was possible for her smile to grow more, but it did. "Such a sweet talker," she said as she put her hand in his and stood.

Slowly, he led her out to the dance floor as the band cued into another ballad. "How about you, Nana? Are you enjoying yourself?"

"It's been an almost perfect day," she told him. "Everyone I love in this world is here."

"Then how come it's not completely perfect?"

She was barely five feet tall and she looked up at him with a sad smile. "Elliott, I've been watching you all night and you rarely smile. It breaks my heart."

Well, damn.

"I'm sorry, Nana. I didn't realize I was doing it," he said softly, kissing the top of her head.

"Are you sure you didn't know? Because you looked positively furious when all your handsome friends were dancing with Skylar." She gave him one of her sweetest smiles. "If I didn't know any better, I would swear you were jealous." Then she shook her head. "But how could that be? You've known her for most of your life. She's like family."

"Yeah," he murmured. "Not really."

"Elliott," she quietly demanded, and when he looked down at her, she looked pretty fierce. "You're not fooling anyone. If you want the girl, go and get the girl."

"Pop said something similar to me earlier..."

"That's because your grandfather and I are one," she said, back to her sweet, demure tone. "We're old and wise."

Leaning down, he kissed her on the cheek. "And I love you both."

"Then what are you doing dancing with this old lady? Go and tell her how you feel!"

"Nana, I can't do that here. And besides, we're dancing."

"Not anymore," his grandfather said from beside him. "I just saw Skye go into the kitchen." He nodded in that direction. "I'm going to be giving my speech in five minutes. It would be nice if the two of you were out here to hear it."

Then he nudged Elliott out of the way and took his wife in his arms.

Hint taken...

It would have been easy to wander around and pretend that he needed to think about it, but...he didn't.

He missed her.

So much it hurt.

And his damn beard itched like wild.

So with some intent in his stride, Elliott made his way to the kitchen and spotted Skye in the far corner eating something. The closer he got, the more his smile grew.

Frosting.

She didn't notice his approach, and it wasn't until he was behind her that he leaned in close and whispered, "For shame, Skylar. They haven't even served dessert yet."

A small scream was her first response as she jumped and dropped the bowl of icing and the spoon.

It reminded him of the day she dropped his phone.

"Dammit, Elliott! You scared me!" Bending down, she scooped everything up. When she straightened, she glared at him. "What are you doing back here?"

Taking a step back, he slid his hands into his pockets and just drank in the sight of her. From that sleek ponytail that she only wore for events, to the sexy-as-hell backless dress, and even the slight smear of chocolate icing in the corner of her mouth, she was perfect.

Everything.

But did he really want to proclaim his love for her and beg her forgiveness in the middle of the banquet hall's kitchen?

Um...no.

Instead, he took the icing and spoon from her hands and placed them on the counter. "I came here to get you."

"Get me," she repeated. "For what?"

That was a loaded question and he mentally congratulated himself for not going with the obvious responses.

"My grandfather is getting ready to give a speech and he asked for everyone to be out there."

"I don't think that includes the staff," she murmured. "You should get out there so you don't miss it."

Shaking his head, he stood his ground. "He specifically asked for you, so unless you want to ruin the moment for him, you need to come with me."

Rolling her eyes, she crossed her arms over her chest. "Somehow, I highly doubt that."

"Are you really willing to risk it?" he challenged.

Her shoulders sagged and he knew she wasn't going to argue with him. "Fine." And before she could change her mind, Elliott took her hand in his and led her out to the dining room.

And she only tried to pull away a few times, so he considered it a victory.

Standing in the far corner of the room, he saw his grandfather smile in his direction. Elliott gently positioned Skye in front of him and gave his grandfather a thumbs-up.

"I really don't know why I'm out here," she whispered, and he bent down until they were cheek to cheek.

"Stop arguing and just listen. Please."

His grandfather walked up to the bandstand and took a microphone. "Does everyone have a glass of champagne?" he asked and then watched as the staff finished handing them out. "I want to start by thanking all of you for coming out today to celebrate this wonderful day." He turned and smiled at his wife. "Sixty-five years ago, I was lucky enough to say 'I do' to this amazing woman, and she looks just as beautiful today as she did then."

There was a collective round of "aww" heard throughout the room, and Elliott stepped in close behind Skylar and slowly wrapped his arms around her waist. She stiffened, but she didn't move away either.

"I never thought I'd be so lucky," his grandfather was saying. "You see, a lot of marriages don't last. We don't have many friends who have lasted as long as we have, so every day we have together is a blessing. We've raised four beautiful children who blessed us with ten grandchildren." Then he glanced around the room. "And it wouldn't kill you kids to give us some great-grandchildren! We're not getting any younger, you know!"

Everyone laughed and Elliott smiled as Skye relaxed against him as she laughed.

"So, what makes a marriage last this long? I'll tell you," he said with a wink. "We fight, we disagree, we talk, we laugh, and at the end of the day, we always say 'I love you.' Have we gone to bed angry? Of course! But I know, for me, when I wake up in the morning and look over at my beautiful Millie, that she is it for me. There isn't another woman alive that I would have wanted to share these six-and-a-half decades with." He looked over at his wife again. "You are my love, my angel. You taught me to follow my heart." His voice caught with emotion and he took a moment to compose himself. "And it's a good thing you did because it's always belonged to you." Turning, he picked up a glass of champagne and held it up to her. "You're the best part of me and I love you. Thank you for loving me all these years." And placing the microphone down, he walked away so he could kiss his bride.

The whole room erupted in raised glasses and cheers and yet Elliott managed to keep one arm around Skye. When he glanced down, he saw she was crying and immediately took her glass from her hand and put it down right beside his.

"Hey," he said softly, turning her in his arms. "You okay?"

She burrowed against his chest as she nodded. "That was the most beautiful thing I've ever heard."

Wrapping both arms around her, he held her close and simply reveled in the feel of her there. After a moment, she pulled back and wiped at her tears. "Sorry about that."

"No need to apologize. I thought it was an amazing toast, too."

She nodded and went to move from his arms, but he wouldn't let her go. "Elliott..."

"I want that," he said gruffly, staring down at her beautiful, teary face. "I want what they have."

It looked like she was going to say something, but he continued on.

"I honestly thought I was doing the right thing–embracing that ridiculous embargo and telling myself that I was happy being single. But I wasn't." He paused and reached up to caress her cheek and wipe away one wayward tear. "The only time I was happy–truly happy–was when I was with you."

"Elliott..."

"I'm so sorry for what I did, Skye–for the way I treated you." Leaning forward, he rested his forehead against hers. "Tell me I'm not too late. Tell me I didn't ruin everything."

"It's been a month," she said with a slight tremble in her voice. "A whole month, Elliott, without a word from you."

"I know," he said firmly. "Again, I honestly thought I was doing the right thing. Doing what everyone wanted me to do. And I thought I was doing what was best for you. I meant what I said that day, Skye. You deserve to have a life with a man who can make you happy and give you the future you want." He swallowed hard. "I want to be that man."

She was crying softly as she shook her head. "I can't do this with you again. I don't know that I can trust you."

"Skye, I'm standing here telling you that I love you and that I want a life with you!" his words were quiet but fierce.

"We're standing here in a quiet corner in an otherwise noisy room, where no one can hear us," she reminded him. "I don't want to be your little secret, Elliott."

"You're not, Skye. I swear!"

"What about your family, huh? What about the embargo? What about...?"

He instantly released her and took a step back. "You're right."

Her look of confusion was utterly adorable, but he'd wait to tell her that later. "I...I am?"

Nodding, he took another step back. "I never should have done this."

Skye's expression went from confusion to fury, and he

was pretty sure she called him a bastard as he turned and walked away, but...it was going to be worth it very soon.

Walking across the room, he strode up to the bandstand and picked up the microphone his grandfather just used and waited as the band slowly faded out.

"Excuse me," Elliott said to the room. "Can I have everyone's attention please?" He waited a moment until all eyes were on him.

Especially Skye's.

"Some of you may remember that a little less than a year ago, I was supposed to get married." He waited for all the murmurs to die down before he continued. "You also probably remember how that all played out and how after being left at the altar, I was told that I–a grown man–wasn't allowed to date or get involved with anyone for at least a year."

There were some murmurs and a few laughs, but he expected it.

"Anyway, I hated the way things happened that day, but it turned out to be the best day of my life."

And cue the gasps...

"You see, it was a wake-up call for me. I've always been in love with being in love, but apparently, I wasn't always great at recognizing love in others–hence the four failed engagements."

A few more laughs.

"I was heading home that day, totally intent on being alone for a long time, when something incredible happened. Skylar Jennings broke my phone," he said, staring right at her and grinning. "She was snooping and I caught her, and she dropped my phone. Like I wasn't already having a crappy day."

Even from where he was standing, he saw her roll her eyes.

"Now here's where the second wake-up call of the day happened–Skye drove me home. She was the designated babysitter for me, I guess, and we ate some of the food from the canceled reception and just sat and talked for hours. For those of you who don't know Skye, she's one of Josie's best friends and also her business partner. She's been in our lives for almost twenty years and it wasn't until that day that I really got to know her."

No one laughed. There were no murmurs. Suddenly everyone was hanging on to his every word.

"Skye has a degree in psychology and I really thought she could help me figure out what was wrong with me–like why did I keep making such bad decisions? She reluctantly agreed to help, but..." He shrugged. "Things didn't exactly go as planned."

Stepping down from the stage, he walked to the middle of the dance floor.

"Friends and family, I broke the embargo," he stated firmly. "What started out as two friends hanging out together turned into so much more. I tried to tell myself it was casual and that it didn't mean anything, but I was lying to myself." He turned and faced Skye. "But mostly, I lied to and hurt Skylar."

Slowly, he made his way over to her and saw there were still some tears flowing, but she was smiling.

"So, I'm standing here in front of my entire family to tell you, Skylar Jennings, that I'm sorry I hurt you. I'm sorry that I didn't trust what we had. And if I learned anything from my extremely wise grandparents today, I learned that I should have followed my heart. I love you. I want us to be together. I want that four-bedroom house with the yard big enough for a jungle gym for our kids. I want the SUV so we can take everyone to little league and soccer practice."

Skye was crying in earnest now, so he knew he needed to wrap this up.

Looking over his shoulder, he asked, "Am I supposed to wait out the rest of this ridiculous embargo or am I allowed to publicly declare my love for this woman right here and now so we can start planning our lives together?"

The entire room cheered them on and he smiled as he turned back to face her.

"I don't want to wait," he told her. "I want to give you everything you've ever wanted. I want to be the man who makes all your dreams come true. Will you let me?"

And before he knew it, someone took the mic from his hands so he could finally reach out and take Skye in his arms and kiss her like he had been dying to for a month.

CHAPTER 16

*True love is when you put someone on a pedestal,
and they fall—but you are there to catch them.*

UNKNOWN

As MUCH AS Skye loved and adored the Sullivan family, right now she couldn't wait to be away from them. Even as Elliott continued to kiss her, she was planning a way to get them out of there.

Fast.

They finally broke apart and everyone in the room was on their feet and clapping and her face felt like it was on fire. "Oh my goodness..."

Elliott's big, strong hands cupped her face as he smiled at her. "I think my family's okay with all of it. What do you think?"

She couldn't help but laugh. "It does seem that way."

Glancing around, she saw nothing but smiling faces. "I kind of feel like we totally upstaged the guests of honor."

"Don't worry about it. They were the ones who convinced me to stop waiting, and considering how long they've been together, I figured it was okay to take relationship advice from them." He put a little space between them and reached for her hand. "How about a little dessert, maybe a dance or two, and then we get out of here?"

"Can we take the dessert to go and dance at my place? Or yours?"

His laugh was loud and hearty and the greatest sound in the world to her right now. "I don't think we can be that lucky. There's more than a few people looking anxious to talk to us so...let's get that over with and I promise to get us out of here as soon as I can."

"And where did we land on the dessert?"

He kissed her thoroughly. "That's my girl. I promise to get as much cake with icing as I can get my hands on." He kissed her again. "After we mingle for a few minutes."

She sighed dramatically. "I guess that will have to do."

They hadn't gone more than a few steps when Josie practically tackled them both to the ground. "That was amazing! Oh my goodness, Elliott...my heart nearly burst listening to you! And that was after Pop gave the most perfect romantic speech in the history of the world! How did I end up being related to such hopeless romantics?"

"We all ask ourselves the same thing," Elliott teased, and Josie simply rolled her eyes at him.

"And you!" she said to Skye. "You are the luckiest girl in the world because my brother is amazing. He's a bit of a doofus at times, but I know you'll keep him in check." Then she hugged her and whispered in her ear, "Just know that I am going to want to know all the details over coffee and bagels Monday morning."

"Consider it done," Skye whispered back before they pulled apart.

Grinning at her brother, Josie wagged a finger at him. "Thank God you finally did something. I don't know how many more single guys I could've thrown at Skye to dance with her!"

"You...um...what?" he asked.

"Yeah, what?" Skye repeated.

"Oh, please," Josie huffed. "You're welcome. Mission accomplished. Anyway, I'm sure the two of you don't want to hang around much longer so I'll make sure to keep an eye on things here."

"Jos, no. I promised I'd be here so you could enjoy the party and I meant it."

"Oh, please! Like I'm going to be the reason the two of you don't get to have makeup sex? Hell no!" Then she paused and shuddered dramatically. "Ew. I cannot even believe I said that knowing full-well that included my brother. Ick!" And then she was gone.

"She'd going to be a handful. You know that, right?" Elliott asked.

"I think we can handle her."

Together they made their way over to Elliott's grandparents, who both jumped up to hug and congratulate them.

"This was the best present we could ask for!" his nana said as she hugged Skye. "Although I do need you to promise me something, Skylar."

"Anything," she replied.

"Make him shave that beard off as soon as possible! I miss his handsome face!"

Looking up at Elliott, Skye grinned. "I completely agree. I miss his handsome face too."

"Then go, you two! What are you still doing here?"

"Nana," Elliott chimed in. "We wouldn't leave in the middle of your party. That would be rude."

"Well, you have our permission to be rude," she told him. "Grab some cupcakes and get out of here and go be happy." She smiled at them both.

"I'm sure my folks still want to talk to us..."

"We'll handle them," his grandfather said. "Seriously, go." He hugged Elliott and then Skye.

"And I hope someday the two of you are standing here doing the same thing we are—celebrating decades of love."

It almost made her cry again, but Skye hugged them both one last time before Elliott took her by the hand and carefully led her through the crowd and back to the kitchen. "Wait, what are we doing back here?"

"Snagging us some cupcakes to go and your secret stash of icing for later." He gave her an exaggerated wink and she couldn't help but laugh. And it felt so damn good. For the last month she hadn't laughed at anything and felt so sad and hopeless and now...

"Oh, Skye! There you are!" Patricia said as she walked over with a big smile on her face. "Leanna told me to give this to you if you came back here with Elliott." She handed her a large takeout bag. "It's dessert to go."

"Are we that predictable?" Elliott teased.

"No," Patricia responded with a small laugh. "We were all just hopeful. So...go and have a wonderful night!"

You didn't have to tell her twice...

Now it was Skye's turn to lead Elliott out of the kitchen and out to the parking lot. Pausing, she looked around. "Where's your car at?"

"I'll pick it up tomorrow, so..."

"Perfect! Come on!" They ran like two little kids to her car, laughing the whole way. She tossed him her keys so he could drive, and when they were pulling away, she let out a sigh of relief.

"Your place or mine?"

"Yours," she told him. "Definitely yours."

Taking her hand, he kissed her palm. "I was hoping you'd say that."

There were so many things she wanted to say–to ask about how they had finally gotten here–but there was going to be plenty of time for that later. So instead, they made small talk about the party. Luckily, Elliott's house was less than fifteen minutes away, and when they pulled into the driveway, she suddenly felt nervous.

"So, um..."

Turning to her, he caressed her cheek. "I know we have so much to talk about, but..." Then he gave her a bashful and sexy-as-hell smile.

"Maybe we could save the Q&A for after?"

His laugh was low and gruff. "After, huh?"

She nodded, biting her bottom lip. "Yeah. After."

"You know, this all sounds very familiar to me. It's a little like déjà vu."

"Why mess with a proven thing?" she teased, leaning in and kissing him.

Cupping her face in his hands, he kissed her back, and it was wild and frantic and as much as she hated to stop because she missed this so much, Skye knew they'd be much happier if they took things inside.

Fast.

Like now.

"Elliott..."

"One step ahead of you," he said as he placed a hard kiss on her lips before climbing from the car. Skye grabbed their dessert bag and quickly followed him to the front door. And once they were inside, it was pure chaos.

The dessert bag was the only thing handled with care. Skye placed it on the entryway table right before Elliott scooped her up in his arms, strode through the living room, and didn't stop until they were in his bedroom. She let out a small giggle as they each tried to get her out of her dress. There was a small hook at the back of her neck and it was too much for four hands to deal with.

"I got this. You work on you," she told him, and then they both laughed during the least sexy stripteases ever.

Sprawled across his bed, Skye knew she was smiling from ear to ear. Elliott was about to climb over her when he stopped.

"What's the matter?"

He ran a hand over his jaw. "Should I shave first?" he asked and then shook his head. "I should totally shave first, right?"

"Hmm...I don't know. I've never been with a guy with a beard quite like that..."

Grinning, he finally did crawl over her. "Well then, I guess we owe it to ourselves to try it at least once."

"Yeah, we do." And curling her hand around the back of his neck, she pulled him down and kissed him until they were both breathless again. In the back of her mind, she couldn't wait for him to shave a bit, but for now she was more than happy to take him exactly as he was because she loved him.

Had always loved him.

And after today, she knew she was always going to love him.

"I think that was too much."

"Pfft...no such thing."

"I'm serious. I have a headache from it."

Skye turned her head and looked at him with amusement. "Really? All that delicious icing gave you a headache? How is that possible? I ate twice as much as you and then licked even more of it off of you, so..."

"Hey, cut me some slack. You've been training for events like this. You eat icing the way most people eat fruit."

"Although I bet I'm much happier when I'm done."

Pulling her into his arms, Elliott kissed the top of her head. "I'm sure you are too." He let out a long breath and felt a contentment like he'd never known. They were quiet for several minutes before he said, "This is good."

"I agree." She kissed his chest and snuggled closer. They were naked and in his bed and wanted to stay there for as long as humanly possible.

"No, I mean it, Skye. This is really good–you and me."

Raising her head, she smiled at him. "I know. I feel the same."

"I was so happy with you before, but it feels different now. Better."

"Because we're not sneaking around. It's all out there for everyone to know about, and judging from the round of applause we got, I'm guessing they're all happy about it."

"I kind of feel bad about skipping out before talking to my parents."

Resting her head back on his shoulder, she let out a soft hum. "Well, to be fair, they're kind of the reason we were sneaking around."

"Yeah, but they're also the reason we're here now."

Her head popped up again. "How do you figure that?"

"Well, if they hadn't put me on the embargo, you wouldn't have come home with me that day. And you certainly wouldn't have kept coming around to make sure I stayed away from dating. So if you think about it..."

"Wait, wait, wait..." Now she sat up and pushed her long hair away from her face. "That's not true at all. I still would have gone home with you that day because you were still going to need a way home–embargo or no embargo. And I think we still would have been drawn together because of it."

"Maybe."

"Definitely," she said firmly before leaning in and kissing him. "Either way, we're here now and...it's after, so..."

Right. The Q&A...

Gently, he tugged her back so she way lying beside him again and then took a moment to collect his thoughts.

"I don't even know where to begin," he admitted. "Every moment of our time together–from that first one after...you know...to the day we came home from the mountains–I really tried to tell myself I was okay with it being casual. It was like I had to keep giving myself pep talks to stop myself from over-romanticizing what we had and for that, I am so sorry. We wasted so much time because of it."

Quietly, Skye's hand skimmed over his shoulder and down his arm and then up again.

"Say something. Please."

"I wouldn't say it was wasted," she said slowly. "If anything, I think it gave us time to get to know each other in a way we never had before."

"You mean besides the sex, right?" he teased, hoping to

lighten the mood, and when she gave him a playful shove, he knew he succeeded.

"Yes, besides the sex. Ugh...men!"

They both laughed, but he sobered quickly. "I know what you're saying, and I agree. It was nice having that time without the pressure of..." He paused and shook his head.

"Come on. Out with it. What were you going to say?"

"I was going to say without the pressure of trying to impress you, but that's just wrong and it makes me sound awful."

"Just a little."

He met her gaze and saw she was smiling. "You know what I'm saying, Skye. This is the most relaxed I'd ever been with a woman, and I couldn't tell if it was a good or bad thing."

She shrugged. "A little of both, maybe? But there were extenuating circumstances. It's moving forward that we have to worry about."

"Do we?"

"Um...yeah. Are you going to turn into that guy who is all crazy obsessed with doing over-the-top stuff to impress me? Or are we going to go back to being so chill that we're just sex buddies?"

"Somewhere in between," he said confidently. "Definitely somewhere in between. And you know how I know that's the way it's going to be?"

"Um..."

"Because it's you, Skye. You know me and I know you'll reel me in and keep me grounded. And I hope you'll indulge me a little and let me spoil you because I've been dying to for so damn long. That weekend in the mountains was so not what I wanted for us. Next time we're going to the beach and I want to see and do all the things you've talked about."

She smiled. "I would love that. And I think we'll eventually find a good balance."

Swallowing hard, he took her hand in his. "I love you, Skylar. And I meant every word I said at the party. I want a life with you and I don't want to wait. If that makes you uncomfortable and you're afraid I'm reverting to the old me, then I'll understand and we'll take it as slow as you want. But just know, if we could, I'd move you in here tonight and marry you tomorrow."

"Oh my goodness," she whispered.

"You're it for me. And if you can handle everything that goes with marrying a guy like me–knowing my history and how I'll forever be the butt of a lot of jokes–then know that I'm right here waiting for you." He kissed her hand. "I'll wait forever if that's what it takes."

His heart was hammering hard in his chest and he realized that this–*this*–was what it felt like to be in love. All those other times had been infatuation, convenience, and just plain wishful thinking. But what he felt right here, right now, in this moment, was so much bigger than anything he'd ever felt before. And knowing it was with Skye–and for Skye–just made it feel that much sweeter.

And he knew he would wait for her because she was worth it.

But he secretly hoped and prayed she didn't want to wait too long.

Glancing at her, he saw she was studying their hands–undoubtedly thinking about what she was getting herself into–and he wished he knew what was going through her mind.

One minute turned to two, and that's when panic started to set in.

Do I say something? Nudge her? What is the protocol here?

Yeah, he was slowly losing it when she finally smiled at him.

"What if...what if I said I would move in here tomorrow," she said evenly.

"Then I'd say let's go see about renting a truck," he replied in the same tone.

She gave him a curt nod. "I know we can't get married tomorrow because...well...it's too quick to invite anyone..."

"There's always next weekend."

"Elliott, be serious!" she said with a laugh.

"I am serious, Skye. Personally, I don't care what anyone thinks anymore. I know what I feel for you and I know that I can truly be myself with you. It won't matter if it's tomorrow, next week, next month, or next year; I am still going to be the luckiest guy in the world because you want to be with me!"

Her beautiful eyes went a little wide. "This is crazy! I mean...there's still so much we need to talk about!"

He sat up. "Okay, then let's talk about it," he challenged. "Ask me anything. Tell me anything! Yell at me for all the ways I screwed things up. Whatever it is, we can talk about it and be honest with each other."

She stared at him for several minutes and he was sure she had a list of things she wanted to say. And when she finally spoke, she blew him away.

"I'm going to want to have a baby," she blurted out. "Sooner rather than later. Does that freak you out?"

"Not at all. The thought of a baby with you is just icing on the cake."

Her expression softened, and she sat up and wrapped herself around him. "That was the perfect answer, and I love how you included icing in there."

His arms banded around her as he held her close. "We may need to ask Leanna to make us a couple of gallons of her best stuff to keep on hand. I want you to be happy."

"As long as I have you, Elliott Sullivan, I'm going to be happy."

Those were definitely the sweetest words.

Pulling back, he rested his forehead against hers. "I don't have a ring, but...Skylar Jennings, will you put me out of my misery and end my embargo and marry me?"

Nodding, she reached up and cupped his face. "Yes! Oh my God, yes!"

And this time when he lowered her back down, he loved her the way she deserved and promised to love her every day for the rest of his life.

EPILOGUE
THREE MONTHS LATER...

Don't marry someone you can live with. Marry the person you can't live without.

UNKNOWN

"HMM...THIS one's good, but...I think I need to try that second one again."

"Really? Because I think the third one was the winner." Dipping his finger in the icing sample, Elliott held out his finger for Skye to taste.

"Oh my God, you two!" Josie cried. "Get a room! And keep your freaky sex stuff out of the office!"

"I think they're cute," Leanna said with a big grin.

"You realize you're simply providing them with edible sex toys, right?"

She blushed furiously. "Oh...um...yeah. No." Then, glaring at Skye and Elliott, she said, "Knock it off, you two!

We're trying to finalize your wedding plans so...keep it in your pants!"

"Oh, good grief," Josie murmured. "That was like being yelled at by a Muppet."

"Hey!"

"Okay, okay, okay," Skye said, sitting up straighter. "Sorry. We'll behave."

"Finally..."

"So we were talking last night," Elliott chimed in, "and now we're thinking that we need to take away the sushi bar at the cocktail hour and replace it with a pasta bar."

"O-kay..." Josie said, making notes in their file.

"And can we add pigs in a blanket too?" Skye asked. "With the honey mustard dipping sauce? I love those things!"

"Good call, babe," Elliott agreed. "And for the cupcake tower, I think we should do a variety of all three icings, just to play it safe. But for the cake, we want to go with the devil's food with the cannoli filling."

"You two realize the wedding is less than two weeks away, right?" Lea asked. "You can't keep changing things. This has to be the final version."

They both nodded.

"But just on the menu, right?" Skye asked. "I mean, we've made last-minute adjustments for other couples without it being a big deal."

Lea and Josie looked at each other and sighed. "Was there something you wanted to change for the reception?" Josie asked wearily.

"We were thinking of maybe switching the flowers..."

Josie stood up. "No. Just...no. We sat down and planned a fantastic wedding for the two of you on super short notice. I made calls, Lea made calls, hell, Skye! You even made them, and we called in a bunch of favors to get everything you guys wanted! So I'm putting my foot down! No more changes! Everything stands as-is! Understood?" she cried before storming from the room.

Skye and Elliott exchanged glances before looking at Leanna. "Um...what was that all about?"

With an apologetic smile, Lea sighed. "I think she's feeling a little left out."

That was...not what she expected to hear. "Why? We've included her in everything and she swore she didn't have a problem with us being together."

Another small smile. "It's not that. Not really. I think after your engagement party when she saw that pretty much everyone there had a date..."

"You didn't," Skye pointed out, and her hands immediately flew to cover her mouth. "That's not what I meant. I mean...I didn't mean that in a bad way! I swear!"

Lea waved her off. "Oh, I know. Don't worry about it," she said with a laugh. "But Tyler was there with his girlfriend, Jared brought a date, and Alex and his girlfriend stopped in before he left for the airport so...I think it just hit her that maybe she might like to have a plus one, too."

"I still can't believe those guys have had girlfriends all this time and no one told me," Elliott grumbled and Skye simply patted his knee.

"I know, baby." Then she looked back at Lea. "So what are we supposed to do? Is there anyone we can fix her up with?"

"I don't think so. Besides, you know how she is. She'd want it to be her own idea or she'd feel like we were pitying her or something."

"Maybe," Skye replied with a frown.

"Oh, come on," Lea told her. "I think you know better

than anyone that you never know when and where you'll meet your perfect someone. Look at the two of you! Twenty years and it was only this last year that you realized how perfect you were for each other. Josie just needs to get out more and meet some new people."

"I can't believe none of you have ever met a guy at one of your events," Elliott commented. "I would think there would be plenty of single guys at the weddings you handle."

Both Lea and Skye shrugged. "It's not like we're out mingling with the guests," Skye explained. "It's not like that."

"Oh, but how I wish it were," Lea said with a grin.

"So, what's next on your calendar? Don't you have a consult for a dessert weekend or something?"

Lea's smile was instantly gone. "Yeah. My cousin Charlene just got engaged and she's having this ridiculous four-day engagement party extravaganza." She groaned. "Her future husband's family is mega-rich and they live on this huge estate in Chapel Hill."

"What do they do?"

"I think something with hotels and corporate convention centers." She shook her head. "Apparently the groom's family is handling all the food and all the arrangements for the party, but Charlene only wants me doing the desserts."

"Oh, well...that's nice, right?"

"I'm not sure yet. Charlene's a bit of a handful on a good day and I have a feeling the groom's family is going to be a bit challenging to work with. I'm not a fan of being treated like the hired help when family is involved, and that's exactly what's going to happen here." She paused and let out a long breath. "Maybe I should tell her I'm not available or..."

Reaching across the table, Skye squeezed her hand.

"Or...you can meet with her and feel her out first. And no matter what you decide, Josie and I will support you, okay?"

"You're right. I'm getting myself all worked up before I've even met with them. Silly, right?"

"I'm sure it's all going to be fine, Lea."

With a nod, Lea stood and told them she had shopping to do and when she was gone, Skye leaned against Elliott and let out her own long breath.

"You okay?" he asked.

"I'm just worried about my friends and feel guilty that I've been a little MIA for them lately."

"Well, to be fair, we're planning our wedding and...have had a few other things on our plates."

Her hand immediately rested on her stomach. "I haven't told them the news yet."

He laughed softly. "If you wait a few more weeks, a month tops, maybe they'll figure it out for themselves."

Glancing up at him, she gave him a bland look. "This is big news and I was trying to find the right moment, but it seems like they're stressed enough. Maybe I'll just wait until after the wedding to tell them we're having a baby."

"We were planning on waiting to tell everyone until then so...it wouldn't be the worst thing in the world." Tilting her face up to his, he kissed her. "Although if it were up to me, I'd be broadcasting it everywhere. Do you have any idea how excited I am about this?"

"The fact that you already ordered a jungle gym for the yard was a big clue," she teased, kissing him.

"Ugh, we get it! You're happy!" Josie called out as she walked by the room.

"I think that's our cue to leave," Elliott said, helping Skye to her feet. "Come on. Let's go home so we're not flaunting our love all over the place."

That made her laugh. "Well, we had to hide it for so long so I think we're entitled to a little flaunting.

"In that case..." he reached out and scooped her into his arms and strode through the Meet Me at the Altar offices, making sure everyone saw them.

And that was more than okay with her.

She'd waited long enough for her happily-ever-after, and every moment she and Elliott shared told her it was all worth it.

WHICH MEET ME AT THE ALTAR
GIRL IS GOING TO FIND HER HAPPILY
EVER AFTER NEXT?

WITH THIS Cake

It was eight-o-five on Monday morning and Leanna Baker was already stressed.

Not a great way to start the week...

As she pulled up to the Meet Me at the Altar office, the only thing keeping her sane was the fact that one of her business partners and best friends, Skye, was back from her honeymoon and they were going to hear all about it over breakfast.

Which Leanna was currently going to try to juggle to bring in.

Climbing from her car, she almost sagged with relief

when her other business partner and best friend, Josie, came walking over to help her.

"Good morning," Lea said, feeling a little breathless as she started handing things to Josie. "Sorry I'm late."

"Late? It's only eight o'clock."

"Eight-o-nine to be exact."

Groaning, Josie took the tray with their coffees and then the bag of bagels from Lea. "Stop being such a stickler for crap like this. Skye's not here yet and no one's waiting on us, so relax."

Easy for her to say, Lea thought. She hadn't been harassed all weekend by her bridezilla cousin Charlene.

They walked into the office and set their breakfast up at the conference table like they did every Monday morning. "Have you heard from Skye since they got back?"

"Only a text thanking me for watering plants and for handling the appointment with the electrician last week. As far as I can tell, she should be here any minute."

"Good. Good. That's good," she murmured as she moved around grabbing napkins and knives for the bagels. It was their standard menu for their weekly meeting and Lea could probably have it all set up blindfolded, but she found a certain amount of peace in the mundane task.

"What's going on with you?" Josie asked after a minute.

"What do you mean?"

"You're scurrying around here and you're acting a little twitchy. What's up?"

Maybe she'd feel better if she just talked about it–especially before Skylar arrived and the conversation turned to her fabulous honeymoon.

Grabbing her chair, she collapsed on it. "My cousin is a nightmare," she blurted out. "Like the worst bridezilla I've ever dealt with! I thought it wouldn't be so bad for this engagement extravaganza, but it just keeps growing and taking on a life of its own and it's too late for me to get out of it!" Slouching down in her seat, she let out a long breath. "Oh, my goodness. It feels so good to say that out loud!"

Taking the chair opposite her, Josie gave her a sympathetic smile. "Okay, what can I do to help? Seriously, just name it and I'm there for you."

"Thanks, but...I think I finally have it all worked out, I'm just going to have to make sure I have several backups ready just in case."

"Why?"

Sitting up straighter, she explained. "It's a four-day event–Thursday to Sunday. Thursday afternoon, people will start to arrive at the groom's family estate in Chapel Hill. There's going to be a casual dinner–they're having some famous Pit Master come in and do a barbecue for them. I'm doing the cupcakes for dessert. A hundred of them."

"Yikes! Isn't this just an engagement party?"

She nodded. "Yup. There's fifty people confirmed for Thursday and then another fifty coming in Friday and then an additional hundred for Saturday and Sunday."

"Seems a bit excessive for an engagement. I can only imagine what the wedding is going to be like."

"It's going to be a three-ring circus, I imagine. Fortunately, I'm only doing the cake for that one. Although it's going to be like nothing I've ever done before. They're expecting five hundred people. Can you imagine? So it's going to be a six-tiered cake with two giant cupcake towers on either side. Just thinking about it gives me a headache."

Josie nodded. "Okay, but back to the weekend thing. You're doing cupcakes for Thursday night. What about the rest of the weekend?"

"Friday night will be more of the same—lots and lots of cupcakes—plus a cake. All Tiffany themed."

"Tiffany? Like the jewelry?"

"Yup. I finally got the fondant the right color and I was practicing with it all weekend. I swear, Josie, I ate way too much cake while trying to figure out the design. My pants are very squeezy today."

"Damn. You should have called me. I would have loved to have some cake rather than the bland vegan dinner I was forced to eat."

"Since when are you vegan? Have we talked about it and I forgot?"

Josie shook her head. "No. I had a blind date Saturday night and he's vegan."

"Oh, um...how did it go?"

"I went to the Burger King drive-thru at midnight and scarfed down a Whopper in the parking lot. There won't be a second date."

"Wow. Sorry."

"Don't be. Even without the whole vegan thing, we weren't particularly compatible." She sighed. "But back to you. Again. What's after the Tiffany cake and cupcakes?"

"We're doing a dessert bar Saturday night and fortunately, I was able to sub out a lot of it. I've got someone doing cookies, someone doing the sundae bar, and then we'll have a chocolate fondue station, plus cupcakes."

"I'm afraid to ask what happens on Sunday..."

"I have to prepare two hundred goodie boxes," she said wearily. "One cupcake, one cookie, some assorted candies, and a little bag of those Jordan almonds." She sighed. "I've got a team coming in starting on Wednesday to start prepping and assembling as much as we can in advance."

"Good grief, Lea! Is there space for you at their estate to work?"

She nodded. "They've set up a trailer for me as well as a tent specifically for setting things up and assembling. Plus, they're giving me a room in one of the houses on the estate so I don't have to commute back and forth."

"It's only a forty minute drive..."

"I know, but it will mean I can sleep a little too. It's going to be exhausting, but I've got a team of six coming to help, so it should be okay. Just a lot of work."

"O-kay...so tons of baking, but that's nothing new to you and not enough for you to be this stressed."

Rather than respond, she groaned and slouched a little further down in her seat.

"That doesn't sound good."

Letting out a long breath, she forced herself to sit up. "Charlene invited me to brunch yesterday so I could get a feel for the layout and walk around and check everything out. Basically, she wanted to make sure I was going to have everything I need for the weekend."

"Well, that was very nice of her. No surprises, right?"

"Everything looked great."

"But...?"

"So we're in the middle of eating in this massive dining room where the table could have easily fit fifty people and..."

"What did she serve?"

"Um...what?"

"The brunch?" Josie prompted. "What did she serve?"

"Oh, um...we had lobster eggs Benedict, fresh fruit, and chocolate croissants. Very yummy."

"Nice. Okay, go on."

"We were eating, and she was going on and on and on

about how fabulous her life is when somewhere in the house, people start yelling. Like seriously arguing."

Josie's eyes went wide even as she smiled. "Who was it?"

"Apparently, the groom has two older brothers. One is married and–according to Charlene–the nicest guy in the world. But the other brother..."

"Was the one arguing, right?" she asked excitedly.

Nodding, Leanna couldn't help but laugh. "Yup. Things are supposedly so hostile, that he's not part of the bridal party."

"Yikes."

Nodding again, she went on. "So they broke the news to him Sunday morning that he was out of the bridal party, but then the father chimed in that he still was expected to be at the wedding and all the wedding and pre-wedding festivities. And on top of that, he had to be on his best behavior or they were going to fire him from the family business!"

"No!"

"Uh-huh!" Lea said, her heart beating a little faster just like it had at brunch. "I asked Charlene about it because... you know...we were overhearing it all, and she told me that she wanted five minutes alone with him to threaten him that if he did even the tiniest thing to ruin anything, that she'd personally lead the charge to have him thrown off the property!" Shaking her head, she sighed. "At that point, I kind of felt bad for the guy."

"That's because you never like to believe anyone is bad and believe me, sometimes, people are. It sounds like this guy sure is. If the entire family is ready to throw his ass away like this, then you know it's serious."

"Yeah, but...maybe he has his reasons..."

Josie held up a hand to stop her. "Don't. Just...don't."

"Don't get involved, Lea! This whole weekend is going to be enough of a circus without you getting involved in their messed up family dynamic. Go and do the cupcakes and the goodie boxes and whatever else, and steer clear of this brother person."

"It's not like I was going to actively seek him out or anything. And besides, I don't even know what he looks like. There was a lot of yelling, but no one came near the dining room." She shook her head and laughed softly again. "Seriously, the house is so big, I could have walked around it for hours and never found where the fighting was coming from."

"Sounds like they're going to need it for this whole weekend party. Where's the wedding going to be?"

"Their signature hotel–the very first one they built–is located just outside of Charlotte. It's a massive hotel and golf resort and according to my cousin, it's the most magnificent place for a wedding."

Rolling her eyes, Josie snorted. "Please. We hear that from every bride, don't we? She just loves it because that's where she's getting married and I'm sure they're bending over backwards for her."

"Probably."

"And you're doing the cake for that?"

"Unfortunately," she murmured.

"Lea, it's okay if you tell her you can't do it. After all, it's three hours away. That's a lot to ask when you're transporting a cake for five hundred people."

"I know, but if I don't do it, my family is going to throw a lot of guilt my way. As it is, I'm already hearing the usual remarks because I'm not bringing a date to the whole weekend thing."

"Sadly, that's nothing new either, and I'm sorry. The

good news is you can hide out in the trailer and ignore them and pretend that you've got way too much work to be socializing at the party."

"That was my plan," she admitted and felt her cheeks heat. "I'm such a coward where my family is concerned."

"I think we all are in our own way."

They grew silent, but it didn't last for long because Skylar came breezing into the room carrying two giant gift bags and smiling from ear to ear.

"I'm back!" she cried happily, arms in the air.

After that it was nothing but squeals of happiness and lots of hugs for several minutes and it was exactly what Leanna needed. Maybe listening to her best friend gush about how lucky she was to finally marry the man of her dreams was exactly what Lea needed to snap her out of her own funk.

And maybe if she was really lucky, this engagement party wasn't going to be the nightmare she was already envisioning it to be.

The phone beside him chirped with yet another reminder that he was expected in hell in one hour.

Okay, technically he wasn't going to hell—not yet anyway—but his brother's marathon engagement party was pretty damn close.

Reaching for the phone, Brody King dismissed the reminder as he leaned back in his desk chair and groaned. There were a million other things he'd rather be doing than spending four days celebrating with his family and two hundred of their closest friends.

Hell would be preferable.

Raking a hand through his dark hair, he blew out a long breath. As much as he needed to get going, he knew he needed to get into the right mindset first. He'd already been warned numerous times that he had better be on his best behavior ever second of every day of this ridiculous four-day engagement party.

"Why does anyone need that long of a celebration?" he murmured, even as he felt his blood pressure rising.

The whole thing was just beyond crazy to him. And to make matters worse, he was being attacked for simply being honest.

Well, his brother had called him a callous jackass and rude, but Brody preferred to call it as stating the truth.

For starters, no one needed a four-day engagement party.

And no one needed to create such a spectacle and waste so much money in the process.

But the straw that had pretty much broke the camel's back for him, was the fact that this was all taking away from time that would be better spent at work. They ran a billion-dollar business and in order to keep it that way, someone actually needed to work.

Something his baby brother couldn't seem to grasp.

Ever.

An extended weekend may not seem like much to most people, but to Brody, time was money and four days of pointless celebrating was going to grate on his last nerve.

Sooner rather than later.

Brody knew he was the workaholic in the family. His grandfather had started King Hospitality more than fifty years ago. Then his father had joined him and they branched out into corporate convention centers and took their business across the U.S. Once Brody was old enough to join the team, he took them global.

Maybe it was middle-child syndrome, but he had always felt the need to work as hard as he could to stand out–to make an impact. His family didn't mind when he was making them millions, but as soon as he speaks up against something his brothers are doing and suddenly, he's the problem.

Groaning, he wondered how he was supposed to handle everything.

Or rather...the next five days.

Even though the party didn't technically begin until Thursday evening, the entire family was told to show up today–Wednesday. He didn't have a part in the wedding–thank God–but for some reason, he was still expected to be there for everything as if he did.

His backup reminder chirped and Brody knew he had stalled long enough.

The drive to the family compound in Chapel Hill would take him less than twenty minutes. King Hospitality's main office was also located there and it was a fairly direct route. His own home was in Raleigh–which wasn't that far away and it seemed silly that he wasn't allowed to sleep in his own bed for the next several nights–but again, he was trying to do what everyone asked.

No matter how inconvenient.

Fortunately, he had a suite of rooms at his family's home and knew he could retreat to them at the end of the day and have more than enough privacy away from the throngs of people who were going to be staying there.

He shuddered at the thought.

There was a knock at the door and he looked up as his father walked in.

Great.

"Brody," he said in his usual booming, commanding voice. "I expected you to be gone by now."

Standing, he stretched. "I was just getting ready to leave," he replied respectfully. Walking around the desk, he slid his phone into his pocket.

"Good. That's good. I'll follow you out."

For the love of it…

"Dad, you don't need to do that. I really am planning on leaving. I just need to grab my laptop and some files and I'll be on my way." To prove his point, he gathered up his belongings and put them in his satchel.

"How's the training going?" his father asked as he stood and watched his son move around the office. "You were here pretty early this morning."

"I came right from the gym and showered up here. It's preferable to doing so in a public locker room."

"When's the triathlon?"

"Eight weeks," he replied. "And if I keep up this pace, I should beat last years' time."

"Good for you, Brody. Personally, I don't know how you do it. Don't you ever just sit and rest?"

"What for? I don't see the point in simply sitting around the house." It was true, he hated to be idle, but what he wouldn't admit to anyone was how his current training was kicking his butt just a little bit. He was even considering not training next year.

"Maybe you'll relax this weekend at the house and do a little less training." He paused. "You tend to go to the gym at night, too, don' you?"

"I do, and before you ask, I'm heading straight to the house and don't plan on going anywhere, so you don't have to worry."

"Yeah, about that…"

Brody stopped in his tracks. "Is there a problem?"

"Charlene's cousin is staying in the house this weekend. She's in charge of the desserts."

"O-kay…"

"Her room is in your wing so…please be on your best behavior and don't scare the poor girl. She was at the house Sunday and heard you having your meltdown and…"

"It wasn't a meltdown, Dad," he said with more than a hint of annoyance. "I was simply giving my opinion. Last I checked, that was still allowed."

Pinching the bridge of his nose, Marshall King tensed. "We're not doing this again. Just…please be nice to her. If anything, be overly nice to her. Do I make myself clear?"

It was pointless to argue so he simply nodded.

"Excellent," his father said, his relief palpable. "Now let's get going."

As soon as they were out of his office, Marshall talked about all the plans for the party–as if Brody cared–and all the preparations that were currently underway. It sounded like there was going to be hundreds of people there setting up, and again he had to wonder why his presence was needed or required today.

It felt a little like walking to his execution and Brody knew he was dragging his feet a bit–literally and figura-tively. Still, by the time they were down in the parking garage, he was more than ready to be alone in his car. "I'll see you at the house, Dad," he said with a small wave, and once he was seated behind the wheel of his Aston Martin DB11, all the tension left his body.

"And I've got all of twenty minutes to enjoy it…"

Glancing up in his rearview mirror, he spotted his

father's BMW idling and knew the old man was waiting for him to pull out of his spot.

With a muttered curse, he obliged.

"So much for relaxing," he muttered and slowly drove out of the garage. It wasn't until he was out on the highway that he forced himself to forget about who was following him and why. Turning on the radio, Brody let himself indulge in some loud music from his youth. A little Foo Fighters was exactly what he needed to clear his head. By the time he turned onto the long, tree-lined drive of his childhood home, he felt like he just might survive the weekend.

Then he spotted the long line of trucks and vans lining the driveway–caterers, electricians, florists, linen rentals, tents...his shoulders tenses and he had to remind himself that he could be in the house and up in his wing in just another few minutes. Being that he wasn't part of the bridal party, none of this chaos had anything to do with him.

So he parked his car and grabbed his satchel before getting out. He waved to his father as he walked toward the house, and once inside, he kissed his mother on the cheek while she talked to the florist about her displeasure over the color of the flowers.

Just another day in the King household...

He was halfway up the grand staircase when his little brother and groom-to-be came jogging down toward him.

"Hey, Brody! You made it!" They met on the landing and Travis gave him a brisk hug. "I was afraid we were going to have to send someone to force you to leave the office!"

Brody knew he was teasing, but it still was enough to make him have to roll his shoulder and force himself not to negatively respond.

With a smile, he shrugged. "Well, Dad came in and walked out with me so..." They both laughed. "So where are you off to?"

"Oh, Charlene's down at tent and doesn't like the lights they're installing. I'm going to go see what we can do about it."

"They're just..." he started but noticed his brother's glance hardening and simply bit his tongue. "They're just doing their job," he corrected mildly. "If they don't have anything they can swap out, maybe see if the florist or someone has something that can dress them up."

Travis's jaw dropped slightly before he smiled. "Wow, thanks, bro. I never would have thought of that!" Then with a clap on the shoulder, he took off down the rest of the stairs and Brody was blessedly by himself.

Jogging up the stairs to the third floor where his rooms were, he whistled. Once in his suite, he shut the door and placed his satchel down on the coffee table in his sitting area. Loosening his tie, he wondered what he should do with himself. There was no way he was going to go down to the tent or risk running into anyone who might want his input on anything. The brief conversation with Travis was enough.

"So now what?" Yanking his tie off, he tossed it onto the sofa before unbuttoning his shirt. Walking over to the French doors that led out to his balcony, he looked out over the property and sighed.

People. Everywhere.

At least...over on the east side of the property. To the west, there was one trailer set up all by itself, but other than that, it was nothing but acres of green grass, a paved path his parents used to get to the tennis court, the lake, and the nine-hole golf course.

It was also a great spot for jogging.

The thought of going for a run put a smile on his face because it would be a great way to let off steam, relax, and stay out of everyone's way.

And that last one was for everyone's benefit; not just his.

Plus, it was a way of keeping his word about not going to the gym but still getting his training time in.

With a renewed sense of purpose, Brody stripped down to his boxer briefs and rummaged through his chest of drawer to find a pair of shorts, a t-shirt, and some socks. Next he pulled a pair of wireless earbuds out before pulling up a playlist on his Apple phone. Sneakers were in the closet and once he was dressed, he spent a few minutes stretching before heading down the back stairs that led directly to the kitchen. Once there, he maneuvered through the crowd working there, grabbed a bottle of water and made his way out the door.

After that, it was pure bliss.

The sky was still blue, the temperature was in the sixties, and the best part was that no one was around.

He started out walking across the yard–around the pool, the pool house, and the large outdoor kitchen. Once he passed them, he started with a light jog and within a few minutes, he had a great eight-minute mile pace going. Brody had been a runner since middle school. He'd been an all-star on the track team, and normally he only managed to get his runs while on a treadmill. Being outside was a total game changer and he made a mental not to himself start getting up earlier so he could get a run in before work.

But for this weekend, he knew he was going to utilize this path as much as humanly possible.

Music played, the perfectly manicured scenery passed him by, and by the time he was approaching the house, he had a good sweat going on and felt invigorated. If it was a little warmer, he would consider going for a dip in the pool and doing some laps, but he'd have to settle for a shower and possibly a few minutes in the sauna or something.

While he walked around to cool down, he drank the rest of his water and looked over at the lone trailer, frowning.

Why was it on this side of the yard? Why wouldn't it get placed with all the rest? What other unnecessary attraction was being added to this spectacle?

"Brody? There you are," his mother called as she walked outside and spotted him. "We were wondering where you were."

Sylvia King may be the mother of three grown men, but she didn't look a day over forty.

Which is what she told her plastic surgeon every time she saw him.

"I'm not late for anything, am I?"

"No, of course not, sweetheart. Dinner's in an hour and no one knew where to find you. We're having Italian tonight. Lasagna. I know it's one of your favorites." She looked up at him with a big smile and he couldn't help but smile back.

"I guess it's a good thing I went for a run, huh? Now I can have two helpings," he said, winking at her.

"Oh, stop. You could eat a whole tray of it and not worry. Run or no run."

"I'm not so sure about that."

"Oh, and we have some very decadent dessert! Charlene ordered some tiramisu and a New York cheesecake, and I had Mrs. Grayson make her famous chocolate lava cake. You know how I love something sweet after we have Italian."

Brody made a face. "You know sweets aren't my thing,

Mom, but you enjoy them. Actually, you can have my dessert."

Shaking her head, she made a tsking sound. "I don't know how my own son doesn't eat dessert. It's not right!" It was a conversation they had all the time and he knew she was teasing. "Just know that I love you anyway." She went to hug him but pulled back. "But you really should shower first so...go."

Kissing her cheek, he grinned. "I'm on it. See you in an hour!"

Get your copy of with this cake here:
https://www.chasing-romance.com/
with-this-cake
And keep up with the meet me at the altar
series here:
https://www.chasing-romance.com/meet-me-
at-the-altar-series

ALSO BY SAMANTHA CHASE

The Magnolia Sound Series:

Sunkissed Days

Remind Me

A Girl Like You

In Case You Didn't Know

All the Befores

And Then One Day

Can't Help Falling in Love

Last Beautiful Girl

The Way the Story Goes

Meet Me at the Altar:

The Engagement Embargo

With this Cake

You May Kiss the Groomsman

The Enchanted Bridal Series:

The Wedding Season

Friday Night Brides

The Bridal Squad

Glam Squad & Groomsmen

Bride & Seek

The RoadTripping Series:

Drive Me Crazy

Wrong Turn

Test Drive

Head Over Wheels

The Montgomery Brothers Series:

Wait for Me

Trust in Me

Stay with Me

More of Me

Return to You

Meant for You

I'll Be There

Until There Was Us

Suddenly Mine

A Dash of Christmas

The Shaughnessy Brothers Series:

Made for Us

Love Walks In

Always My Girl

This is Our Song

Sky Full of Stars

Holiday Spice

Tangled Up in You

Band on the Run Series:

One More Kiss

One More Promise

One More Moment

The Christmas Cottage Series:

The Christmas Cottage

Ever After

Silver Bell Falls Series:

Christmas in Silver Bell Falls

Christmas On Pointe

A Very Married Christmas

A Christmas Rescue

Christmas Inn Love

The Christmas Plan

Life, Love & Babies Series:

The Baby Arrangement

Baby, Be Mine

Baby, I'm Yours

Preston's Mill Series:

Roommating

Speed Dating

Complicating

The Protectors Series:

Protecting His Best Friend's Sister

Protecting the Enemy

Protecting the Girl Next Door

Protecting the Movie Star

7 Brides for 7 Soldiers

Ford

7 Brides for 7 Blackthornes

Logan

Standalone Novels:

Jordan's Return

Catering to the CEO

In the Eye of the Storm

A Touch of Heaven

Moonlight in Winter Park

Waiting for Midnight

Mistletoe Between Friends

Snowflake Inn

Wildest Dreams (currently unavailable)

Going My Way (currently unavailable)

Going to Be Yours (currently unavailable)

ABOUT SAMANTHA CHASE

Samantha Chase is a New York Times and USA Today bestseller of contemporary romance that's hotter than sweet, sweeter than hot. She released her debut novel in 2011 and currently has more than sixty titles under her belt – including THE CHRISTMAS COTTAGE which was a Hallmark Christmas movie in 2017! When she's not working on a new story, she spends her time reading romances, playing way too many games of Solitaire on Facebook, wearing a tiara while playing with her sassy pug Maylene...oh, and spending time with her husband of 30 years and their two sons in Wake Forest, North Carolina.

Where to Find Me:
Website: www.chasing-romance.com
Facebook: www.facebook.com/SamanthaChaseFanClub
Instagram: https://www.
instagram.com/samanthachaseromance/
Twitter: https://twitter.com/SamanthaChase3
Reader Group: https://www.facebook.com/
groups/1034673493228089/
Sign up for my mailing list and get exclusive content and chances to win members-only prizes!
https://www.chasing-romance.com/newsletter

Printed in Great Britain
by Amazon